EX LIBRIS

Alice Spencer

RAZORBILL

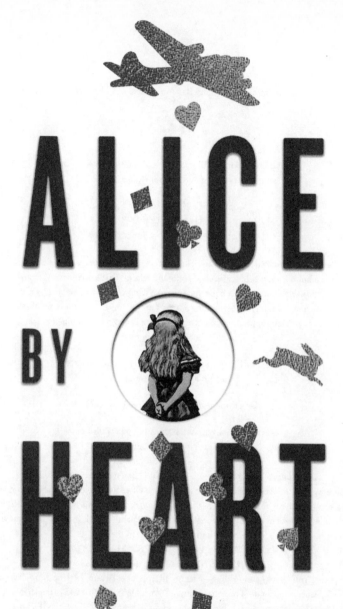

AL·ICE
BY
HEART

STEVEN SATER

RAZORBILL

RAZORBILL

An imprint of Penguin Random House LLC, New York

First published in the United States of America by Razorbill,
an imprint of Penguin Random House LLC, 2020.

Visit us online at penguinrandomhouse.com

LIBRARY OF CONGRESS CATALOGING-IN-PUBLICATION DATA
Names: Sater, Steven, author.
Title: Alice by heart / Steven Sater.
Description: New York : Razorbill, [2020] | "Based on the stage musical
Alice by Heart." | Audience: Ages 12+ | Summary: Fifteen-year-old Alice confronts grief,
loss, and first love with the help of her favorite book, *Alice in Wonderland*, as she shelters
with other refugees in a London Tube station during World War II. Includes photographs
of underground shelters used in the war.
Identifiers: LCCN 2019036447 | ISBN 9780451478139 (hardcover) |
ISBN 9780451478153 (ebook)
Subjects: CYAC: Books and reading—Fiction. | Orphans—Fiction. | Friendship—Fiction.
| Subways—England—London—Fiction. | World War, 1939–1945—England—
London—Fiction. | Great Britain—History—George VI, 1936–1952—Fiction.
Classification: LCC PZ7.1.S2649 Ali 2020 | DDC [Fic]—dc23
LC record available at https://lccn.loc.gov/2019036447

Printed in the United States of America
1 3 5 7 9 10 8 6 4 2

Design by Maria Fazio
Text set in Carre Noir Std

For my Gemini women—Emily, Jessie, and Jill . . .

AUTHOR'S NOTE

—

For a long time, books were my everything. It was from books that I learned all the things that seemed worth knowing. In a world of parents, teachers, and friends who seemed uncomprehending, it was, always, only books who understood. Books like Edith Hamilton's *Mythology*, like *The Little Prince*, like *The Poems of Emily Dickinson*. Books, unearthed from our school library, which I'd pore over so continually, they came to read like diaries of my own feelings. And indeed it was only to those "diaries" that I could bring my truest self, could reveal my aspiration, could entrust my darkest secrets . . .

Alice by Heart is a book about a book. About the power of books to help us through the hardest times—to help us restore to our innermost selves what has been lost and found and lost again.

To be fair, I had a rather unusual childhood. Due to respiratory ailments, I was regularly shuffled from home to the hospital (my plastic-covered room at home coming in time to resemble the oxygen tent I revisited so often). In the meantime, I rarely went to school. Instead, my older sister became my teacher. Each day when she came home (the eternity of waiting till 3:00 p.m., each day, for her!), her lesson plan became my plan; and when she read to me, books *were* my world.

Thankfully, by age thirteen, I'd emerged from that plastic-covered room, only to suffer through high school like everyone else. But then, just after my twentieth birthday, a serious accident left me hospitalized again: strapped onto a Stryker frame, which resembled an ironing board, and which turned me from my back to my front every two hours, night and day. Banishing all film and TV, I taught myself ancient Greek, and read every novel I could fit my page-turner into. (Nineteenth-century British novels primarily—Jane Austen, the Brontës, George Eliot, Charles Dickens . . .) The truth is, when I look back at all that now, I tend to dwell less on my hospital bed and more on the time I spent in *The Iliad*.

It's telling about me, but despite how formative those years have been on the rest of my life, and of course on my writer life, it never occurred to me to write about them, or even about what all that reading had meant to me—until . . .

In the spring of 2006, in the first flush of *Spring Awakening*'s success, my esteemed theatrical agent proposed that, like others before us, Duncan Sheik and I try adapting *Alice's Adventures in Wonderland* into a piece of musical theater. Of course I knew and loved the book—and the subversive gust of childhood which breathes through it. I had read it to my own children. But given the singular form of its dreamlike narrative, I resisted. My strong instinct was not to turn the story into something it wasn't. Not to try to craft a

Wizard of Oz–like fable out of its hallucinatory sequence of "curiouser and curiouser" incidents. (For, what was the book really but a series of marvels coming and going—phantasmagoric visitations upon a charming, if cipher-like, young British girl? And all the other characters—those unbridled, id-like figures—seemed to appear only to disappear, leaving only the hint of a Cheshire grin.)

Hardly the stuff of a musical, I thought. Rather, what excited me was to dispense with a theatrical form altogether, and create a music-only project: a series of songs, with an accompanying set of music videos; each song an attempt to capture the magic-carpet ride of its particular chapter.

Then one night, something in me caved. My beloved friend, and sometime writing partner, Jessie Nelson, invited me to see a group of self-proclaimed high school "theater geeks" perform a concert of *Spring Awakening* songs. Watching that fresh-faced cast, just the age of our casts when we first began workshopping *Spring Awakening*, it struck me that we might craft a viable musical from *Alice* by centering it on the evergreen conundrum of how to leave childhood behind.

It was at that moment, nine years ago, that Jessie, Duncan, and I began work on our stage musical *Alice by Heart*. And it was Jessie—forever Jessie—who first encouraged me to incorporate elements from my life into our narrative—to draw on what classic works of literature had meant to the younger me, in the story of our own Alice and her beloved friend Alfred.

And so we began, and began again. At every subsequent stage of our musical's development, it's been Jessie who has inspired, conceived, coerced from Duncan and me, and crafted with us every beat of our musical story. It's also been Jessie who has repeatedly urged that we incorporate more and more of the original text into our script.

This afternoon, in a glacial New York January, as I sit beneath a tiny red work light, in the unlit house of our theater, rehearsals for the New York premiere of *Alice by Heart* are nearing a close; and the image of a treasured book—a book that's found and lost and found again—now permeates every aspect of the piece.

On a rather more golden afternoon, one Southern California day in the summer of 2016, the brave, believing producer of our musical called with a fresh bright idea. "Wouldn't it be cool," he pitched, "if you could write an *Alice* book? A picture book, maybe?"

Honestly, Kurt's suggestion left me cold. Why ever would I attempt to transmute our musical monster-in-progress back into a book? To try to craft from it some fresh convincing narrative? A book meant to sit on a shelf—or at least on *my* shelf—beside Carroll's classic, transgressive text?

And yet, as time passed, against all my better wisdom—against every good reason I could muster—as the ever-intrepid Kurt raised again and again the idea of "a picture book—or something like that," something about the idea began to stick. Something I heard in that inadvertent echo of Lewis Carroll's text . . .

At the beginning of *Alice's Adventures*, the impatient young heroine famously wonders, "What is the use of a book . . . without pictures or conversations?" Pictures for a book based on our *Alice* musical I could well imagine. Fresh illustrations, to be sure. But also there were so many heart-stopping photographs, which Jessie and I kept uncovering from our internet research: Londoners taking shelter in Tube stations during the Blitz of World War II.

So, pictures there were—plenty. But the idea that genuinely sank its teeth into me, that began to live within me, was of a book as a kind of "conversations." A new *Alice* book in conversation not only with the original *Alice* books but also with so many books I had loved—books which had gone through hard times with me. A testament to what those stories had meant to me.

From the beginning, I envisioned this book as a kind of mosaic. Or perhaps as my own sort of web—a stitching-together of all I wanted to keep myself from forgetting. After all, that was the brunt of our story, really. That in the midst of war and destruction, when all our dwellings can be turned to dust, there remains still what we carry with us. The memory of all we've felt or understood. Something like a book we've learned by heart.

My favorite novelist, Marcel Proust, writes unforgettably about what goes into the making of a good book. And he trenchantly observes that a novel is like a cemetery, where the names have been effaced from all the former loves who actually inspired it. For me, *this* book was to be a different sort of cemetery, one where the headstones represented those books I'd loved. And while the authors, like Proust, were not explicitly credited, still their names were not to be effaced, but meant to be legible for those who cared to look.

S.S.

January 2019
New York

CHAPTER I:

—

MY STORYBOOK ALICE

London, 1940
The Underground

ALICE was beginning to get very tired of lying on her flimsy cot—within this barrack full of cots, this musty world of makeshift hammocks strung between Underground tracks. But, here she was—*whoever* now she'd become—in the same old shape of her old familiar self—in a cold that kidnapped her from everything else. Everything but the drip, and the drip, and the drip of some thankfully still-unburst water main, high overhead. (Each drip like a word in some un-known tongue, reiterating how irritating Alice's presence was.)

Something—each drip seemed to insist—she had to do something. Couldn't merely lie in the gloom here forever, running the parched palm of her hand over the burlap strap that bound her cot to the world of these tracks. *No*, she could not just lie here. Not at age fifteen—without even a shred left of her irony! No—no more pretending. *Not now.* She had to go, had to know: how was Alfred? And so, she thrust herself up—*bye-bye, stuffy cot.*

Upright, she started—one step, on. For, despite how far it might feel, despite how disruptive to those other Tube-creatures her trundling by might be, it was only a few meters, she knew, between her cot and his quarantine.

But then, all at once—there *She* was. (As always She was.) That Red Cross Nurse. She, who was always and forever monitoring their every wayward move, policing every breath, suppressing every joy, their slightest wish. Keeping every one of them separate and alone, on separate, lonely beds, with only their broken thoughts to keep them company—those, and their bruised or wounded limbs.

Just hold still, Alice told herself. Soon, she knew, that dread Nurse would be gone—soon, moving on. Passing out blankets to those homeless souls of London. She, the would-be Soul of Charity, clothing and visiting, tending to the drippy-nosed and sickly. Any excuse, Alice surmised, to barge her way in. To bark out orders in that rasp-addled accent of the failed (or faux) aristocrat. Handing down her imperial decrees: "Chilly night, tonight!" Her petty commandments: "You naughty elf! Wipe your nose on someone else!" This High and Mighty Nurse, forever talking *down*, never *to*, them—and rarely to some *one* of them—rather, to the one *them*: this one, lowly, incurable Tube-station crew, who dared exist beyond Her whim. All their orphaned minds like perfect blanks, awaiting her beige-crayon words to color them in. "Do you have any idea, any of you, how many tired girls in floral prints labored to cut those blanket threads to regulation lengths?"

So the woman would bark—so she'd instruct—and then, on she'd go. With that prominent nose, protruding from those tweezed-out, painted-on brows, and that prehistoric raven claw of hair. Leading, of course, with her no less prominent chin. Declaring herself incapable of fatigue with her every wary step. Demanding room for herself, wherever she went.

"Dr. Butridge!" the Good Nurse rasped. But no word answered. "Lyman Butridge!" she bellowed, as if swallowing the sorry truth that she could not, even through such vocal grandeur, summon a somewhat grander man. No, only him. Him, her minion. In rank, the woman's superior; in fact, her subordinate.

"Doctor, this instant," she persisted.

"What?" he quacked.

Poor Butridge. Had he lost his hearing in the bombing? *Or something?* In any event, here he was, doddering on, on his interminable nightly rounds. *Really,* thought Alice, the man must have been here, must have done this, must have spewed out his spittle and prescriptions since the ducks got seasick riding Noah's ark.

"Doctor, come see," the Nurse yawped. But that Doctor doddered on. And on. Exasperating the would-be-unflappable Nurse: "Dr. Butridge! The *Hallam* boy."

"The *Hallam* boy"? *Meaning, Alfred?!* But why was she summoning the Doctor to him? *Why again?*

Duty done, the Nurse flapped the quarantine curtain shut and hastened on—to examine her next suspect.

Alice shuddered, snapping to attention. She had to see, had to know, what those medical thugs were planning. Couldn't they just let be? Why this infernal need to *Do?* After all, what was Alfred to them? Just another stop on the Good

3

Doctor's nightly perambulations. The truth was, for medical men, war meant business.

On, Alice. One step. No Nurse around now. And that Doctor? He's a Doctor, he won't even look up. Certainly, he won't look back.

Beyond all that, she thought, he wasn't a mean man, Butridge. No doubt, deep down, he wanted to help Alfred. She knew that. Still, let her step the slightest step toward her friend's quarantine, the man would virtually thrust himself before her—like some ministering Minotaur in this labyrinth of cots. (Or like that nonsense-spewing beast from her Alice-book, *Through the Looking-Glass*. The Jabberwock— but grown so wonky!) Splattering the dingy world with his doomdealing words, diagnosing this and that. Confusing this patient with that one. Prescribing that one this, and this one that. Spilling his Medical Commandments onto the platform like jacks. An incompetent, querulous quack, deciding what was what, and who got what—who was permitted to live, and who not. As if he bore the Clipboards of the Law in his ecstatic, twitching hands.

All the more reason she could not back down. Must not look back. And so, forward she inched. Vigilant. As, in his never-soiled medical robe, with those pleated short sleeves and that drooping button wagging from its mildewed thread, that antediluvian Doc clambered behind Alfred's curtain. Clipboards clattering.

On. One step Alice went—clocking the Doctor through the sheet. His lean, shoulders-wobbling silhouette.

"Hallam. Alfred Hallam," he mumbled. Mere words, she knew. Some mere name, soon to be ticked off from an indifferent, half-rusted clipboard. (One more Element, merely, on his official Periodic Table—another human life reduced to isotopes and neutrons.) But Alice leaned forward, intent. *Now what?* Not a breath. Not a thump on the chest. And then, some Roman-sounding phrase, like a verdict: "Superventrical . . ." something? "Tachycartoonia . . ."? Mere gibberish. As her most-beloved book, *Alice's Adventures in Wonderland*, would say: "*I* don't believe there's an atom of meaning in it!"

Ridiculous, really. Could he never just say, "Your friend will be all right, thank you." *No, always and forever, that Doctor used only the most inscrutable terminology.* As if only to show you how scary words really were. Why else did doctors and priests always speak in such a way, when they knew you knew no Latin? Why, except to show how much you needed them, Goodly Robed Men, to intercede with God or some Bacteria on your behalf.

Another step. *Very nearly there* she was. She could almost duck, could almost join that Dodo Doctor and Alfred, on the other side of that silvery curtain. *Maybe she could—maybe she just would.*

She set her hand on the curtain. Finally, there. But was she there, she wondered, while he remained unaware of her? Half-stooped already, she cast one last quick look about. And *there*, zooming toward her—from where?—that Nurse! God's one Cross Nurse. A Fascist if ever there was one (though of course she wasn't). A woman like a coil ever coiled, ever ready to spring.

"*Alice?!*"

Never had her name felt shorter or squatter or more spat out upon her. As if she were hardly worth the time it took to name her.

"*ALICE SPENCER!*"

This time, her full name. Which, of course, took that much longer. Which, of course, gave Alice such a tremor, till she felt herself frozen—in those two extra syllables of fear. Caught, with that snatch of sheet in her red hand. *Nothing left to lose, then, was there?* Better just to yank open that curtain—to be with him, a moment. All at once, she tugged the sheet . . .

And there he was. In one keen glance she could grasp it: his cheeks, his throat, so red and swollen; his eyes sunken in hollows; his forehead matted with sweat—as if he'd been feeding only on the fever now. *Poor Alfred!* The Doctor bent over him; some press-down stick, some beastly twig in that hypocritically Hippocratic hand, pressing down, down, down—as if he'd leverage Alfred from his tongue. Over him, that Doctor darkly murmured some pseudo-truth, some mumbo jumbo: "Due to Hypovolemia, and concomitant Hyperhydrosis—severe night sweats . . ."

Alfred trembled as her eyes passed over his. Over his lips, his strained neck, throbbing. Breathing. *Oh, touch me, sad eyes. Soft eyes. See me, Alfred.*

Through the fringe of dark fluttering lashes, he saw her— he must have! He tried to utter something—"*Alice*"?—but his bloodshot blue eyes washed full of tears, then fluttered shut again. As if someone had just closed the blinds on her view of the sea . . .

"Yes," she whispered. "Yes, still here. I'm here."

And with that, a stab of rage came ripping through the curtain. Stout rutted hands grabbing, thrashing her. Gripping and suffocating her. *"Let me go!"* Alice shrieked. "He needs me." But, those barbed-wire arms clenched tighter, piercing their cold thorns into Alice's flesh, as that Monster Nurse lugged the girl like a sack of guts toward her cot.

"Please!" Alice protested. "You're hurting me."

"No. *You* are hurting you. I am merely moving through."

So, is this what Nurses do? Keep everyone apart, for fear their mental flu will spread? As if words and thoughts and looks were somehow germs?

"And button up that blousy, Mousey," the Red Cross Nurse groused.

Ouch! If only she were in Wonderland now, Alice thought, she could fall—flat on her fat Alice-face—like one of those shamefaced Playing Cards, humiliated by the Queen of Hearts. Not being there, but here, within this grimy Tube station, she merely lowered her *eyes* and took in her guilty blouse again. Yes sure, it bulged—a bit. *But it had unbuttoned itself, it had!*

"Button it," that dour Nurse pronounced. Then, with a brusque peremptory shove, she dumped Alice onto her deadly cot.

"Back! To! Your! Bed!"

CHAPTER II:

—

SO MANY GUTTERING CANDLES

NIGHT Nine, was it already, she'd been here? That she'd bunched herself up and tossed herself about and just generally lain here? Tossing and tossling not only her head, but also her (adjacent) shoulders and neck. Trying to scrunch herself into some spot, in this god-awful cot, that felt like sleep.

Nine nights, yes. All of them crowding together, as only nights can. All of those nights settling in beside her, like ghosts cuddling in, on the cold platform with her, breathing this thick-with-breath air. All of those ghost nights, restless, sleepless, fidgeting, as she was, beneath the drip, the relentless drip.

Sleep, Alice, sleep—it will all seem truer, if stranger, after a sleep. Or so she told herself, this less-familiar self, while she struggled to yawn out her arms without battering into some neighboring cot. Failing at that, she gathered them back, ignoring the still-tender burn spots along her forearms and chest, doing her best still to resist the itch of her raw, scraped knees. Better, she knew, not to breathe a word about them (the last thing she needed was someone doctoring *her*).

And what good was Mercurochrome, anyway? Better to try not to fret. Better just to lie here in silence, dodging all these thoughts (these thoughts like wasps in mid-August, issuing in endless hissing swarms, stinging, assailing her, louder and louder, the more she kept trying to swat them away). Better to breathe, to lie still and keep trying, *trying*, pretending to sleep (what *they* call sleep) (they who were *truly* asleep). When all she wanted, really, was to escape from this shadowy Underworld, from this imbecile Tube-station hell, to lie in her warm room again—her room, as it once had been—before the wailing cries of drones, before the fearful humming from her anxious windowpanes—to lie, warm as warm, in her old familiar sheets again, and read.

Good God, just to forget herself and read!

But where were they—her bed, her soft Witney blanket, her so-long-slept-on, rose-embroidered sheets? All the lovely bed-lamp world she'd known? The "me" she'd been? Forever smelling of lemon and lavender soap. The *me* she'd simply taken for granted she would always be. Forever immersed in her book or out on the lawn, enacting whole chapters with Alfred—departing to Wonderland with him; chattering with the Magpie; grousing with the Gryphon; bantering with the Mad Hatter and the March Hare while sipping their own mad, imaginary tea. But now—where was all that now? Their homes, their common garden? Her mother, sister—Papa, too, of course. Poor Papa!—*where were they?*

Gone. All gone. As if, in some few months, the world had grown so old in death. So old in bombs. In dark-bright fires screaming from the sky, cracking the heavens across, leaving them gaping, night after night—Death in his black leather jacket, shaking London from her streets. And with his feckless gloved hand, ripping, clawing the heart out of Bromley; battering out every window, each shopfront, mowing down flats, making a smoky O of her broad, gabled school.

And it wasn't just Bromley, of course. Out there, right now, Alice knew, beyond this trembling Underground, the entire city, her proud lovely city, had been brought in rubble to its knees. Strong, unstoppable, eternal London—so many people unbowed, and yet so many undone, now bending, weeping. *Can't someone cry stop? How can this be?*

And yet, for all that had been lost, *all* was not lost. And never would be lost. So much still there. It *must* be still. Her loved London Bridge. Still standing. Thankfully. Luminous a moment, from the passing beams of searchlights; then, soon obscured again. A phantom bridge, but no less solid; as it lifted the night, unglimpsed, within its arms. And there, there must be still, some score of gas-masked toddlers skipping rope on heaps of earth, on someone's bedroom turned to rubbled street. There, a sorry, gazeless girl with her blinking-eyed doll, both of them staring at nothing, merely perched on a pile of debris; the Thames still flowing, running softly, on. There, a radiant young bride walking through broken streets, with her glorious satin train in her daintier hand.

And . . . *there*, from that above-earth, another siren. Up there, no doubt, with the sound, every dog would run bounding home, as those Messerschmitts went screaming, went crying, dropping their shells from some surreal rosy sky. The crowds—you could almost hear them, scattering—running, taking cover under the Blackfriars Bridge—so many! Huddling beneath the broken altar of St. Paul's Cathedral. Watching as their lives, their homes, their loved ones all went up in flames.

And here? Down here? In this cavernous, clammy old tunnel? In this querulous cell, with its dirtywhite walls. (Where some lost soul seemed embalmed in every last tile.) Only those endless, cylindrical walls—if walls they could be called—looming round and above, speechless and cold. Below, just there, up and down those implacable stairs, only the bundled-up sleepers: fellow pilgrims in this make-do shelter, sojourners of the night, who could find no room on the congested platform. Stair-dwelling semi-regulars they were; smelling of infection and disinfectant (which, admittedly, she did, too) and camphor and urine; breathing themselves, the smells of all the London dead, while resting their heads (and the occasional attaché case) on those same stairs. And, below them? A space hardly larger, if longer, than her room (her old, lost room, where she'd been free to read, and think, and just generally be as miserable as she pleased). But here: only this flat concrete platform, strung with unsleeping cots—a landscape of open eyes, looking out on those colder steel tracks.

How, she wondered, how had she ever managed to find herself here? To settle Alfred here—in this ward of ailing and wounded youth. After all those fiery nights. A conflagration of September nights, like a blank in nature and time. Nights when she'd run like a stray dog, skulking about the streets, hiding with Alfred. Ducking the bombs, jumping gutters, until he had stumbled—had fallen—*Stop! Alfred!*—caught

in an avalanche of brick. In a whirlwind of gravel and mortar. No fireman near, no tin-helmeted warden to help him,
scarcely conscious, to his feet, to lead him through those
blighted streets. No. On, alone, she'd led him. Through heaps
of ruin, toward an ashen queue—no end to it, the children,
with dust-covered suitcases, the women and men, laden with
bags and blankets, like some wandering tribe in captivity, desperate to find shelter in this Tube station. No one willing
to risk their spot in line to help *them* down—him, wounded
and limping—down those cramped, crowded stairs. Not one
sleeper rising, not one waking to aid them. Too accustomed
they all were, by now, to cries through the night. To wounded
bodies scuffling by. Like so many contorted limbs of trees and
scattered leaves, those abject sleepers lay bestrewn on those
stairs, both guarding and blocking the way to this Underworld
realm. To this below-world, this makeshift shelter, where so
many had settled, where they still huddled: evacuees, as she
was, of their city at siege. Their hearts resigned to a state of
sempiternal sleep. Like so many guttering, indignant candles,
refusing to give up their flames.

So, too, Alfred and she now huddled. Fellow squatters on
the common concrete. *Yes.*

With some touch of envy perhaps, Alice looked again at
all those separate sleepers, finding themselves within the one
sleep. *That must be peace.* For, here *she* was, whoever now she
was—asleep but not asleep. In this hole that was her sleepless mind. Down this hole, upon a platform, which, unlike
those somnolent stairs, was filled with only the most rowdy,
waking crowd: all these strange sad displaced children, to say

nothing of that hopeless, opium-smoking older lad, and those soldiers—that one soldier, wounded, with artillery fragments littered through him. And there, her dearest dear, her injured friend, her Alfred. Roped off, curtained apart, alone with the alone.

So unfair. Disgraceful, really. There, they kept him, so rigidly kept him, so far from her—bandaged and iodined, laid out on a sort of stretcher, continually inspected and tended, behind those makeshift hospital curtains. And she, consigned to this dismal, distant cot. Compelled to lie, no longer beside him. To see and know him there, so many—five? six?—cots away, and in quarantine! To what end? For how long? *Her Alfred!*

Here. Upon the chill, damp platform of some shadow-riddled station, her sole friend, her loved friend, coughing up blood and moaning, ailing. *Alfred!* Here, where once they'd ridden the train to school.

CHAPTER III:

—

ANOTHER ACTUAL ALICE

"*O*H dear! Oh dear! I'm late!" *he'd so grandiloquently exclaimed. The five-year-old Alfred, yanking his moonfaced watch from his plaid-ish pocket. Running past, then dashing back, then past and back again, until Alice had nearly gone racing after him . . .*

Oh dear, thought Alice again now, crowded into this Tube-station realm, all these years after, remembering . . . Invoking for herself again those well-worn words of her treasured *Adventures in Wonderland* book: "Curiouser and curiouser!" Sometimes it struck her (though, still, she'd deny it to Mum), just how much of herself she had given, and still would so willingly give, to that book. Their book. All those pages, those luminous sentences, reread so often, they'd grown clearer than her own thoughts . . . Sometimes indeed, it seemed, those Wonderland words were the whole of her world, the sole place she found her truly strange self. She, who so often was two—both the doer and the looker-on— could become, there, so solidly one.

Alone on her usual bench, beneath that gnarled black mulberry, full of the near-illicit joy and fear prompted by all those storied scenes, she'd pore over page after page (in the classic crimson volume Alfred had given her), retrieving all the reveries she'd known there, remembering, too, all the accidental sights and smells, the tics of life surrounding her on all those gorgeous stolen afternoons. That is, until some Banal Disrupter would come crying, exasperatingly enough: "Dinner!" or "Come, Alice—tennis!" Dragging her back to that dreary land, that actual lawn, in the actual, colossal, stifling sun, that primitive country of Philistine family and cavemen friends, who dwelled outside her mind—and so, outside her book.

And of course it was also that book that had served, from their earliest childhood, as her chief recreation, her source of the purest joy with Alfred. Indeed, it was Alfred who'd first told her of Wonderland, beneath that ageless white afternoon sky, in the common garden that united their houses (that broad, tree-lined, and rarely mown lawn, which bound all the homes of their street with the lane of houses just behind). There it was she'd first seen him, beneath the pale May blossoms of a wild cherry tree. Him, already so him. Already playing the White Rabbit, both chasing after and bolting from his own shadow. Scattering pigeons from the neighboring brick path, rattling on, to the calm indifferent daisies and the still-green daffodils, as he thumped and skipped and jumped, his head half-flung back—in the likeness of a bounding hare!

"Dear dear! So much ado! Adieu, adieu! I'm late, so late, so late!"

"For what?" she'd naively called after. Never having heard of such an anxious, articulate (and perhaps bilingual) Rabbit.

"The Queen, the Queen!" he'd blazoned back. "She'll have my head! She will, you know? I must be there, beside her royal side, to play her Herald at the Trial!"

And off he'd dashed again. Past that mossy toolshed, that leaf-strewn rookery fountain, which he seemed to tag, in passing, with some giddy sense of Wonderland . . .

How lost she'd stood—and puzzled. And yet, rapt in wonder. All the more so, as the boy remained so unselfconscious, carrying on with utter aplomb. As if it were thoroughly ordinary to be thumping about, wriggling pretend-paws like mad castanets, practically yanking pretend-whiskers out, in the guise of a character from a storybook. How warmly, how simply he'd invited her in—to join that Rabbit-him in Wonderland. And then, his unutterable joy! His disbelieving sense of all it meant to be *him*, now that he'd welcomed an actual *Alice* in!

"Why, it's positively everything," he proclaimed, panting for breath. The spring air surrounding, seeming so enamored with him.

How soon thereafter—that same day, was it? or one later?—he'd allowed her the secretest peek at his most treasured treasure. His paperbound, pocket edition of *Alice's Adventures in Wonderland.*

"Just imagine, Alice," he'd announced, his face so proud, "the book was written for another actual Alice. Alice Liddell. Actually."

"Another actual Alice?" she'd teased.

"Absolutely. My Dad told me. It's all from stories this mad maths professor told her—over the course of one summer afternoon, as he rowed her and her sisters down the Oxford river . . ."

How he'd grinned! As if he'd just become part of the book's royal lineage, because he, too, was letting an actual Alice in.

How long they marveled over each illustration. How eagerly he read out his most favorite passages, adopting a wild antic voice and the most definitive gesture for each of those most particular characters. (Boldly displaying, in the meantime, the full, virtuosic range of his vocal register.) Until it seemed the book had been written for his voice (much as music may be written for a particular singer). Thus was the book granted its deepest wish only in being read aloud by him.

"*The Caterpillar,*" Alfred instructed, "*being the Caterpillar, was, is, and always will be first to speak.*"

"*I see.*"

"*Indeed.*"

And so, adopting the Caterpillar's dreamsmoky catch in the throat, he addressed her as the Storybook Her: "*Just what size, Alice, do you truly wish to be?*"

"*Oh,*" she hastily replied (doing her best to follow the script), "*I'm not particular as to which size.*"

"*Or not particularly?*" he extemporized dryly.

"*It's just that one doesn't like changing so often, you know.*"

"*I* don't *know,*" that Caterpillar-Alfred concluded, most conclusively.

Naturally. Given how "sacred" the text, and how much care he'd already invested in performing so punctiliously each of its characters, it took some few days for Alice's full initiation. And yet, from that very first day, she was entrusted with the sublime, with the role of a lifetime. She was starring as Alice! (While coached on her lines, she was also encouraged to improvise—but only so long as she remained, as he did, within each scene's arc and classic story line.) In the meanwhile, he explained delightedly, he'd be playing every other role. The King and Queen of Hearts, the Dodo, the Mad Hatter, the Dormouse, and the Mock Turtle. And, while she balked initially, before the end of that lazy blue day, she couldn't imagine anyone, ever, doing them better.

For Alfred so completely disappeared into each tic, into each transmuting timber of each distinctive character, it was less like watching a display of his dramatic artistry and more like looking through some series of Wonderland windows into his unchanging soul.

And so it began. A summer of afternoons. And two summers thereafter. The intervening autumns and winters, too; all day, every day, always late afternoon. The two of them, in those frostier seasons, perched in his sitting room. Reading aloud, leaping up, acting out all those scenes, reveling in all those harlequin characters. Falling down, down the hole, together, to such mad adventures.

So it began; so it went. So they lived—summer to summer, battening themselves for the pageant of winter. Their shadows aglow on the wall by his fireside, like coconspirators, racing as they raced their Caucus Race, dancing as they danced their Lobster Dance. She, forever chasing and chasing her brilliant White Rabbit, without ever truly admitting (to herself or him) how much she longed to hold on.

But all that, so suddenly changed. All that, already changed—long before the air-raid warnings. More, well more, than a year before the Nazi incendiaries began burning holes in the sky, leaving whole villages in flames . . . All so irrevocably changed, on that soft-dying day, when the stark pain first raked Alfred's chest; when that racking cough, like some scrawling wind, cast its dark signature over him; his lifted arms, feverish, battering back—

"Are you all right, Alfred?"

Overcome, coughing so loudly, so long—he nearly lost consciousness.

"Are you?!"

Trembling, he fell—fell for real—coughing still. Till, it seemed, his breathing had stopped.

"Mrs. Hallam—it's Alfred!"

Immediately, the housekeeper, Mrs. Austerlitz, bounding in—Alfred's brother, next. Finally, his near-frantic Mum, dropping to her knees, trying to breathe her heart into his.

"Alfred, darling—it's Mummy. Talk to me!"

And still he did not, would not talk. Would not look up. As if some negative integer of him kept canceling him out, annulling him.

And yet—Alice knew—he still was, he must be still, all that he was.

All at once, that lunkhead brother of his lifting him—so carelessly. Alfred's feet dangling so lifelessly!

"But where are you—"

"To hospital," his Mum briskly instructed. Her stacked-square heels following the hoisted Alfred across the wine-dark carpet.

"I'm going, too," determined Alice.

20

"No no, darling." Without even a rearward glance: "Mrs. Austerlitz, ring her Mum."

"No—please—Mrs. Hallam!"

That terrible slow door shut. Locked shut. She hurled herself senselessly against it.

"Alfred!"

No one there. Not a sound returned. She tried calling, screaming, pleading. Not a sound.

She tried knocking banging pounding. No one.

It echoed within her, haunting her: "There's no sort of use in knocking," as their book said. (A thing Alfred, playing the Frog-Footman, had so often said . . .)

Gonegonegone.

There she stood. No one there. For how long? Just stood and stood.

Shuddering, wary. Unsure how even to move. Unsure that there she even was, that any of this was—she'd stood. Merely stood. Beside that senseless slate fireplace, suppressing some weird sense that she'd always been waiting for this, had always dimly known she'd be left by this slate, alone as it. (This slate, which seemed to shrug, "So it goes," as though it shared her sense of abandonment.)

But she was, she remained, alone. All those months, him in hospital. The winter and spring of his illness. She, never allowed to go visit. Never allowed to be near him. She, at school, or shut in her room—unable to bring herself to open their book. She, seated stiffly at dinner, receiving false-cheer talking-tos from Mum: all these mad gabs about enlarging her world (as if anyone else had half-nearly so large a world), about making new friends (as if that would help, to be staring in the face of some healthy someone *else*).

Till finally, that too-tardy July, months after he'd come home again, and only after the most rigorous, soul-sickening talks with his Nurse and Mum, she was once again let in his room. How washed-out, how emaciated, he'd looked; and yet, so demonstrably him. How glad he'd been to take her hand again, his eyes mirroring hers, welling with tears.

And how many more months from then . . . ? Till every day had become afternoon once more. He, as she'd sit with him, always so ready to leap up and act out each chapter. To sing out—in full-throated ease—their Mock Turtle song. To wave, wave his flappers—or what were they, *forepaws?*—in time to that boisterous "Lobster Quadrille." She, always struggling to coax and cajole him just to lie still, to let her read to him.

So it was, so it went—they, so themselves again—till the terrible rain of night-fire began—the bullets tearing holes in the sky, night after night, all the desecrated stars falling through—till that harrowing night, that abysmal gap in time, when both of their houses were hit, and she went running prowling searching howling . . . till she found him, wounded, led him through those desolated streets, and settled them, finally, down here. She, no longer by his side, but still holding on, making him her whole mind.

She had to. More now than ever, she knew. He had no one but her now. No one else to look after him. No one who knew him. Up she sat again, and peered round. Nothing she could see of him but the dimly shimmering curtain surrounding him.

CHAPTER IV:

—

ON SUCH A NIGHT AS THIS

ONLY a month, a little month ago, was it? On a night like this, on such an autumn night as this, I sat beside you, Mummy. In our sitting room, behind the blackout curtains. You, beside the heater, counting shillings—every shilling meant another egg, you said. "Black market eggs, is that our way? It isn't, Alice. Thank God, your Papa's been spared the seeing it. But what's a body to do, since the rations began? Not an egg—not an orange—to split between your sister and you. And say we get hold of one, who can enjoy it? Knowing how we got our guilty fists around it. Honestly, love, these days, we've forgotten how to feel the joy of anything . . ."

At your knees beside you, Mummy—all that gravy-browning painted up your legs, since now there were no stockings . . . I sat watching you not watching . . . from your corner of the sofa, from your throne of paisley cushion—with the ever-fraying tassels. You were reading T. E. Lawrence, or no longer. Rather, setting him aside, those smudged old vellum pages open by the window, while you retrieved your darning. "Tell me, Alice," you said, "how is Alfred? Was this another good day?"

Can we not, not—just please not? Can't you hum me something, Mummy?

"Alice?"

"Yes, it was a wonderful day. They are all of them, such wonderful days."

"Oh"—*you would not smile*—"I hope so, darling."

Can't you please not? Can't you just lean in and say again: "Mr. Churchill? Well, he's always Mr. Churchill. I've never seen a man so much himself, I tell you." *Tell me. Tell me that, Mum.*

"You are spending every day again there, Alice. It was one thing when you were seven—or even ten. But you're older now, love. A boy's a boy."

Excuse me?

"I don't need that look, thank you," *on you went, Mum.* "My main point is: that boy's remained your only friend."

"He isn't. He never has been. And, what if he is? Why shouldn't I spend every day with him?"

"What happens if he goes away again?"

"To hospital? He won't. He's better. Everyone, they all agree."

"Pray God, he is—and will be. It's you that I'm concerned about."

"For what, Mum? What can happen? Nothing, nothing bad can happen. Nothing will. Not again. Not to him or me."

"There's a war on, Alice."

Yes. No. No more, please. Just sit with me, and hold me. Let me set my head against you once again, our room suffused with you again. Not like before the war, I know—you in your gorgeous French perfume—but like on all our summer evenings,

*you in your lovely Yardley water. All that lavender that was
you, as you'd hold and rock me near. Come, hold me. Tell me
once again, Mum: "Alice, when this blackout ends, we'll see our
evening star again—our ancient star, in that most ancient sky.
Our British sky. And that star will be our inner light, I tell you.
Like the word of God that willed it and does still."*

"Back to your bed," that dread Nurse had commanded. As
if those were the wizardwords, and her merely *saying* them
would somehow resolve the witless mystery of everything.
Would wipe some nursical sponge over a world in tears.

But how? How could Alice just be back to bed? When he,
her friend, might be wondering where she was. The truth was,
she could *feel* he was, despite the fact he might be resting—
and although he might need her now less than rest.

"Thinking of him still, Miss Drooping Head?"

"Him? No. Absolutely," Alice answered. Without a clue,
really, whom she was answering.

Whooo? Seeing without feeling, she peered about, scanning the dim ambiguous crowd. (Once again, with the dismal, dizzying sense that everywhere she looked boiled down
to nowhere in particular.) Till, *there*, she spotted her listener
across and above the track—beside the glowing orb of that
cracked Tube-station clock—that street-tough Tabatha. Poised
in her perch on high, her long, unbandaged legs sometimes
dangling from that cavernous nook, sometimes disappearing with her into that wide toothless chink in the tile. There,
where the mosaic mold of the ceiling had split its mortised

25

seams and crumbled away. She who, like Alice's kitty, had accustomed herself more to the house (here, the tunnel) than to the people living in it.

But how ever in the world, Alice wondered, had that unearthly girl discerned the slant and droop of her head? From such a distance—and with *her* eyes all bandaged to boot? That Tabatha—always so aloof, maintaining that comfy-kitty distance from those "cracked-egg souls" (as she called them) on the platform. So accustomed to distance in general, and to that perch in particular, it seemed like she, so early abandoned, so long an orphan, had probably been living there for years.

Though Tabatha's trek—as she'd detailed it to Alice—had not been so simple as that. Consigned as she'd been, reassigned as she'd been, from one orphan-asylum to another. From that Home of Poor and Abandoned Children (where the ultimate lesson had been that she herself was to blame for being born poor and alone) to the East London Orphan Asylum, where blank-faced teens sat on long blank pews. ("All of us," she'd said, "in uniform. To teach us, I suppose, that we, too, were uniform.")

From those pews she'd gone on, to the care of two caretaker-women in Devon, where a febrile young orphaned girl had clung to her like a sister. Had attempted to spend every moment with her. And then, when Tabatha broke free, had simply insisted on running off with her. And she had. Such a hallowed sort of soul-time those two had spent, together in London. Haunting the streets, crouching nights under bridges. Finding themselves so serenely indifferent—like the

moon balanced over them—peering out on the ruddy pande-
monium of anti-aircraft fire.

Telling themselves such truths, and such patent untruths,
night after solitary night; till that "scraggly ginger of a thing"
had been lost in a sudden air raid—only a single tree left,
where once Milton Court had been. There the poor girl lay,
windpipe fractured, suffocated. Her fingers sunk limp into
the dust heap beside.

So, Tabatha had found her way here, to this shelter below-
ground. Had perched in that crack in the tile—on her own
again. Cowled about that cracked and opalescent clock, as if
it were her truest mirror.

And yet. No matter how remote she might seem—
crouched on her high ceremonial perch—never did she
refrain from making pithy observations. Just as now (like
some local, nocturnal oracle), through that preternatural grin:

"So, Alice. *Not* thinking of him?"

"Not thinking. Period," rejoined Alice, lifting her chin in
defiance. "And certainly not about him." With a studied "I'll
show you" on her face, she pulled back her shoulders, careful
not to droop one bit or let her pooling eyes confess.

"But"—submitted Tabatha—"aren't we always thinking
about precisely what we're *not* thinking about?"

"Certainly not."

"All right, then," Tab concluded. Threatening, with a pout,
to remove herself from such petulant premises.

Arrgh. *But no arguing it.* "*One* moment. *Please!*" Alice
called after. Then, dropping her sorry grey gaze, gave in: "If I

could only be near him again, could merely sit and watch him . . . I'd be good, so good, at keeping quiet."

"Ah yes. You would be good at *that*," hummed Tabatha slyly. "You, so long familiar with the quiet . . ."

And how did she know that? The truth was, even before all this, Alice could sit so long, so silent, she sometimes could lose track of where she ended and where the evening quietude began.

"Besides," Alice hazarded, "I know well, from my kitty, how to let a body sleep."

"While you dream on about him?" Tabatha hazarded back. Her legs folding, disappearing into that shadow-cranny with her.

"Stop. It isn't that," Alice called after. Then considered, "To watch someone asleep, it's more like . . . Like accepting that you're never with them, really—not in that other room inside their head."

"Ack, ack! Anti-aircraft! Hear that?" someone cried out, elbowing Alice. "Shall we have a flyboy row, then? Shall we?"

Who, now? Who else but Harold Pudding—the inimitable Pudding—that poor, traumatized soldier. He, a gangly seventeen, who was meant to be lodged on the cot to her left, except that he rarely could sit still long enough. No, he was always jerking about, jolted about—just as now—as if in some wild, head-wounded flight from the pain. With some desperate message to impart but no word, no way to say it.

"Pudding. Harold Pudding," Dr. Butridge decreed, flailing at laying a hand on the lad. "Hypnagogic Hallucinations—i.e., ungodly visions, obscuring that last fraying state before sleep—due to Subdural Hematoma, Cerebral Edema . . ."

"Dr. Butridge, please!" the Nurse bawled balefully.

There, hear them? All of them. All one merry muddle. Soldier. Doctor. Nurse. Each with their own voice, and yet each dissolved into one voice. Like they were the voice of night, mused Alice. The one-voiced night, which murmurs on, below the continual cries of the sirens: *No, Alice, nothing we articulate can ever bring relief from all the pain.*

But enough of that, Alice thought, and cast her glance back to that chink, hollowed out of the tile high above. Namely, Tabatha's throne. Now, not a hint of a grin, nothing but shadow—and cobweb—there. While *here,* just before her, came Private Harold Pudding again, clambering out from under some other cot, like a golden Lab surfacing from a pond, shivering off scores of melancholy water drops. "Shall we have a riddle? A roomy riddle—with no answer? Shall we?"

Had he plucked that riddle—that unanswerable riddle— from her precious book of Wonderland? And, having learned the riddle, had he somehow *turned to* riddle? Hoping, praying, that by asking (by becoming he-who-asked-it), he might find that (like most askers) he already knew the answer?

Or perhaps there was no answer. For surely, the real riddle was: why was it he—a simple northern lad, who'd signed up, who'd enlisted, who'd been so proud to be an infantryman— why was he the one who'd ducked the bomb but split his skull, and yet who, unlike his mate Freddie, was still here? And why, being here, could he not be still, not sit still? Not stop himself from jitter-jumping, as-as-asking: "Shall we have some tea? Tea for two. For him and me—with me. Say, shall we?"

Such a kind soul, really. And how, Alice asked herself, how and when, had Harold learned to do those glorious drawings, those elegiac sketches on his sketchpad? And why was he always trilling those riddles? And had he not been split, would he still be asking?

Barely could Alice ask, let alone answer, herself on the matter, when Harold dove, all at once, as if under a bunk. Shivering, suddenly sweating and trembling, clamping his palms firmly over his ears. Crying out, to his lost comrade, "Duck! Duck, Freddie! Quick!"

Oh no. Not again!

Settled contentedly upon that same cot (just to the right of Alice's cot), lost in some content-free thought, sat the ash-and-dusty Angus Wilkins (*how could anyone—Angus or not—accumulate such ash, so much dust, so young?*). Breathing forth a surreptitious, blue opium smoke-stream (terribly debonairly, from his antique ivory pipe); not bothered a bit, not a whit, by the threat of that pipe being taken from him, nor by the bellowing soldier below him. Bemusedly, he fixed his realm-less eyes on Alice. "Harold Pudding, hmm. Loses his wits on the front, then comes home to the Blitz."

"Misplaced wits!" Dr. Butridge abruptly declared, some unswallowable lump arising in his throat, as he went battering, clipboards clattering, past. Just as abruptly, he paused, and pivoting, seized hold of Angus's wizened wrist. Hearing again there something low-pulsed and familiar: "Wilkins."

"Him I am, ma'am," Angus Wilkins quipped, his vision seemingly as blurred as his speech was slurred. "Wilkins, yes. Formerly the punter teen in Leeds, dreamin' all the usual dreams. Believin', I did, that once in the Royal Air Force, life would be so jolly good. Such adventures I'd have, yeah? No longer pitchin' in weekends cleanin' litter boxes in my Dad's pet shop. No, I'd be risin' high. In some single-seat Spitfire—or highfalutin Hurricane—whirlin' through the bloomin' blue. Never dreamed I'd be spendin' these raids wipin' windows, cleanin' tires—till I'd barely see the inside of a plane. Meanwhile, spendin' my nights in some bloody Tube."

O-o-o-o, from his resinous mouth, toward Alice's ear, nose, and throat, the wolfish Angus Wilkins let those smoke rings bluely go. Each one breasting the air bravely, a moment, then smaller and smaller, one after the other, as if their successive diminishment mirrored the tale of his own disillusionment.

But Butridge, of course, saw nothing, knew nothing of that. Indeed, he barely bothered with that human instrument in front of him, too intent on diagnosing it: "Opioid Dependence in the Nucleus Accumbens—namely, that grey, pre-optic area in the frontal lobe . . ."

It's like he talks in riddles, really! Alice barely had time to observe, when . . . seeing Butridge tarry, the Red Cross Nurse erupted: "*Dr. Butridge!* Come, this moment! Listen to the hacking of the Hallam boy! We must move him immediately."

Move him? Why? Because he'd taken a fall? Had cut himself, had punctured his rib in a flurry of mortar and brick?

Because he'd been coughing and pale, his same old miserable illness, ever since? *Ridiculous!* Alice leapt unsteadily to her feet: "Who? Alfred? No!"

But as she lurched forward, to lodge an objection, that militant Nurse pressed on, with dark conviction: "Summon the Orderlies. Send that child to the end of the line."

In a fury, in a frenzy, Alice started toward the quarantine drapery. But the goodly Doctor had preceded her. And already had his goodly nose down Alfred's throat: "Tonsillar Pseudomembrane—a viscous yellowish coating over the throat, you see?—consisting of coagulated Fibrim—"

"What does that mean?" Alice demanded.

"Mean? What it says it means. With complications due to Corynebacterium Diphtheriae—*meaning*, the pathogen transporting Diptheria—and Mycobacterium Tuberculosis—"

"*Which* means," the Nurse spewed, with a pitchfork glance at Alice, "catch that cough, he'll be your death."

"Alfred?! Never. No. Please don't move him. He's my friend. He's always been. My dearest friend."

Winding a flick of unruly fringe behind an imperious ear, Nurse Cross took her cue from Stalin then: "Today he is your dearest friend; tomorrow, a statistic."

"Don't listen to them, Alfred," cried Alice—toward his quarantine. "I'll read to you."

"Alice Spencer, get it through your head. Thirty-seven nights straight of bombs—and this is just the overture."

With a heinous snap of her heathen fingers, that Nurse barked: "Ward D!"

"Ward D"?! The words alone, so cold. Alice knew what they meant: that dire ward where the wounded went. What they called the "good-as-dead." Children whom you never saw again . . . But Alfred was not, and never would he be one of those. Not for Ward D.

No no no no. "He'll be safe down here. With me. He'll get better near me," Alice declared.

"Back! To! Your! Bed!"

And with that, that Nurse—no, not just her—no, the entire eighty years of Red Cross Nurses, dressing all the wounds of all the world—seized hold of Alice and brazenly hauled her across the insomniac platform, till the girl tripped, near-toppled, but finally broke free. And arighted herself. Herself, once more!

And with that, and a splat, upon the floor beside her cot, down down down our Alice went.

Down down down. Yes—just like in her treasured book. Where her lovely Storybook Alice fell *down down down* the hole to Wonderland. Or so Alice thought, steadying her forearms on that gloating floor, resting her head against that callous cot.

But in the storybook, Alice remembered, her lovely Story Alice fell, and fell so slowly, *she* had time to ask: Would her fall never end? *She*, she tumbled past such child things—cupboards, maps, and empty jars of marmalade. And she played such sweet-sad word games ("Do cats eat bats? . . . Do bats eat cats?") as she fell fell fell right past. Asking herself, wonderingly, that sweet Story Alice: Did it matter with a question, how she asked it, if either way she asked she couldn't answer?

She, that ever-lovely Story Alice, with her daisy chains and sweet White Rabbit, how could she know what it was, what it had been, to wake up from the sleep of life and find yourself within some dream of death? To find your door blown off, embedded halfway up the stairs; your bedroom crumbling about you, the rubble blasting down. Could *she* have stood, stood fast somehow, teetering, trembling, but not falling? Could she have stood and seen—yes, *seen*—her sister's scream? As lovely lovely Cathy fell, bleeding, screaming, fallfallfalling, sprawled and crying, down that staircase, flailing in a gulf of crumbling banister and raging black-fire ceiling beams.

Run! Alice had. She'd run straight to her sister. *Catherine!* Had grabbed her hand—still pulsing hand—*hold on!* Till that strong-arm man, that fireman, had heaved her off, had dragged her screaming into night. No air, no sky left in the sky. Cathy carried out, her arms charred, her chest all sunken and awry. Some rescue worker thrusting her into an ambulance, one in a line of waiting ambulances—each with its war-widow, volunteer driver—as Alice wailed *Noooooooo*, and Mum gone crawling after. Screaming, crying—as if from some earthquake life. Grabbing for Alice: "Darling, quick!" But Alice . . . could not. Could not. She'd just . . . stood, silent, mouth wide open. As if some tree (which lacked the intelligence of trees) had begun growing, spreading from its rough trunk into branches straining from her—no talk, just brittle

37

barren leaves. Not a word she had to offer. Not to Catherine, not to Mum; not to them she lovedshelovedsheloved. Not while down through her tongue, those dark roots dug. Small wonder, she could not budge. Could not *see* them, really. Only darkly, through some inner, annihilating mirror: Mummy crying, "Alice, please! This minute!" But she could not. *God my God, so sorry, Mum.* (Papa, had he still been with them, he would have understood. *She knew.*) She just . . . she had to run. From them. To hurtle herself through this Nowhereland. Past the children covered in blood, the dogs lying helpless or stiff, the mothers, bandaged, wailing, covered in dust. Had to run from all that—on, past that broken bank of blurred neighbor faces, all their features erased from them.

She had to rush. Had to run. Even as policemen cordoned off lawns and piles of loose brick and shattered streetlamps, all the burnt ruined emblems of her street, her home. She had to run, to see . . . where Alfred was. To know he was . . . still there.

How could her lovely Storybook Alice ever know what that was? To bid *good night, good night,* to everything once you, once yours? To run on, as the moon lugged out, like some blank-faced rat just crawling from the rubbish heap? To run and run, through rubble-streets? Past the steeple of their ravaged church, the steeple which always had spoken for the church, scorched and burned—the nave and altar reduced to a heap of dumb nothing—embers of nothing. Shriveled, charred prayerbooks alight in the flames, bits of print scattering into the night like black butterflies . . . How could that Story Alice know what that was, to run on, regardless, past still-live bombs just covered with sand and earth?

And what of the library? Those wood-paneled chambers, more full of thought and mystery even than their church . . . Their beloved library, where she'd huddled so often with Alfred. All of those mullioned rose windows. All those immaculate aisles, where they'd knelt, where she'd let her heart run shelf over shelf, over *Anne of Green Gables* and *Captains Courageous*, where she'd gingerly thumbed through already-thumbed pages, wondering just who had passed there before her. All that, all those, gone up in smoke. A holocaust of words.

And everywhere else, everywhere that she looked—nothing but dust, ash, and litter. As if everything truly human—everything of the mind, of the spirit—had been stripped from the world. Leaving only one ruined, material shell. Only death. Only fear, as they said, in a handful of dust.

How could that pinafored Storybook Alice know what it meant to find, in that empire of dust, that the neighborhood shelter had also been hit—to fear her friend was trapped within and then to dig and dig for him? Her Alfred! To dig through the black-pit rubble with her own bare hands while hearing those terrible moans from within, and the only light she had was from the shells exploding overhead? As all those wounded ghosts ran, screaming through the fiery brimstone streets—like the graves had cast out all their dead.

Alfred—where was Alfred?

Then, someone calling—neighbors shrieking—they had found his father. Mr. Hallam. No! Buried in debris. But he was such a good man! Always so good to her. And here he lay, no breath. No heartbeat. No life left.

What could she do? What else could she have done, if

not to run to find her friend? No matter what they screamed at her, she knew she had to keep on—keep running. Through the naked desolation that was London. Running who-knew-where. Where *where* was Alfred? . . .

So alone she stood, as if she'd somehow stepped outside her mind, and had no map, no guide to help her be here *with* herself. Though, in truth, her Story Alice had been there too. There, in Alice's hand. Within the book.

Still with her. Her storybook Hero, calling to her: "Run, and I'll run with you. You'll find him—come, you have to. You can't imagine life without him."

No, she couldn't.

"We'll find him. Come. We must."

But how? Where?

"Come, now, Alice."

CHAPTER V:

—

A PORTRAIT OF URBAN CONTENTMENT

HOW long had it actually been since Alice had finally straightened her knees, since she'd climbed from that timedulled floor onto her cot again? She couldn't say. *Long enough*, that was all.

Sometimes, it felt like she was one of those (fabled) prisoners in Plato's Cave. Chained to her cot, like her fellow inmates—and all she knew were those shadowy walls and the secondhand sounds from above.

And, as for the world *below*? Only the circus surrounding her. Witness the sideshow: that myopic, and mean-spirited, Miss Mamie Van Eysen. Also aged fifteen (but going on a flirty fifty). She, who barely deigned to inhabit the common air. She, seated, thankfully, two woolen cot-thrones to the left, but so omnipresently there.

How, Alice wondered, *how* had that golden-haired girl, the transparent belle, no doubt, of every debutante ball (where the dance floor undoubtedly brightened beneath her, wherever her petticoats roamed)—how had that same Mademoiselle Van Eysen found her way here, to this random and plebian platform? And how how *how* did she find herself now, lolloping out of that moth-holed bit of burlap; rising in tattered majesty, barefoot and stocking-free? Without even (choke! gasp! scream!) a governess?! As she intrepidly set aside her chipped, chipping teacups (the sole treasures she'd brought with her) to wade through the slatternly fish-and-chips wrappers toward Alfred's quarantine? For *what*? All the while, fanning her delicate self with her debutante fan? *How could the Nurse allow that?*

How indeed. Alice knew by now (by this, the ninth night of this Underground-now) exactly how that privileged Mamie would answer—with a sigh of fatigue, so grand it could only be known by that languid, leisure class . . .

"You want to go, then go," counseled some rough-magic voice, high above.

Tabatha? With a turn of her head, Alice pried into the gloom. Only the barest hint of that enigmatic grin. (As if the one-behind-the-grin felt that was enough of her and so she let no more of her appear.)

"Go," said the grin.

"Oh, but," Alice stammerstalled, "he already has a guest."

"Careful," admonished the grin. "When you act too stupid, you turn into stupid."

Alice frowned. "But I'm not . . ."

"Acting?"

"Look at her," the frowning Alice persisted, with a discreet nod toward Mamie. "With all that weariness tutored into her from the moment of her silver-spoon birth."

"The question is," countered Tabatha, "how will those tattered airs serve in this war-leveled world? In this strange new world, where a Princess Starlight lies cradled next to those Unthinkables—the Poor."

"Meaning, me?" deduced the frown. "A girl like me?"

"Alice, *take in* the world. We weren't all born with a Mum and a home and a warm cottage pie after school. Nor is this war merely what it is to you." With that, that brightness disappeared, like the gleam of a wick going out. (Or like vision, itself, falling darkly away.)

"Yes, of course," Alice silently mouthed, and in silence *felt*. Till gradually her eyes settled once more on the Underworld war zone she now knew as home. She breathed, *all right*, take *that* in:

All those toddlers. Tied to the rails and hovering over those blank, night-mirroring tracks, the youngest and frailest children hung, suspended in hammocks (like so many baby Moseses in bulrush baskets). What a picture they made: like some portrait of Urban Contentment, really, or some advertisement in Sleep's tourist office. For, those children did not appear stricken but, rather, at peace—as if lifted in the rough grasp of that burlap into an otherworldly calm. An ignorant bliss: this being the only world they had known, it was good enough for them to forget themselves in. This bare platform night-world, which they'd been so rudely shuffled into. What, what would become of them, when they emerged, Alice asked—how would they do, when they woke, in the dark arms of sleep, to the war-ravaged daylight again?

Alice shook and shook her head. As if to loose every last riddle out of it. Really, what a surfeit of thoughts, what

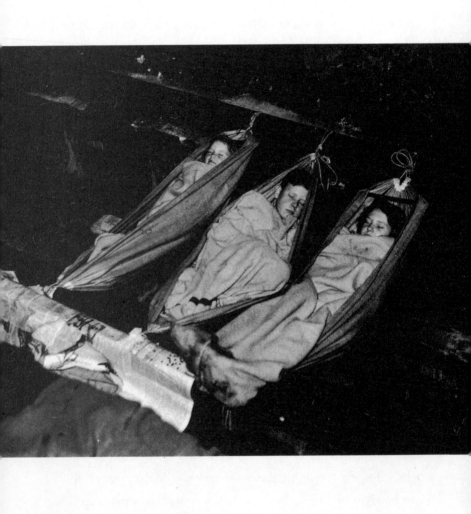

a surplus of feelings she near-always had! The question was, what was the purpose in *having* them?

Rousing herself, drawing her still-scabby knees to her chest, she glanced toward that quarantine curtain. *Drawn open a bit. Yes!* But there skulked that Splintered Princess, Mamie. Slanting her pretty, freckled self in, *fanning him?* Cooing to him? Making him laugh? (As though merely by speaking to someone she conferred such superiority upon them that all others only could envy them.)

"Nothin' to be done for it," some throaty voice concluded, just over her shoulder. Presuming, it felt, on just what Alice felt. *Who?* Who else but that loll-about, ever-near mouth in its nodding, smokeblue cloud. The unstoppered Angus. Regaling, with one of his tales, someone beside him but not listening to him. Someone too muffled by their own thoughts to be bothered with *his*.

Someone. Someone else, who mumbled merely: "I'm beginning to come around to the opinion. Yes." *Who?* Who but that daft and (indubitably) dapper whippersnapper, Dodgy.

An Eton schoolboy formerly, Dodgy had been posh as posh could be—from his patent leather slippers to the primrose boutonniere in his neat crop jacket. Or so Alice imagined. But, here he was, below earth now, seemingly allergic to this, that, and everything; like a creature who could thrive only in artificial light; his pallid arms shivering—as he ducked the common dust. The next moment, with a Vaudevillian flourish, he'd drape himself like some grande dame, in a fraying shelter blanket, donning some "borrowed" earring, and

45

fretting his complexion in a suspect hand mirror. This ever-bickering, cross-dressing lad, drawn near, no doubt, like some hungry calf, longing for that whiff of class that Mamie still possessed. His Roman nose held lofty in the close and musty night air.

Past that notable profile, Alice let her gaze wander toward Alfred, only to recoil at the touch of a rough, uncustomary hand, at the sight and the smell of all those vagabond smoke rings. "All bloomin' Leeds," blathered the dust-strewn Angus, proud owner of that rude-rough hand, "it was one wrecked shell . . ."

"I'm, uh," Alice tried, "a little busy . . ."

"Feel it with me," roocoocooed a rogue, throaty ring. "The black-eyed remains of the church—my dead Mum's church—where my best mate got married. The pub from their brilliant reception no longer there. Blue o'clock in the morning it was, and the whole infernal sky, pink as pink could be."

"I'm sure," Alice offered firmly, attempting to wriggle her shoulder free (after all, she was rather accustomed to having it).

"All the windows pink," Angus blithely continued, "the pavements pink, even the breeze. Brisk and cold as a wolf tit, it was."

"Tit, indeed," observed Dodgy. With a connoisseurish eye, browsing Alice's breast: "Well, a cad like Angus wouldn't bother, would he, if that blousy wasn't such a snuggly fit."

"Stuff and nonsense!" Alice retorted. *Really.* Never before had her growing chest been such a nuisance as this. Surely, there were bigger things to dwell on than her blouse. To Angus she turned imploringly: "Unhand my shoulder, please."

But Angus held tight. His clenched hand straining out of that seeming dust-heap of his outfit. Waxing irascibly on: "Those Nazi swine, flyin' low, black crosses on their wings. Droppin' their damned incendiaries, dottin', dribblin' their poisonous spunk down the night; those magnesium flares climbin' back up the sky. And all I could think was: *See? Now, you satisfied? Knobheads!* Throw yourself a bleedin' war and not let me play a part in it? We all could be gettin' a night's sleep, if you'd only let me fly . . ."

Almost, just almost, Alice could let herself entertain empathy for the stunted hopes of this still-aspiring lad. Were it not that . . . his own rogue eye kept roving her chest, as if he were staking a claim on her just-budding life . . .

"Hehehehe," came some fresh lowlife laugh, from behind, someone else crowding in. *Who?* Who but that sad-sorry, shape-shifting tyke, Nigel, who'd been drawn like a moth to Angus's cot (from his own, further on). A young man of thirteen, or so he claimed, though seeming about nine—in any event, such a child. So snooty one minute; the next, so broken-and-scattered. And always so oddly in denial, forever fidgeting with his battered schoolboy hat and his dusty, pockets-ripped navy-blue jacket, with the ink-bleeding pen clipped to the faded breast pocket. Still dismissing all this Blitz as phooey, just some Phony War. Although the poor thing had already lost his mother, his father, all his brothers to it—and somehow missed his teddy most of all.

So sad, really, Alice thought, hearing that boy heheh-ing on, mocking his surroundings to console himself, for the loss of everything he'd known as himself.

"My Mummy's coming for me today," declared Nigel to everyone and no one in particular. Plugging his mouth shut with his ink-stained thumbs.

What, what would he do, when his Mum did not come?

Thankfully, a (rather nonplussed) pause ensued, and Alice managed to slip free from Angus's grasp. Unencumbered, she retreated—head, neck, and shoulders, thank you—to a more discreet space on her cot. There she settled, sighed, drew in a breath. She gnawed a bit on her stiff nether lip, determined to get back to something, to somewhere the world still made sense. "The necessity of living," as Papa had said, "in some upper air."

"I only wish you'd known your Dad before his illness did," Alfred's Dad, Mr. Hallam, once had said. *"What a prince of a man he was. For him to be taken, with you still so young . . ."*

A prince, yes. With her signature sigh, with a stubborn stretch of her unbruised hand under the burlap, Alice dredged out her nub of a pencil and yellowing school pad. And through the bars of mothy light, she reviewed those Wonder-landy rhymes she'd been writing (and rewriting) through all those nine, unending nights:

> *How sweet-sad-sadly does Miss Mamie*
> *Glance up from her dress,*
> *And mock my now-familiar pain*
> *With her faux-posh "Ah yes."*

Ah yes. Tilting aslant on her elbow, Alice snuck another look. But she saw no Mamie there, at the quarantine bed.

Only Alfred. Through the opened skirt of dusky curtain, Alice could see him, propping his weakened form on his pillow. And she rose, in response—couldn't help it—rearing herself from her cot. That moment, everything stopped. (Or perhaps it was only that everything within her stopped.) How he looked at her! As only he would. With something of his old rascal smile. As if taunting her with some secret . . . ?

Abruptly, a brusque, gruff hand slung his curtain shut. Slap-bang—duty done. The Nurse! Alice shuddered, then nested her forehead in her hands, if only to secure that wink still within her—in the face of that Stalinist medical glare. *Enough.*

Forward she lunged. She would go, she'd demand a moment with him. One solitary moment only. Surely, no true Nurse—no volunteer for some Humanitarian Organization—would deny her that. Digging her blistered fist into the cot, she pushed herself up—but there, before her, *there,* Miss Mamie went. Casting her disapproving shadow on Alice's bed as she (just so accidentally) sauntered past, with a once-dainty hand on her soot-sullied dress. A daub of what—jam?—on the bodice. As she nibbled on something crumpet-like—fig biscuits? *Really?*

"My Aunt Millicent says," that oncegolden girl said, "the Savoy's the shelter to be seen in, these days."

What a pleasure, Alice thought, to be proven right in instinctively disliking that girl so much. It was as if, however tragic the circumstance, however much all the majesty of London—all the temples, domes, and theatres—might be crumbling around her, somehow some few gilded crumbs always clung to Miss Mamie's maidenly lips. For, she (as she was so fond of reminding them), *she* was the daughter of the Duke and Duchess of Such and Such; *she*, the doted-on niece of the seventh Earl of Sandwich of Such and Such; she, the granddaughter of the Baroness Beaverward of Such and Such.

"My Auntie Maude says she's just dined at the Dorchester. What with the bore of the bombs, all the pommes frites went rattling right off the table. And every grasping waiter expected his fair shilling, just for picking them up again. Gave her such a fit of indigestion!"

Go! Alice knew she should go, must go. She looked again, one brisk look. But there, that Nurse remained—in stubborn vigil beside his closed curtain, surveying the ward with a crude and cruder leer. Squelching the hope of all who came near. *The futility, really.*

Back Alice turned—to that foundering gossamer girl— with some answering sense of sympathy. Whoever, whatever the girl was, Alice had to interrupt, had to reach out a hand. Had to ask: "Tell me, please. How is he?"

At the touch of Alice, Mamie drew back, as if not wanting it known what she felt like. "He? Who?"

"Alfred."

"Oh, him. Silly me! Obviously." With a spry turn to that navel-gazing Dodgy, and those select few Tubees whom she deemed worthy of speech, Mamie heaved forth a sigh so profound it seemed to shatter what little was left of her: "Good God! Her, and her consuming love for that consumptive boy."

Then with a cold, wandering scorn, eyeing various curves and dark corners of Alice's body: "What a relief it must be, never having to think about having a family."

To Alice's surprise, not a sneer came back from Dodgy, only a quick nasal twinge to indicate the lack of an impression Mamie'd just made on him.

Unsurprisingly, then, Miss Van Eysen's tone lightened, and she cast her fishing line again: "But beyond all that, and all them, haven't we had a marvelous war?"

CHAPTER VI:

—

PIG AND PEPPER

MIDSUMMER, *had it been? Just some few months ago, when their world was still one stream of af-ternoons? (Before the Luftwaffe—with its howling worms of the night—had come to feed on all their loving, secret life.) How contentedly Alice had been seated, couched in that plum-cushioned seat, by Alfred's canopied bed . . .*

"Chapter Six," announced Alice, reading aloud from her ver-milion, gilt-edged storybook, that gorgeous rare edition Alfred had given her. With a voice like a clarion bell, she proclaimed its title.

"'Pig and Pepper'!" Alfred cried in delight, despite the strin-gent warnings that Alice and he had received: that he must remain calm as they played (if they were to be allowed to play); that he must relax on his bed—no major laughs, no tumultu-ous crying out—he must stay put and breathe.

But all that warning, Alice hardly remembered—so absorbed she was. So otherwise she was. For the light that fell from his eyes, and the glow on his cheeks from his reddening mind, seemed somehow more rose-tinged, more permanent and human a sun-set than that soon-expiring early June light. That near-forbidden light, which streamed through the mostly closed blinds, like some unwanted messenger from the world outside. The world where Alfred's stouter, robuster, and years-younger brother was playing badminton—whacking the shuttlecock da da dum da de dee.

But never mind. Clapping his hands, Alfred made a brilliant grab, gripping his pillow—like Wonderland's Duchess, near-suffocating her infant. Even as she so violently tossed her snout-nosed baby about, he began tossing his pillow, riffing on verses beloved from the book:

> "Speak roughly to your little boy,
> And beat him when he sneezes.
> Then he, plump pig, can well enjoy
> The pepper when he pleases!"

"Wow! Wow! Wow—" Alice began to howl.

But even before her last wow, Alfred was seized by one of his coughing fits. Nothing serious, she knew, or told herself she knew. Still, it was a thwarting reminder that she must exert a calming influence—or else be sent home again.

"Come, silly," she cajoled. "At the beginning, we begin."

"The Fish-Footman!" heralded Alfred.

"Of course! But first, let's rest a bit while I read on."

So saying, Alice resumed reading, to the relief of that rather neglected-feeling book: "For a minute or two, she stood looking at the house, and wondering what to do next, when suddenly a footman in livery came running . . ."

But Alice broke off, seeing Alfred already upright, his bare feet astride his bedding as he struck the most supercilious

Fish-Footman pose. Producing, from under his arm, his afore-mentioned pillow (in place of a royal letter "nearly as large as himself"), he carped: "For the Duchess. An invitation from the Queen to play croquet!" And Alice was too charmed to dream of trying to tame him.

For now he seemed to claim the entire world stage—leapfrogging to the opposite end of the bed, then unbending, valiantly upright again. Scooping out his chest, tapping his shoulders as if to straighten those bizarre epaulettes. The very picture of a proper Frog-Footman. Making a kind of bulge out of his eyes, and a snout out of his mouth, he drew forth an equally large pretend letter, bowed low, croaked lower, and pre-sented it: in the near-exact fashion it had been presented to him: "From the Queen. An invitation for the Duchess to play croquet." And then, with a mad dexterity, alternately wiggling, then wriggling his head, then snatching, then catching the hair on that head—in order to mime how the powdered-wig curls of the Frog entangled so ringlingly with those of the Fish.

Alice laughed so much at this, and as she laughed, she wondered: Had she ever been so charmed? Had she ever felt so fond of anyone, anywhere?

Caught on the thought, she'd forgotten to talk. Prompting Frog-Alfred to leap ahead, to plop down seated on the bed. To prompt her, with an insistent psssst: *"When she next peeped out, the Fish-Footman was gone . . ."*

Alice listened, merely. Marveling.

On he psssst'd: *"And the other was sitting on the ground near the door, staring stupidly up into the sky . . ."*

"Oh, right," she remembered, but let him continue.

And so he did: "Alice went timidly up to the door, and knocked."

Rapt in the marvel of His Frog-Footmanness, still Alice said nothing. Until, with a nudging nod toward the door, he rapped at the air with a white-knuckling fist.

"Alfred!" she crowed. "You know it by heart."

"Shhhh. Do knock."

With a penitent nod, Alice leaned toward the rosewood tea table and knocked.

"Sorry—no use in knocking," the Frog-throat croaked. "And that, for two reasons."

Here, Alfred looked up. As if allowing his adoring throngs a glimpse of the lad behind the Frog-mask: "Guess."

"Oh, come on."

"Two reasons. Guess."

Knowing well that Alice knew (equally) well the answer to that, and indeed the entire script, he pressed on again, his would-be-frog-like eyes rolling back in his head. "Two reasons, yes. 'First, because I'm on the same side of the door as you are: secondly, because they're making such a noise inside, no one could possibly hear you!'"

"Please, then," said Alice, adept with her line, "how am I to get in?"

Scarcely had Alice let out that question, when—

An actual knock on an actual door came sounding, announcing itself.

Alfred's blank mahogany door looked blankly back.

A second, more obstreperous knock followed.

With a wild zeal, Alfred dropped onto his covers—striking a pose as motionless as some marble-sculpted Roman Cherub Reclining.

A sudden, vociferous "Answer me" knock—

"Yes?" he addressed the door, ingenuous.

Mrs. Austerlitz's ageless voice replied, as her ageless, peek-a-boo eyes peeked in: "Would Mr. Alfred care for some liquid refreshment?"

"Some orangeade," he replied, "would be just enormous."

"And Miss Alice?"

"Please." Alice smiled. "Smashing. Thank you."

"You will allow Alfred some rest as you read to him?"

Look the woman straight in the eye, Alice reminded herself. Trust me. I will.

"Of course she will, Mrs. Austerlitz," Alfred replied. "She always does."

"Then why is it, sir, I am always sent to look in?"

Before there was even time to reply, the ever-efficient Mrs. Austerlitz had caught his eye, had smiled her ever-morose, mournful smile, and with a dire air stepped out again.

"Always so Out of Sorts, that Mrs. Outofsortz," Alice quipped, recalling their dry, familiar line.

But this time Alfred did not smile. No, he seemed only to inherit that woman's mournful gloom. And sighed, as if he too had gone out. Or some light in him had.

"Come, Alfred," Alice tried, and waited, but knew, knew well, he would not look up again—not for some time yet. Sighing her own sigh, she looked through the windows' eyes, onto those ochre clumps of crocuses, where once they'd run, and now only that uninterrupted badminton.

CHAPTER VII:

—

SOME SPRUNG MONKEY

STILL there. Those same, unheeding eyes. Mamie eyes—brimful with assurance she'd had the last word. She had Come (those eyes declared), she had Seen, she had Conquered poor Alfred! And now, with a satisfied toss of her weddingbell curls, that Mademoiselle drifted back to her bed. Like some amber-plumed bird, in her lone-remaining dress—that pale-canary party frock. She, whose every outfit must once have expressed its own rainbow-slant of her soul, now molting a bit as she collectedly fluttered back to her Underground cage. Her main mating call done for the day.

Ah well, Alice mused, carefully observing the palefreckled girl. Knowing that, one day, when this war ended, and Alfred came home again, some laggard afternoon she'd be *playing* Miss Mamie as part of their afternoon game. And Alfred, he would do such a dead-on impression of that dastardly Dodgy. Would huff and puff himself up, just as that proud boy was, just now. Seated high on his would-be throne (which was to say, high on his folded coat on his own bunklike bed), one cot past where Miss Mamie sat. "Poor Alice-Thing!" the scamp yawned, too bored to say more—until he did: "Playing Miss

Forlorn—with those scabby knees. Meanwhile, bursting at her blouse's seams!"

"Excuse me?"

"Didn't I tell you: button up the blousy?" came the raucous Red Cross cry, echoing out of the undercover nowhere.

Like a guilty thing surprised, like a ruddy cactus pear, Alice prickled: "But, it is. All buttoned. It's just grown smaller, really."

From behind those bandaged eyes, Tabatha weighed in: "Funny how that happens, when the boys start growing bigger."

Ouch. "What do you mean?" inquired Alice.

Tabatha sighed, with the graveled voice of a street grown impatient with some dreamy-headed flaneur: "Blouses—they're like flowers, aren't they, love? They only really blossom when the young men stop to look at them."

"Sorry?!"

But no word, no purr, was forthcoming.

"Tabatha?"

Not a wag of that cat-cophonous tongue? Nothing? Alice pursed her lips: "It's just my body—growing. Not much I can do about it, is there?"

Still no answer to that. Only the drip drip drip of her own soul's November. Echoing the loutish, soulless drip of that water main overhead.

Had she gone then? That itinerant Tabatha? Or had she merely receded, like a phantom, into her personal shadow canyon again? Where an occasional glint from the cracked clock face, mysterious as twilight, sometimes would find her; as if in the velvet gleam of a windowsill on a Rembrandt night . . .

Hard to tell. For, still, on certain nights, she slipped out and away. (Attracted to the danger, was she? Or homesick, maybe?) Alone again, she'd shelter in doorways from the shrapnel falling, "just like you'd take cover from a summer downpour." And indeed the shrapnel wounds remained visible, up her cheeks and down her forehead. The burns as well. Until, these past few days, the bandages had so consumed her face, there was nothing much left, in the high shadows of that scaffold; only the faint, ghost-bright glint of a grin. (Like some slim light shining in darkness, which the darkness could not comprehend.)

What was left of *her*, then, Alice asked, though not aloud.

No, merely she looked: down at her self in that ill-fitting blouse. *Was* she—was this new she—these arms? These anemically pale, and yes, perhaps longer, but still-so-spindly things. These hands growing out of them, dangling like strangers beside her; these ever-present hands, of which she always seemed so unlikely a part. (Their bone structure, apparently, the same as a bat's. Thank you, Charles Darwin, for that!) To say nothing of these newly peering-out hips. And these . . . aliens. These breasts. Still forming, yes. But already leaving her so far behind, it was all she could do to keep up with them. She, who (beyond the vagaries of ill-behaved hair) was living within some strange sensation of having exactly the wrong head. This odd box of the nothing that she looked through—onto the nothing much there.

Some solitary whine, some chill unsettling breeze—like rude, cold fingers turning a page—brought her back to this place. And sent her eyes searching about, over the strewn bodies, over the maimed soldiers, and tile walls and iron railings, over the castaway bags and shoes that lay like scattered chunks of masonry . . .

That moment, she knew, knew with the whole of her, something was off, something new afflicting Alfred! She had to be with him. That moment.

She turned, but there, before her, the Ogre. Stooping, high-shouldered, he lurched. He loomed. Good Old Dr. Butridge. Blocking the narrow, cluttered way. A man remarkable in nothing so much as his utter unremarkableness. This bureaucratic medical stooge. Doing his duty to the Sick and Wounded, without really taking in any of them. Transforming all their particular woes into one soulless rote. Did he even know it was Dodgy he tended, depressing that sad, sassy tongue? And then, with a quick indifferent swab, with a muttered *tsssk*, the man was done. Yes! Blessedly done. Once more, he went clittering clattering, like tin over the asphalt, rattling on to the next bacterial suspect. Leaving Alice free to head toward Alfred. Which she immediately did. One stealthy step, on . . .

Only to meet a leg. Directly in her path. But, *whose* leg? Oh, of course—Angus's! With his face gone in a puff of smoke, beckoning her toward his blue-cloud delirium. With a wave of his siren pipe: "One puff—and all this fades away. You're in some other dream."

And with that, Leg 2 swung round and clamped her, just above the knees. All those smoky Os departing from his lips like burp-rings from an openmouthed fish. "O O O, see the pottery frog? On my pipe, that is. O, and I have got such relics to show you: fine crystal stones, and such shrapnel bits—"

"I, please," Alice attempted to plead, when . . . suddenly . . .

Like an answer to her unuttered prayer, Harold Pudding jumped onto Angus's dustblooming cot, and with that plunge, broke Alice free. "Shall we have some tea? Yes? Shall we?"

Mamie, so dislodged and unsettled herself, secured her secret pearls down down her blouse, and nodded most engagingly: "Oh yes, absolutely."

With a flick of her gilded hand and a dash of mordant wit, that tattered Miss dispatched her vanished domestic staff: "With just a spit of jam, James—and perhaps a spot of Spam."

"Sure, every doughboy needs his jam," Angus kindly reminded. "'But armies on their stomachs move, and this one moves on Spam.'"

At which Harold leapt, but all too soon flatlanded, as if on some unyielding trampoline, clapping his battle-scarred hands: "Spam! Spam! What is Spam? Spam is ham that didn't pass its physical. But me, I'm sound. I'm all sound now, me. This time I'll pass . . ."

"You've passed, mate." Angus clapped his back. "It's past."

"I have?!" Harold exalted. Leaping harder, landing longer, than perhaps he ever had. "Sir, yes, sir! Harold Pudding reporting for duty, sir."

Doing her best to suppress the growing motion sickness, Mamie steadied her candytuft-teacup, running a bruised finger over its gilt-edged rim.

"My Royal Albert cup," she observed. "Marvelous, isn't it? If only you'd known its saucer as once we did."

Prompting that dismissive Dodgy: "Oh yes, yes. After the last thirty-seven nights of chip chip chip."

"A world lost bit by bit," Tabatha chimed in.

"My Mummy's coming for me today!" Nigel whined, his weather eye fixed on those unheeding stairs, his inky thumb attacking his ear.

"Hear, hear," Harold cheered. Opening his pad, to show-and-tell his freshest sketch, turning his whole body, whereas once he might have turned only his head: "See *here*, this is *my* here. Here, and heeeeere!" he cheered, as Alice started past.

But that former soldier held her with a bare forked hand: "'Thank Gawwwd,' my Mum said, when my regiment left. 'Thank Gawwd, Harold'll be away at the front—and well out of harm's way in London!'"

Moved by the thought of Harold's sorry Mum, Alice almost met his sorry look. But *no no,* she knew, *I must shut all that out, must shut perception down. Must narrow the world to what I need to do now.* Warily she eluded the soldier's grasp and took one further step.

And that diva, Dodgy, sighed an exhausted sigh. Feeling, at age fifteen, he had already lived five hundred lives: "The endless chain of days, you know."

"Mad, mad," murmured Tabbie, "we've all gone mad here."

And *there*, as if to prove the point that madness stalks, ubiquitous, that Nurse came marching, on her rounds. Like a veritable ambulance, with that awful red Cross on her chest, parking herself directly in Alice's path. Offering up her bad-news wares: "Tin tomatoes tonight. And more of you than rations—not a word about it."

Stymied, stopped, Alice clung to herself. Like some squirrel monkey, sprung from the zoo, stranded in the night on torched London ground. *How, now,* she asked herself, *how to get past? To him?*

And then, like a package from heaven, some bright thing fell from the air: *Cllllllllllllinng!* And then, *cluuuuuuuummph!*

Who? What? Alice looked above her and about, almost as if searching for something known from a past life. *There,* in that vaulted chink, she saw a hand, readying a (second?) fat tin can. Tossing it suddenly, sparklingly, down.

Another: *Cllllllllllllllinng!* Followed by *clumph.* Another something, gone screeching. Screeling. Plopping open. Toward the track.

"Duck, Freddie!" cried Pudding aloud, while ducking for cover beneath Dodgy's cot.

"My nerves, please! Pudding!"

And now, the rations came tumbling. Tins of tomatoes cracking open, spewing red pulp from their seams all over the platform. And with that, the entire global Red Cross, every First Aid Staffer, every black-hatted ARP instructor, every volunteer at each Relief or Convalescent Center—rose up in arms. Positively glaring at that near-invisible trickster, Tabatha: "You! Such a trial!"

And Alice? She stood, motionless, amazed at the space opened by that tomato-chaos. The room she now had to move through, to be near him. From the darkness above she caught a glint of Tabbie's resilient grin. Like some kind of hint from the central mind of the world.

"Go!" said the grin.

Taking the hint, Alice went. Trying her best, as she did, to ignore Miss Mamie's merciless scoffing. Her snickering about that cantankerous tin-can-dropping.

"All *this*," Miss M presumed, "so that woebegone girl can run back to her Alfred? Well, we know who gets that Tabbie's vote for Orphan of the Year."

"Has to save somebody, doesn't she?" Dodgy sniggered, like Snow White's Stepmum, consulting his mirror. "That is, since she couldn't save her pseudo-sister."

Let the choughs chatter, Alice thought—*she* had moved on. Had scooted—*quick, quick!*—behind that dark-shimmering curtain. With a tug, with a robust ducking-under that sheet, there she was—with him, again.

CHAPTER VIII:

—

ONCE MORE, DOWN THE RABBIT-HOLE

SUCH a dank, constricted space—behind that quarantine curtain, in the nightsweat Tube-station air—and yet, to her it seemed so grand a room . . .

Alfred's face. Every time she looked at it, she'd remember another part of it—how many details, how many contours she'd forgotten—as if she'd never quite taken in this or that. And so, each look brought her again some lost part of him . . .

And yet, to him, she reasoned, his face must seem so outside himself. Like a mask that still surprised him, a familiar ghost he met in every mirror. Whereas, whatever world he knew in sleep must seem so much more *him*. So much more where he lived.

And yet. Through that pallid mask which Illness had set on him, she saw again what most she knew *as* him. All the wit, the stubborn strength. The resilience. And, for her at least, the marvel of all he first had been—aglow on their common-garden lawn, as the most-miraculous White Rabbit. (But then, don't we always suffuse our so-desired someone with that supernatural air of all it seemed they were before we actually knew them?)

A sudden wince-inducing thud thudded beyond. She cast about—no fiendish Nurse lurking about. Urgently she whispered: "Alfred?"

Not a murmur. Not a flutter from him. *"Alfred?"*

Something in him stirred. Though what, exactly? "Alfred, please. It's me."

With those words, his eyelids opened—but at once, quite shut her out. *But why?* It wasn't as if she hadn't woken him before—from one of his afternoon naps. *Alfred, please. It's me. Just me.* Or was that just it? Did the sight of her recall too much? she wondered. Did it bring him too much consciousness of where he was, of what he'd become, of all he once had been? Whatever the case, he brusquely turned away. Perturbed. *Ashamed?* Or was it just that her eyes, looking on his, would still long for too much from him?

"Forgive me, Alfred. They wouldn't let me near you."

"Perhaps they have good reason," he contended, some pale light dimming in the blue afternoon of his gaze.

Reasons aside, she drew nearer.

"Alice, please! You mustn't come too close."

"That's the fever talking, not you," she insisted.

But his look resisted still. "Listen to me, I'm falling away. The stars are so bright, they hurt my eyes . . ."

The stars? She paused on the word, unsure. But nodded, nonetheless, reassuring him, touching his shoulder through the bedsheet. *"Come,* let me read to you. You'll feel better."

"Your Mum must be half-mad from worry."

Alice shook her head, quite certain: "She'll know I'm with you."

"Really, you might have left me in that gutter."

"Alfred!"

Those eyes, forever his, become so grave. And still they did not turn away. Merely watched her watching him. The plea within them remaining, unwavering. Slowly, lingeringly, from beneath his thickset pillow, he withdrew a war-scored pocket watch. Through the darkness visible, glimmering. His sole remaining possession—once a birthday gift from Alice.

"You brought it?"

"Tick tock," he intoned, firmly.

"Tick tock," more lightly, still warily she replied.

Over his sloping shoulder, in profound disquiet, his eyes found hers again.

"Just one more night we'll be here," she whispered.

"And you?" he managed. Then, gently jibed: "All comfy on that platform?"

Her eyes pooled, saying no. And he relented, a touch. Half a smile spreading over him, in spite of his firmset lips. "But honestly, how is that concrete world treating you?"

"Quite concrete."

He let out half a laugh. That loveliest, seeing-through-everything laugh, only his. A place, like his voice, she could still find shelter in.

"And all our . . . fellow pilgrims?" he asked. Growing playful once again—as once he so had been—he aped that blue-blood girl's precise, sparrowlike intonation: "Your Mamie Van Such and Such Eysen?"

"*Your* Mamie," Alice archly replied, matching him.

As if to spite the nose on his own exhaustion's face, he

put on a bit of Mamie's posh-exhaustion: "Summon Dotty—darling, do—she's the only one who even remembers how we take our tea. All the rest have fled or are dead—and so much for steeping our chamomile properly! My Auntie Maybelline says, she's locked herself up in the Tower of London. Times like these, it *is* the place to be."

With a wink, he slipped a pretend-posh hand beneath his pretend-cotton sheet and withdrew two dark-swirling fig pinwheel biscuits. Pale pale his fingers, offering them: "Aren't they mahvelous?"

"Most mahvelous," Alice posh-said, her smile declining, in spite of the rich, dark fruit interior. "She meant them for you."

Once more he extended the smuggled confections. With half a brag: "Sweet as our past."

"Well, when you put it that way." Alice reached—but as she clasped that worn brown-sugar sweet, he cupped his free hand over her hand. Locking it between his. Seeking, it felt like, some world he'd known within her. Some part of himself he could recognize still as himself. Some part of himself still there. Tingling (more than she'd care to admit), Alice looked into his mild mocking eyes.

"And Angus?" he asked, pretending, Angus-like, to rise from an ashen heap of his outfit and exhale a fictive, blue smoke plume. "Has he been utterly captivating, with his tales of the phosphor-pink sky over Leeds?"

He'd been listening? "They're all he has, those tales," she opined.

"Tales, *sure*," Alfred murmured, "they can be wonderful things."

He passed his hand over his lips; something, some further sigh, festering still within him: "But in the end, what are they—tales? Distractions, Alice. Diversions, merely. From seeing what we have to see, from thinking all the terrible things we cannot help but think . . ."

"Alfred!" she called out—couldn't stop herself.

And with that note of alarm, his look shut down. And he folded in on himself, removing himself. A glaze, like over those Tube-station tiles, closing over his eyes, as he rested his head on the blunt war-bolster again. *Now what?* Say something *else*? Litter him with more her?

Dismay settled beside Alice; a dismay so long familiar, so annoyingly near. Meanwhile, that sweaty fig biscuit, merely sitting there in her hand, ever more awkward, like some odd weight, some dumb lump within her she could not explain away.

"Come, I'll read to you," she tried again, plying him. "I can make you well again. I'll bring you to our world again."

"Our world? What world?" he answered, asking—a sorry smile passing over his lips. "Alice, there's no sky left. Only ash and smoke and ruin."

"There's sky enough in Wonderland."

"Alice," he rasped, the graveled tenor of his voice surprising even him. "I have no time now. Not for this."

"You do. You will," she urged, wanting so badly to rouse him—to awaken too that steadying sense in herself she had only with him. "We'll feast on our Mad Hatter tea and all our grand, imaginary sweets. Like on all our golden afternoons!"

His hoarsened voice rasped words, like so much soot: "Where are they now, those afternoons?"

"Still here," she said, touching her breast. Then, with a gesture toward that manic, makeshift shelter. "All this, we can make it disappear." Her eyes welled with unwanted tears, as she held out her crimson volume of *Alice's Adventures*, the one he'd given her, the one she'd salvaged from the flames and brought here with her: "Come. You can run there. You can breathe there. You'll be well again. Then they won't take you away."

"We'll start reading, I won't even reach The End."

"Of course you will."

He shook his head insistently: "I won't start what I can't finish."

"I know—since forever."

She watched him shiver, his pillowcase wrinkling in time with him. And she saw him again—antic, free, and welcoming—as once he'd been. "Even when you were six," she pushed on, "staying well past dark, ignoring your mother's and my mother's calls. Poring over every picture, each comma, impersonating every single moment of our book. You just so had to finish it."

"I've no time left—you understand?"

But she would not. "Don't believe them. You can't let them take *this* from us. Not this, too. It's all we have. It's Wonderland."

"You go there without me now," he urged.

"You can't lose heart."

"Oh really?" he asked so plaintively. "After everything else we've lost?"

But with that plaint, a heaving cough racked Alfred's chest. A rattling chain of phlegm and blood. His fists, his ribs, his cheeks convulsed with vehement breaths; as if he were recoiling from the stigma of his consciousness.

From just the other side of that quarantine curtain, a wheedling voice could well be heard: "No coughing on me, thank you." *Dodgy, it must be.*

"Have some compassion on these frayed nerves, please." *That mahvelous Mamie,* assuredly. From her perch of proper ruin.

Alice tugged at the stubborn, clinging curtain. Which still disdained to shut. *Enough.* Her determined hand clasped Alfred's hand. But before she could even . . .

"Please," his voice pleaded. "Don't try to hold me, too."

"But I will—"

"No. Alice, let me go."

No no no. Another tremor, yet more violent, erupted from him—like a blistering string of nononos, fresh black-red blood sprinkling his pillow, with the guttering aftershock of each successive, jerking cough.

And with each jagged cough, the affrighted Nigel cried out like a damaged toy, cradling himself upon his cot. He and his thumb in shock. "No more, no more! My Mummy's coming for me today! My Mummy's coming for me today!"

"Oh, do you think?" purred Tabatha. Through the half-open curtain Alice could see her, effusing feline irony, as she skeptically took in the motley platform-crew, singling them out, one by one with her barbed tongue: "Just like mine, and yours, and his, and hers . . ."

And *hers*? Alice pondered. If only Mum could leave Cathy's side and come find them, could stay a night down here with Alfred and her, could run her work-roughened fingers through Alice's hair, whisking out the dust, critiquing the ends . . .

"Hear that? It's the end!" Nigel yelped, uncradling and cradling himself. Rocking forward and back.

"Sprengbombe 250, is it?" the deep-toking Angus posited.

He listened. They all listened. Only the low hum of the nothing-to-be-done. The anxious hovering hmmm . . . Till the waiting (nothing yet), the listening (nothing still), grew too disconcerting, and there rose from this ill-kept company a reflexive, quick cacophony. A bantering. A banging. A snatching-up of rations.

Angus, it was, who'd hazily managed to zone in on Alfred's discarded dinner, and had sidled close as close: "On a hunger strike, is he? I can use that boy's bacon, thank you."

Like a dervish, Dodgy whirled about, chiding: "You pig— that's my pig!"

"Charming," added Tabatha dryly. "Rationing out the world he had."

At that, Alfred began wheezing—more harshly still. His wasted body, cowling, his bulging chest racked by stertorous breaths.

Springing straight up, Dodgy tossed his gauntlet at Angus: "Bit of shrapnel says that boy doesn't last the night."

"Bit of bacon says he's gone before this bite," wagered Angus, wagging that esteemed bit of bacon against his lips.

Can you, please? No course left for Alice, *none*, she thought, but to rise above. To *read* above. She opened her treasure-book and recited aloud: "Chapter One: 'Down the Rabbit-Hole.' Alice was beginning to get—"

"Alice, no," Alfred urged. "I'm not listening."

But Alice pressed on, knowing him: "—to get very tired of sitting by her sister on the bank—"

"Alice!"

"Once or twice," she continued, "she had peeped into the book—"

Startling and abrupt, a gruesome cry slit the narrative mist—and the Underground air: *Alice Spencer!*

Shhhrrrghkk. With a frenzied, near-maniacal grab, the Red Cross Nurse snatched that tome from Alice's hand: "Thirty thousand dead up there—and you, with your head in Wonderland. No wonder they are burning books."

With that, that savage Red Cross Nurse ripped Alice's book, shredding rending chucking hurling it—

"Don't!" cried Alfred.

Startled, grateful, Alice looked to him, revived. She cried at that Nurse: "It's all I have—or had. He gave me that!"

"Then she can't take it from you, can she?" Tabatha purred. "No one can."

At those words, at that probing look, Alice caught on a breath. *No, they can't.*

Too late. *Look*, the spine, the binding, breaking—all those gorgeous dusty dog-eared pages, scattering now across the track.

And with those pages, all the gorgeous, cloudless hours; all the notions, all the playtimes; all the impish daydreams Alice still retrieved; the memories still triggered by revisiting those pages, all those long-familiar phrases, each like another golden key upon another three-legged table, another way out of the "dark-hall" self (namely, that feeling of being too big or too small for every door to the world) into that welcoming, word-lovely garden—with all its gossiping flowers and crisp sapphire fountains.

She lunged. But the Nurse grabbed hold—tearing the distraught girl from herself, and him. Imprisoning her within steely, practiced arms, dragging what was left of Alice, those few meters back—to her four-foot cell, her sad, constricting cot.

All the while, the dogged Dr. Butridge clumped doggedly on—further away from the still-stricken Alfred. Disdaining (it seemed) to help in any way, to offer even a jittery hand. No, nothing to be done—only more clipboards to clank, more Latin to spout. *(Were we supposed to feel somehow grander, hearing ourselves diagnosed in Latin?)*

The while, Dodgy jeered about Alice: "Clinging to some kiddy book?"

"Appalling," mocked Nigel.

"Duck!" cried Harold, with a sudden duck. "London Bridge is falling!"

"Falling sickness," Butridge expatiated. "Disequilibrium, due to Narcoleptic Cataplexy—i.e., fitful sleep paralysis—"

"Dr. Butridge!" wailed that Nurse.

"Whaaaaaaat?"

And—as ever—from nowhere, Harold Pudding leapt to claim the air, bounding like some fraught gazelle (who'd smelled the cheetah near) from Mamie's to Dodgy's, and then back to Mamie's, to Alice's (hello!), to Angus's cot. And with every mad leap was chaos come again. "More tea?"

Prompting Dodgy, who could not *not*: "Shut *up*!"

"Pay up," Angus demanded, "the boy is dead."

"*Almost* dead," Dr. Butridge coldly corrected.

"Don't you dare!" Alice cried. Spinning about, she started toward Alfred. Only to meet that Fury of a Nurse, that brutal Red Cross Queen, bulldozing toward her:

"*Off! Of! That! Bed!*"

"No!" Alice cried, pinning that Curse of a Nurse, making that bloated butterfly squirm, with every last word from their book: "Off with your head!"

"Braaaaa!" the Nurse bawled, extending those ravaging arms, grappling for Alice.

Stopstop it!—*Stop!* Alice ducked. Skittering over the grime, breathing hard, down the platform she ran. Clamping her hands, clap clap, over her ears: "Stop! Stop! You—and you—and you!"

Now now. Alice pivoted, her forefinger extended. Marking those cots and those cowards, one after the other: "I'll show you."

Round she spun, and caught Alfred's trademark question mark look, her words extending toward him like pincers. "Come. I'll *bring* you. I know it all by heart."

His hollowed eyes stared back, from that paleportrait face. Inscrutable. *On*, Alice urged herself. *On, from the book:* "And so with nothing to do, Alice was considering *what* to do, on this golden afternoon, when . . ."

Those words, so familiar. Like a summons. Like a sound repeated in a summer without end. Their daily incantation to Wonderland: "Suddenly . . . a White Rabbit ran close by . . ."

Not a flicker from those eyelids. *Come, Alfred.* Not a breath. Her urgent look solicited his.

Slowly, measuredly from under his blanket, the boy pulled forth—on a slant, like a rabbit from a hat—an antique . . . fan? *Mamie's fan!* He dangled it. Faintly, frantically fanning himself, mustering a wry smile.

A sigh so profound issued from Alice: *Thank you, yes. I'll bring you. Done.*

For, she knew, she knew well, exactly what she believed; all she had to do was to hold on to that. To stay in that. To be there, with him again.

She shut her eyes, completely shut. And—down, down all at once, she found herself . . . falling down suddenly down doooooowwwnnnnn the hole to Wonderland. (Some voice somewhere within her, echoing through her, those fateful words from her book: "Never once considering how in the world she was to get out again . . .")

But *what* hole, in what *world*, exactly? And where was Alfred? Had she succeeded in bringing him? *Open your eyes,* she told herself. *No, no!* that self said back. Not yet.

Reciting, contriving, to keep herself tumbling. Down as she tumbled, on on she went: "'Well, after such a fall as this, I shall think nothing of tumbling down-stairs.'"

Try now, she told herself. *Open them.* She did. But there she saw not Wonderland at all. Only through some widening skirt of light, a darkness beyond darkness.

And, *there*, from somewhere, she seemed to see again those fat tin cans—*cllllllllllllinng clllluuuummmph*—careening past. She must be under the tracks?! What with those ageless dust-whiskered rats tumbling past—suspended, as she was, between future and past.

She shuddered, doubting herself. A shudder between worlds. In the midst of all the Underground gloom, could it help him? she wondered. Would it? To go there, to their world again? To run through that mystical garden again? To "manage" their Flamingos in a game of Royal Croquet? To *imagine*? It had to. Otherwise, they both would die of too much concrete. Yes. *But was there time enough?*

Stop, stop, she told herself (snapping at herself as if she were someone else). All the doubt, it was locking her out. *On.* She recited, determined to find it, though struggling to summon the passage exactly: "Alice tried . . . she tried to look down and make out what she was coming to, but it was too dark to see anything."

Down down down. Like in her book. Though nothing in her book had ever been like this! *See*, a soldier there, in roomy combat uniform, seated on a heap of broken images. Unstooped, and proud, as perhaps Harold Pudding once had sat, not daring to disturb the universe, taking his tea on a mound of home blown to bits. *But no,* Alice thought—this was all too odd. Something was off. She couldn't be falling *into* and *out of* the same somewhere. Couldn't be falling *down* into London, not with that same London *above* her.

Into that world tumbling by, Alice peered again. And there she made out, just like in her storybook—yes, it

79

was!—that tyrant Queen of Hearts, surrounded by a cowering crowd; full-grown Playing Cards throwing themselves down, muffling their coated-cardboard faces, before her. "Idiots!" the dire Queen cried, staring down a quivering Seven and a Five. (But no White Rabbit, alas, behind or beside.)

Too painful to watch! Alice let her eyes scan the violet horizon. There, her milkman, was it? Her own jolly James, with his familiar craft of bottles, who stopped at her house every morning on his rounds? But it couldn't be James—not at her house. There was no house!

She looked again. No, it was not James. Only that dapper Mad Hatter, swanning his way through the ruins, claiming his place at the head of a table—the longest of Churchill-like war room tables (collywobbling as that was). But there too sat that imperturbable March Hare, with the heavy-lidded Dormouse cushioned beneath his elbow. All wry and ready for their Mad Tea Party. (Still no Alfred-Rabbit to be found there. Rather, the lawn and rough hedges beyond seemed to nod and agree: "Haven't seen him, darling.")

But *there*, look—just there, on a towering (three-inch-high) mushroom, rising beyond all the smoking ruin; surrounded by only the loveliest blue cloud, that languid Caterpillar sat, puffing on his hookah. There, beyond him, on a desolate mountain ledge, lolled that fantastical Gryphon, that mournful Mock Turtle beside him, bewailing what his mock-life had done to him . . .

And there, to the west, it was: that loveliest of passages to that loveliest of gardens. There, where the White Rabbit would run. When he was there to run. ("Sorry," those

footprint-like shadows called back, "no Rabbit, not today.")
Still. Just beyond must be those stately rose trees—and those
broad, enormous lawns, like so many aching thoughts just
about to be thought. And there, through the sun-burnished
clouds, the most wondrous of jackdaws, sinking and circling
and sinking, on their dark extended wings. Cawing, and calling her to herself. (Just as she'd dreamed, one day they would.)
All those dawdling streams below them, murmuring. There.

But where *was* here or there? All she'd known, all she
knew, was falling. But where were those fabled cupboards
past which her Story Alice fell and fell? Where, those shelves
with no marmalade? Where the mythic maps of mythic
somewheres? Had Wonderland too been altered? Had it too
felt the wounding of London?

Down down, regardless, down she fell. Unknowing, still
not knowing, where she was—or *what* she was—down the
hole.

And there—with a skid, with a thump, with a somering-
sault into nothingness and some strange sound of sawing
in the air still above—Alice landed. Looked about, blinking,
watching herself look.

Here. Wherever *here* was.

CHAPTER IX:

—

GETTING BIGGER

EYES shut, still shut, Alice saw nothing. Alice knew nothing. And yet, displaced as she was (wherever now she was), she couldn't have been there long. For, she was only just reaching, only just reciting, the very next sentence, from where she'd left off, in her book.

"Alice was not a bit hurt," she resumed, praying she *did* know the whole book by heart. *No, not hurt—not a bit.* "She jumped up on to her feet in a moment; and up up she looked—but all was dark overhead. Before her lay another long passage, and the White Rabbit was still in sight, hurrying down it."

As *she* invoked those long-familiar words, in this senseless new world, it struck her that she'd closed her eyes to see. *Open them.* Warily she steeled herself and did. But there was nowhere there. She peered about—*all* about. Nowhere could she spy that familiar "Drink Me" bottle, or that "long, low hall," or that "row of lamps hanging from the roof"— nor could she catch sight of any White Rabbit. Which was strange enough. But stranger still, she could discern no trace of the Tube station, either. *None of it?* Had she made every-thing vanish? To what end? And if so, where was she now? In some Realm of the Lost? In some Twilight Kingdom of the Unloved? This wasn't good. This was not good. *Hmmm.*

She skipped ahead—leapfrogging past all these compound-complex sentences. Otherwise, utterly motion-less she remained. Fearful that if she took a single step, every-thing might crumble beneath her and another whole house come tumbling down. With a quick breath, on she went: "The Rabbit was no longer to be seen"—*Exactly.* "There were doors all round the hall"—*Not so much.* "All locked"—*Not.* "She came upon a little three-legged table"—*None of the above?* "Nothing on it but . . ."

The tiny golden key!—*Yes.* Just the thing to let her out of this stealthy shade and admit her once again to Wonderland. (When they'd play this scene at Alfred's, they'd had the tiniest antiquegolden cupboard key. Not so much, here. But *all right,* she could mime.) Gamely, into the waste-black space (a space it seemed her memory could not contain), Alice stretched her hand. (Her hand, which, on the old church piano, never could quite reach a full octave. *But . . . so much for that.*) Pretending to lift that missing key, she clinked, or pretend-clinked, and unlatched some transparent door of the air. *So far, so good.*

One, two, three, Alice breathed. She opened her eyes—hoping, at least, to renew her former acquaintance with her mind.

But alas, no table appeared. No key, no doors, no locks of any kind. Nor that loveliest of passageways to the loveliest of gardens, where the White Rabbit and she could wander among those beds of fairest flowers and those cooling silver fountains.

None of it, there. None. Nothing appeared. Only one blankgolden afternoon. Only a sort of shadowless lawn, golden as the clouds and sky beyond. A golden hue so radiant and vast, it was as if it suffused every atom of the land. Just there, Alice stood, without her usual shadow following behind her, or like most mornings, rising to greet her.

But still, she felt very much herself. Even at this new meeting-point with herself. Same (unlikely) hands, same (stumpy, beside-the-point) wrists, same (lonesome) forearms but . . . bare? Not a scar from those corrosive fires, not a bruise from the rubble, or other stigmata upon them. As though some merciful sponge had wiped all the ruin from them.

And look, a puffed blue sleeve—two sleeves! And a pinafore?! Over a pleated . . . something or other—the most unfussed, if flounced, Victorian dress. Just like her Story Alice's dress—but fitted so precisely to *her*. *What*—what was happening to her? Had she unwittingly summoned some Looking-Glass Godmother? Some fairy-tale someone to dress and adorn her, so she'd be proper for Wonderland?

Hard to say. And not a soul to ask. Nowhere to go, really. Alone, she stood. In some straw-colored light, in which everything that was, was meant for her. And nothing, nothing had to be explained.

And, look! There he was—Alfred. Or, rather, her White Rabbit Alfred. The boy she so well knew—the boy with whom she'd played this scene so many times before—but now transformed, as never before, into his storybook self.

His very Character in the Tale. In his fine plaid waistcoat, his elegant whiskers just grazing the collar. So officially his White Rabbit self, she could barely suppress a smile.

And look, that tattered fan. Mamie's fan. He'd brought it! But, *how* had he brought it? It was almost as if she'd transported them both, body and soul, from that noxious Tube station into their storybook. And where once they'd *performed* their first classic bit, now they were going to be *living* it?

Meanwhile, that fan? How anxiously he fingered it, careful as ever to tap the exact same taps, same number of taps, on each palm, on each finger, on each hand. (Surrendering himself to that dread cosmic law of Even-Steven taps.)

She caught his eye: *Ready?* He pulled himself up, his shoulders drawn back, so proper. Readier than ready to begin their scene. With a storysmile, she began: "So, there you are."

He, in his finest, most distinguished Rabbit timbre: "And there you are."

"I'm just so . . . pleased to see you," said Alice politely. "*Here*, that is."

"So pleased to see you, too."

And there, he drew it forth, his war-scored pocket watch. That, too! His silver apple of the Wonderland moon. He tapped it, tap tap—he couldn't not. (What was the wizard without his wand?) "In brief, I'm late, you know?"

"Oh. I know," she replied. "Sorry. Sorry."

But what to say—to keep him? If only for a moment. Just to linger in this moment. *Come, Alice—do say something.* She, always so thick with words—forever in conversation with so many selves, each self so full of so many polysyllables—and *now*? Not a "the," not an "of." Flustered, she stammer-started: "It's, well, it's all—just been ssso . . ."

Tap.

"Of course. Of course," he insisted, growing fidgety. "Oh my ears and whiskers! I must go!"

"*Nooooooooo!*" Alice yelped. Couldn't help it.

"What?" He stiffened, tight-lipped. Tap tap.

Yeeks. Now, what had she done? Why couldn't she ever just look at him without wanting something more from him? *See*—before she knew what, she'd cried out. Had crossed some line—like some wretched, rash, intruding fool! Had broken character, if you will. She could see it in his startled eyes—gone rabbit-pink and all bugged out."

"I don't know," she offered. "Honestly. It's just . . ."

"*What?* It's time," he chided, "it's well past time—you know."

"But . . . here we are."

"Yes—*what*? How long can we spend on this same page?"

This page? Forever and a day. Couldn't they just stay, on this ever-vibrant page, where both text and illustration would say: "We've just begun, in Wonderland." Just here, forever here, they would remain. No earth revolving below them; no cloud, drifting from or above them. As if there existed, for them, neither future nor past.

Say that, then. But all she managed was: "One moment, please."

"And then?" He blinked, a White Rabbit blink, so puzzlingly: "We stop when it's the end. In the beginning, we *begin*."

"But surely," Alice grinned, "books are made to linger in."

Tap.

Now what had she done? (For whatever was *said* was already *done*. Already dead within the heart. And no matter how many times she'd warn herself, no matter how many nights she'd lie awake, regretting every syllable she'd spent, she just couldn't stop herself saying the most shameless things.)

Tap tap, the White Rabbit tapped his watch. And Alice? Virtually tap-dancing she stood, shifting her weight one foot to the other. Time-stepping within. Thinking again on those classic illustrations in their book, wondering: *Do we, too, look like that? Are we, too, being looked at like that?* With someone else forever flipping through, turning us always wayawayaway . . .

"Alice?" he exhorted. Taptapping once again each palm, each untapped waiting waiting so impatient finger.

But how could she speak it, really, the anxiety of *feeling*? Of all she wanted from him. It was like she was forever listening for some key in the door, for some way out of the sensation of herself, that she might touch what was him. Some stupid kiss: was it only that? But was a kiss ever just *that*? Not that she knew, really. But maybe it would be like *not* disappearing. Like tasting yourself on the lips of someone else.

Tap. Tap.

"I only mean . . ." muttered she. But already she could see the refusal, guttering in the pale flame of his eyes. If only she could speak the half of what she felt without becoming so ashamed of herself. "But why not?" she pressed him. "It's still the story. We're still here *in* the story."

"No," he rebutted, with a barely tolerant twitch. "If we're here in the story, we must be *in* the story. And so . . . if so, I'd better go. I mean, that is the story."

"Is it?"

Ah. *See*. Again, she'd done it. Had said so much. Had said too much. Had stammered and stewed, had *interrupted*. And that, after pleading with him to come down here! After turning the poor boy into a Rabbit! Now, she'd stopped him cold—just as they'd begun performing their first chapter. She'd gone off script and left him stranded—and all he had were storywords to try to understand her. Stupididiotly, she'd pulled the storyrug from under them, and put him on the spot—setting them both up for such ghost-responses.

TAP!

She watched him blather, ponder, maunder: "Perhaps you ate a bit more marble cake today, and you grew bigger?"

"And, is that so bad?"

He lifted a strict paw: "The Queen will be just savage. If I've kept her waiting."

And then he did a thing that seemed so sad. A thing that seemed to lock them into place, to make of them an emblem: both of them forever separate, looking on one another but never moving toward each other; both of them, rather, remaining so staid, embalmed in some Victorian Picture book, in a child-pose for eternity. So prim. With such a formal, waistcoat-thrust he offered her that fan and his make-believe gloves: "I believe I . . . leave you these."

She made no move. Just took this in. What what was she to do? To play the churl, and to refuse him? After all, and after everything they'd lost, here they were again. She'd brought him here to do the book, she wouldn't fault him *doing* it. And yet . . .

She made no move. Just nodded. Holding her thoughts hostage. Could she offer some plea bargain?

Tap! Tap! Tap! Tap!

All right. If that was how he wanted it.

And so, she merely nodded, and she took his gloves and fan. And then. Then she watched him disappear. Her whole childhood bending toward her, still too far to comfort her. Just *her*, again, though here.

And she found herself beside a pool of tears.

"Oh, did she?" someone quizzed, puncturing completely the spell of Wonderland. (A spell she'd been working so hard to cast!)

"Who's there? she asked herself—and only herself."

No surprise, then, that no answer answered back. Barely could Alice take in the question. The question of how, once again, she'd been left, beside some slate-colored pool, and no use following him.

"And then?" purred someone.

"And then?" Ah yes. That *was* the question. The dum-dum question bringing her back. Evicting her into the way it still was (and probably always had been)—in this concrete murk, in this Underground ruin, where her eyes remained so downcast. There: all her gilt-edged story pages—all those beloved Flamingo and Lobster engravings—like nose-blown facial tissues littering the coldsteel tracks.

Then again. Perhaps it was only the tilt of her head, or the stubborn slant of her cot, which gave the impression of this Downcast Her. Or . . . perhaps she'd gone too far within, then (so unthinkingly) let herself slip out, and like some imbecile mouse, had left herself only one hole to run back to. Look where that left her now. Stuck in ye olde *world as it was.* Lodged in her old, fatuous self. Wearing this ill-mannered blouse and cement-dusted skirt. *And welcome back, burnspots marking her arms.*

In other words: caught. Yet again. In this dunderhead Tube, in the stupefying midst of this stultifying crew, as she murmuremembered those storybook words: "Oh, I wish I could manage to be glad. Only I never can remember the rule . . ."

"Alice?"

Yes, she thought, through the dirtytile blur: *I must be her still. Alice.* But who was this, bending toward her?

"Have we lost you to the Pool, then? . . . Absent Alice?"

Tabatha, it was. Come from her perch. Gaunt shoulders hunched, beneath a fraying dress, as if to offer some defense for her bandaged face.

"Still here, thank you," Alice murmured. Feeling belittled by the sound of her own voice. "I suppose I've just been chattering on?"

"Like a china cup, yes. But to what end?"

With a sudden self-conscious remembering, Alice looked *out of herself* again—and watched the world lock in around her, like some jigsaw puzzle she once more clicked into, bringing some sense (as the missing piece does) to the whole perplexing thing. *Here* she was—here they all were, still—within the brownblotched encampment. Everyone and everything, appearing like panels in some monochromatic mural. As if the tilewalls and they had been made of one flesh, then slathered with the same dullglaze.

And Alfred? Presumably there—though every fold of his curtain conspired to seclude him from her. And now, two stout Orderlies stood beside, as if stationed there. *Why?*

"He's there, your friend, yes. And we're here. In need of all our courage, yes," Tabatha recapitulated. "Still, it's rather a brave story."

"Oh do you think?" Alice questioned, with a rueful glance toward that quarantine.

"Better and better, the more of *you* in it."

"And the less of *us*, thank you," Mamie lobbed in.

"So," Tabbie batted back, "you have been listening?"

"Be serious," scoffed Mamie.

"But I am," rejoined Tabatha. Her voice, grave as some dark sibyl's, issuing from that mask of wrappings. "It's when you say what can't be said that the dogs snap to attention."

Before the miffed Miss Van Eysen could mutter whatever, Tabbie turned back, her roughsoft hand grazing Alice's: "What next, then?"

"If only I knew," Alice answered.

Feeling lost in something like loss itself. Like some ruined compass, everywhere she looked, she kept failing to find north, failing to find home. *Come now, no time for all that.* Withdrawing into some part of herself where she always was so sure of herself, Alice cast about her mind, to find what next, what next (like some unfamiliar musical phrase she kept struggling to isolate, as it rose into view only to fade away). But it all—all her thought—seemed like some vacant lot, where once, before the air raids had begun, something so good and enduring had stood.

"In the story," prodded Tabatha. The unrelenting Tabatha. "What's next?"

That is the question, yes. But Alice had no answer. And Tabatha kept asking: "She took his gloves and fan, then she watched him . . . disappear. And then?"

And then?

A sudden raw-skinned cough—Alfred's cough! With a jerk of her neck, Alice caught sight of one of those supposed Orderlies, surreptitiously slipping behind Alfred's tent. The next moment, the other Orderly met her gaze. One stark "Don't even think about it" glare.

CHAPTER X:

—

MORE OPEN THAN USUAL

ONLY some months ago, wasn't it? That stuffy, mid-September afternoon, after school. She'd been headed with Alfred to a Tube station much like this one. She, knowing always to remain one discreet step behind, in the event he should slip. As they trod over what had become their new playground—heaps of charred and broken brick, and the neatly swept pile of ocean-green glass. No sky discernible above—only ash from the burning rags, and random bits of flaming stuff. As they traipsed down roads of debris and debris, past the occasional alley of rats, and on—past lone and level heaps, which once had been rows of flats.

And . . . on. Not a chirp from any bird to accompany them, not a sound but their footsteps through the dust. Though, in truth, she could hear nothing much—only Alfred's bare ruined breath, laboring. She could feel him, so anxious, monitoring the raucous tick-tock of it. She could see the red effort fretting his cheeks—after all the nights breathing the sulfurous dust and ash. Dust like the dust rising around them just now, rising from idle depths of the wreck. From the wasteland, the colossal wasteland that was London.

And still on they went. She, saying nothing. Better, she knew, not to stray from their usual trek, better she show no concern (surely, nothing overt) that he could miss a step—or again lose his breath. Better, she knew, that he remain confident.

On. With her shadow even more silent than his. Past a street of homes collapsed like a pack of cards. Spent. Broken pictures and lamps (someone's bedside lamp!) splintering under their feet. He, staring fixedly ahead of him. Finally, addressing the silence as much as his friend: "Just think, Alice . . . all those windows."

"Yes?"

"Behind every one of them, there was a world—just yesterday; mother and father and sister, crazy old aunts with their loud, hungry children and pets. Each of them, caught in a life—however nasty, brutish, or sad. Each of them, roomed in their own thoughts and memories. Where are they now, all those memories?"

"Within them still. Very likely," she offered. "All those displaced tenants, they could well be with their families. In shelters, now. Or settled in the countryside."

"Or heaped in some unmarked street, with the nameless dead."

Must he be so brutish and sad? What what to say to encourage him?

Too late, again. Like a prince in mourning, rebuking the wind that its name had been all but erased: he continued, gloomily, "All the things those people ever saw, all the sweet silent things they ever thought—are those, too, still within them? Waiting to be identified with the rest of them?"

"Alfred, please," she urged. "Don't distress yourself."

"In some way, they're lucky, the ones blown to bits. Must be worse for those under the debris, buried alive but still smelling the dust, hearing the cries of those buried nearby—still muttering. As if being dead were not enough for them."

"Well, it wouldn't be the first life they've taken from us." Her voice rose, fervent as his.

"Maybe not. But at least we're still here. Stumbling over their bones, with homes aboveground to go home to."

"Yes, and yes," she said, alarmed by his ragged, discontinuous breath. "But I'm tired, Alfred. Let's rest a bit. Just there, there's a bench."

But he would not, would not look up.

"Alfred. Please."

Not a nerve in him trembled as she took hold of his arm. As she beckoned him toward what was almost a bench. There sat a blank-faced boy, wrapping his wasted arm in loose pages of days-old newspaper, using its inky print as a kind of tourniquet. As if begrudging the world his endedness.

At the sight or the thought, Alfred stopped. Stood, unmoving. He became his stare. And something so rigid came over him, as if he might never step out of that posture again.

Where, where to look? If not at him? Where, in the landscape of death surrounding them?

Not for the first time since this disastrous war began, Alice found herself musing on those pale, still forms, those ancient Greek friezes her Papa had loved. Those magisterial Elgin Marbles, at the British Museum, worn and wasted from so many centuries of bombings and displacements (and perhaps from all of us, ogling away at them).

What was it Papa'd said? That they stand there as a testament. As a monument which says, despite how fragmented we may become, despite how splintered into how little we remember, still something that is us remains. Something, at the heart of us, does endure . . .

And still, throughout her entire spell of remembering, Alfred had not budged. Beyond him, that solemn brick wall, exposing an empty lavatory, with a lone towel hanging from the rack. A lone, still-standing building, its ragged curtains billowing from empty mouths of rose-brick, where once windows had been. Down the road a bit, an emptied, tottering department store, the front blasted from it, a sign in a door frame, proclaiming: "More Open than Usual." All its tins of food, and bottles of perfume, flat on the street, beside a smattering of corpse-like, rose-pink mannequins.

CHAPTER XI:

—

THAT POOL OF TEARS

"**S**O? . . . Alice?"

Tabatha? It was, trying to conjure the familiar, sentient Alice from the seemingly absent girl. "Meanwhile, back at that 'Pool of Tears'?"

Still no Alice surfaced. However visible, on that ill-lit platform, she (no doubt) remained. *However miserable.*

Lightly, Tabbie assailed her, again: "Come on then—tell us. In that yarn of yours, what's next?"

Barely could Alice hear. Hardly could she bring herself now from the stonegaze of that stout Orderly stationed beside Alfred's tent.

"Alice?"

"Yes?"

"You will tell us?"

Still barely remembering where she'd left off, and little knowing where she'd come out, Alice began to recite, as if to some campfire world (where darkened faces semi-patiently waited): "The Rabbit started violently, dropped the white kid gloves and the fan, and skurried away into the darkness as hard as he could go."

Here, she caught a breath, knowing full well what was next: "Alice took up the gloves and fan, and, as the hall was exceedingly hot, she kept fanning herself . . ."

"How 'bout that Pool?" some smoke-tinged voice drawled.

Angus—from his lazy pipe? Listening? It couldn't be.

A lone cluck—Nigel?—from the ambiguous gloom: "Pool of Tears—yeah?"

Him—listening, too? Well, all right. Once more, she closed her eyes to read, to find herself within the book within her . . .

. . . There, beneath the veiled sun, the Wonderland sun, it seemed Alice stood alone. On some cloudtawny afternoon—reflected, shadowless, within that fabled Pool.

But within that Pool? It was as if all the drops, of all the petty heartache, of all the loss, all the trifling pains that haunted her still, day to day, had joined the unshed tears for all the still-unmourned-for things. As if upon a pool of Wonderland tears, she were meeting some image of her London world, awash. There, *yes*: a pool of her own thought, upon whose surface countless shadows played . . .

Inwardly, she saw again: no Wonderland thing, no. Only that still-unbroken looking glass, swinging like a loose tooth in her sister's bare and shattered room. But she mustn't, mustn't dwell there. *Press on with your story, Alice.*

But . . . there, just there once, in front of that still-familiar glass, within that so sophisticated room . . . her sister had stood. Beloved, lovely Catherine. Still-unscathed, unwounded Catherine. Savvy as ever, lately so tall and surprisingly willowy.

Trying new trousers (the price tag still on them) with her best cotton sweater—the one with the split-pea buttons, picking up the pea-green motif of the collar. Busy, bossy, trendy Catherine. Doing her eyes—as she called it. Readying herself for her Edmund. Meeting him for some High Tea or some such thing. At some smart new café. With some whole new smart set of teens, whom he of course knew. Really, it was all Alice could do not to keep asking and asking about them. (Knowing full well she'd been born with the doom of being too young ever to join them.)

"My advice to you, Alice," Cathy offered. But not as a question—advice was sure to follow. "Keep yourself as is. Everything just as is. One more birthday, perhaps—then, that's it. Never consent to go double-digit."

"Just stay nine, forever?"

"That's when the best of it is," that raven eyeliner vigorously contended. "When you're still free to do as you please. To stay and stay late. To play whatever games—"

"What, with Alfred?"

"Who else?"

Stay nine forever—with Alfred? "What do you mean?"

The light rouge nodded, in sync with the matte-raspberry lips: "Give it a few years. Mum won't even let you alone with him."

"Don't be silly—"

"But she won't, love. It isn't enough to be a good girl, you also have to seem like one. Particularly, since his family has a bit of money . . ."

". . . Pool of Tears?" some brash voice intruded. "Meaning,

like the slosh-pool down here? From the blasted water main? One big bad drip, drip, drip?"

Oh drat! That did it. *Angus, undoubtedly.* Tearing a sudden hole, making a terrible crack in Alice's looking-glass reverie. Yanking her abruptly back, reeling her through some sad fraying portal, back to this grimconcrete world—and Catherine gone.

Once again, Alice looked about—and took in the matte-unrouged Underground gloom. Nowhere to look that could be bothered being looked at. (Certainly not those scattered pages, still scowling in dismay at their own hideous change.) *Trapped.* And somehow sadder and wiser for that. As if she'd reached a sort of puberty in tears . . .

Without so much as a sigh, with only a glance toward her quarantined listener, whom she could only hope was listening, that wordweaving girl took up her Tale again.

Wondering who, or what exactly, she had become, Alice bent to look into that Wonderland Pool of Tears. There, another Alice bent to meet her—a seeming reflection of her, in a Storyblue dress just like hers, in a pinafore just as pristine as hers—but such a strange, ungainly figure that Alice started back from it. It, too, started back, as if she too were strange.

And there, another Image seemed to surface. This one smoother, somewhat slimmer (thank you), soliciting her eye from the watery gleam. Alice bent, for a closer peek—it bent!—and pleased, she fixed her look on it. Pleased, it fixed its look. Like someone Alice had been friendly with, once, but hadn't seen in such an age, she'd rather just avoid her really. (Someone surely Alfred would remember. And had he found her so naive, so needy as now *she* did?)

In any event. Just think how many "me"s she'd already been! Countless "me"s, who'd come and gone. And which of them remained with her, remained *as* her? She wondered . . .

For, with all she'd lost these last few months, with all she'd never dreamed she'd feel, that now she'd come to know so feelingly, she'd had to be continually remembering, stitching together some *new* her, some self who could maybe make sense of all the loss. But then, through the unending night, she'd had to be forever *unremembering*—like some modern-day Penelope—unwinding darkluminous thread, unstitching that new her again. Weaving a kind of tapestry of all she so intended to forget. Of all the fresh hurts. All the loss for words. All the worry for what would come next, what next . . .

Without much noticing she did, Alice shook her head. And *there*, on the pool, another Image appeared. Some younger Alice self, in some petticoaty (yes, god-awful) dress. *How,* Alice thought, *how ever could she have worn her hair like that?* In those awkward braids? Really, had she ever been *that* she—and been content? That idiocritical waif? With all her schoolgirl thoughts and dreams like humbug melodies forgotten soon as played. Some self, some song of herself she'd lost—beyond telling, really.

> *Bite by bite—*
> *Ohhhh you're getting bigger—*
> *Night by night.*

Alice spun about. *Who singsonged that?*

There, within the pool, staring up at her, were all these countless, curious *new* Alices. Spectral, older girls. These smug, shut-down versions of *her*. Mournful *future* "her"s, mock-mocking her. As if they'd known some future shock she could not yet comprehend. Something in her destined to be lost and found, then maybe lost again.

Just look at them. Mocking, clocking her. Some of them completely growing out of—some, just barely squeezing into—others, like overripe fruits, just completely bursting through her exact blue blouse.

Enough. She winced, tugging her blouse and skirt in her own defense. She turned. But where to turn? Everywhere she turned, some *her* was there—stalking her. All those spooky future *"her"s*, so full of themselves *and* her, glaring back at the mess she'd made of the past.

But there—like some would-be White Knight—her White Rabbit charged, thump-thump-thumping by. *Okay!* She reached—she waved. "White Rabbit!" she cried. But on he went. *Without a pause?* Without a look back? She tried again: "White Rabbit!"

"Oh, my dear pink nose!" he fretted (in a White Rabbit—lingo all his own). Utterly preoccupied. "Time! It's time! It's past, past time!"

And with a hop, skip, leap, he was gone.

Well. Good as it was to see him run again, she had to ask: Had he come here only to do *that*? Hadn't they also come to linger together, to take in their Wonderland garden together—all those palefaced roses?

"White . . . Rabbit?"

Nothing. Silence. Only those water-blue shadows of Her Alice-ness, that ever-present, ever-absent *her* who haunted her. All those watery *other* "her"s. Soggy twerps. (Really, it was like she'd been turned into that ancient-myth girl, Echo; everything she heard only fed her regret for something she'd said.)

"Ah, so," some presuming voice chirped.

"Ho, ho," came cackling back. *From the Pool before her?* Some maudlin laugh.

Yes! There, some sunken Mamie-like Image swum, its lank cheeks buried in fast-fading ringlets—like a ruffle of dandelion turning to dust. From those drowned girl eyes, such a baleful look: "Well, if you'd rather thump, thump, thump, don't mind us."

Us? Alice scanned the duntawny nowhere around her. No one there.

"Hehehe," came the titter—from the quicksilver surface of the Pool: "Well, whiskers were always her weakness."

Alice stiffened; her mirror-image stiffened. "Oh, no. Absolutely no," she insisted.

"No?" someone purred. *Some fresh pretend "her"?* Alice scanned the glassy pool. Nothing strange (or, at any rate, nothing new).

She cast about, behind, around, and *look*: within the emerging branches of some newly emerging tree, glimmered that familiar gibbous grin. *Tabatha?* But no, surely. Tab could not have teeth as long as those, nor claws, nor dark fur growing all over her. This must be . . . the Cheshire Cat? Yes, just like in her book! With those feral bulging eyes, and the humped darkfurrowed back, and that knowing smile "from ear to ear." Exactly like that Cat—except that underneath her tummy sat a raft of fat tin cans. But, Alice barely took those in, too caught up in the mystery. Too intrigued by the glimpse into that mystery, seemingly on offer in that grin.

"Cheshire Cat?" she asked.

"Surely, there's no great wonder in that," answered the Cat.

"But why would you be by the Pool of Tears? You're not even in this part of the book."

"So, am *I* the one bringing me here?" Chesh challenged, threatening to shut her piano lid of a grin.

"Sorry?" Alice asked. For her furrowing brow had no answer to that. The question was, like with her kitty at home: was she playing with this Cat, or was this Cat playing with her? "Sorry?" Alice asked.

And now, those ever-feral, ever-mesmerizing eyes seemed to drift from the Cat. "You did say you'd bring us."

"I meant Alfred," Alice contended. Rather assuming that would put an end to the matter.

"Thanks so much," snarled the Cat.

Stung, Alice began, "No, of course—"

But before she could blather on, those arched forepaws departed from the Cat. With a hiss: "Aliccccce. You can always indulge in some Magical Study of Happiness. The truth is, a lot's happened since last you were here. And plenty more to come, before you come back."

"Do you mean, a lot has *happened*, or that it's happened *down here*?" Alice asked.

"That it's happened in you, my pet. You can't be surprised, then," Chesh reasoned on, "that the wonders look so different."

"But what am I to do with that?" Alice asked. "What am I to take from all this?"

"Surely," purred the Cat, letting go of her entire rear, "that too depends on you."

"But all those ghostly Pretend 'Me's?"

"I wouldn't dismiss them too soon," Puss came back, her whiskers disbanding into the brisk autumn mist. "Maybe mirrors have memories, too. If so, who knows what all they hold on to."

Yikes, Alice thought. Feeling frightfully exposed, she looked again: all those Pretend "Her"s—glimmering, grinning so menacingly from the pool. Each of them stinging, assailing her with some "God, is that me?" look, which once she'd cast. See—all the eyebrows she'd squinched! All those faces of "Yeesh." And, beyond all that: what else *had* they seen, all those Ghosts of Alice Past?

Grown quite self-conscious now, Alice turned—but saw no Cat. Only some brooding raft of clouds. There, she could discern a sort of ghostbright crescent mouth—like some odd piano full of too many bright keys. But surely, no Cat thereat.

No, she'd been left alone, just she and this intense distorting Mirror. (Its distortions only exacerbating the endless quarrel with herself she was always and forever finding herself in.) *Really, must a Pool of Tears be so impertinent?* Couldn't a puddle just lie down and feel sad? *Apparently not,* in this bruised new Wonderland.

Now, what had she been just about to . . . ? Something, there'd been, which she'd been about to . . . Before whatever new thought had come barging in. What? *Ah yes.* The question was: What had been going on, down this hole?

So . . . With a restless toss of her sleepless head, she let herself brazenly ask: "The Rabbit. The White Rabbit. Has he met some other girl to give his gloves?"

"Only the mere thousand who come tumbling down each hour," some mirror-self spat back.

"Double that, on Sundays," another mouth mocked her.

"Ho ho. Ho ho," every mock-Alice laughed and laughed. (Every other "ho" concluding in a hiss. As if mere laughter could no longer express her former and future selves' darker contempt.)

And with a merry round of further "Ho ho"s, all the images dissolved. Leaving Alice with no reflection at all. Alone, now, in Wonderland—and with the weird sense that she'd always somehow been expecting this.

CHAPTER XII:

—

AND ALL THE BLUE CLOUDS SING

"**W**HOOOOOO are yoooouuu?"

Those words, so long unheard, yet so familiar. That voice of utter languor seeming to drift right through her.

Alice knew, knew and loved (loved perhaps not wisely but so well) this exact page of her storybook. And here she stood, as never before she'd stood, somehow *within* it! She, the same old she, but leaning against that proverbial Buttercup, surrounded by all those near-transparent blades of summer grass and all the most exuberant flowers. (Which heretofore she'd read of, but only could imagine.) And now here they *were*, just here: all those Tiger Lilies, Larkspur, Dahlias, and Violets, spurting up, flush beside and flushed behind her, like a throng of semi-friendly fellow concertgoers. Maintaining a semi-dignified silence. And there, like some grand dusty proscenium awaiting its main attraction: a large-large mushroom rising, like a maestro, swaying in place, and almost the very same height as she (whatever height this new she might be).

Once she had looked beneath that mushroom, once (as in their book) she'd looked round "both sides of it, and behind it, it occurred to her that she might as well look and see what was on top of it."

Savoring this louche, fantastical moment, one of her favorites of all the storybook bits, Alice took her time, turning longingly round, only to see . . . not her dear, expected Caterpillar. (Namely, Alfred's spot-on imitation of their book's illustration.) But rather, some sort of sultry, lounge-about, slightly older boy, the type whom Mum would tell her to ignore. A boy who rather looked like that would-be pilot, the ponderously-toking, pipe-wielding Angus. *Wait—she couldn't have brought Angus here, too.* What did he care about some silly Tale? He couldn't even be bothered to listen.

But whatever she'd done or not done, there he was. That languid Caterpillar face, just like Angus's face, a blur of thought and smoke. His legs—well, unlike Angus's legs, a corps of countless itsy feet—folded wryly beneath his larva-ly torso and the last few rungs of (weirdly, wartime) belly.

Curiouser and curiouser, Alice thought. And she looked again at that shroom, which seemed now an open parachute, its plume billowing high into the cloudless afternoon.

Upon the most elaborately winding hookah—like on Angus's ivory pipe—that rakishly handsome scapegrace puffed. He pondered. Without a look at Alice, staring her down: "I said: whooooo are youuu? Remind me."

"Well, once upon a time I knew," Alice responded with some misgiving that she even was responding. "But I've changed so many times today."

"Do you mean," he crooned, "you've changed your mind?"

"And body, too."

"Oh, don't I know," the Caterpillar intoned. And now those larval eyes seemed to bore right through her, with a wild surmise: "So, who arrrre you?"

"I'm afraid I'm new to me," she ventured.

"Well, you're looking new to me—"

"No matter really who you are to you," some second voice said. Even as a second Caterpillar head appeared. Purling, puffing up slyly; seemingly young-womanly, and more than a little bosomly:

Now, whooooo? Some *other* Caterpillar? A female Caterpillar? Or a second, unfamiliar head on her fond old familiar? Such come-hither, Smoky-Lash mascaraed eyes, such a strangely dainty mouth, beckoning to Alice through some cloudy-blue perfume.

Joggled, Alice could only question: "But . . . who are *you?*"

"Come, look!" soughed that fulsome Number 2.

Alice looked again: "But are you part of him?"

"Or, is *he* part of *you?*" asked the buxom 2.

"Now, how could that be?" asked Alice, finding herself

oddly drawn to this brave new nubile beast. And yet, also a bit dumbfounded.

All nonchalant, that curvy Caterpillar Number 2 came winding many a wreath alluringly. Issuing, from her sultry tongue, such a satin sound: "Whose head's in the book? Not his."

"Not *hers*," wooed Number 1.

Now that brawny Number 1 came winding, virilely unwinding, round. Terribly cool and friendly.

Alice stiffened, looked again. "Now I'm confused."

She paused, or tried to pause. She looked again. And there, Caterpillar 2 came lolling, like some luxuriant lingerie, wrapping round Alice's unsteady shoulder: "You you you must put put down that book."

"What book?" Alice feinted.

"The one in your head, that is."

"Put put it down," drawled that handsomely lumbering Number 1. "Do."

With a side-curved head, Alice brooded on this odd, alluring Number 1. This rogue, who seemed to tell her, with that languorous grin of his, he knew exactly how it felt to be within her. Within that . . . newly forming her. That newly curvier, there-before-her her. *But but but,* she wondered, *could it actually give her pleasure, growing bigger?*

"You," she murmured, nervously turning to Number 2, "you're not even in the book. Not as I remember—from the pictures."

"A girl can't change the pictures?" Number 2 appended, drawing nearer.

Now Number 1, too, wooed nearer: "Set it down a minute—all the Alice-ness . . ."

"All that By-the-bookness . . ." blued Number 2.

To the uttermost tip of her outermost lip, Caterpillar Number 1 extended the blueing hookah nib. And like that devilish Serpent, offered: "One puff . . . ?"

One . . . what?

Nearer and nearer coiled Number 2, her sultry, mandibled mouth towering above all her mazy folds: "Stops time, it does."

An electric charge ran through Alice—as if those words had flipped some inner switch. "Stops time?" she asked. "It does?"

"To whom Time may concern, it does."

So . . . there it was! The answer to the riddle of why here she was—of course it was! To stop time. To learn the way, the winding way, to make it stop. "But, does it work on . . . other creatures, too?"

"Let's start with you," Number 2 importuned. With a trailing sigh, which seemed to fathom Alice's everything. All those smokeblue feelings rising, seeming to rise, from that Caterpillar's delectable little feet, through every foxy twinge of her lower extremity up to that welcoming breast.

So close those Caterpillars wound around Alice now: another and another mouth, another softsoft breast, another manly chest; wherever she turned, another O-O-O-ing cloud . . .

Roused by the rising swell of those fumes, she spoke more freely: "I have a friend, you know, my dearest friend, spends so much time pursuing time, consumed by running out of time . . ."

"Always thinking forward and remembering backward?" offered Number 1.

"Chasing before," proffered Number 2, "and chasing after?"

Nearer still wound Number 1, beguiling even his fumes, which wafted forth, then back, to his fullmanly lips: "One puff."

"But my head?" she asked. "Will I ever get it back?"

"Then, do you want it back?" some new tongue purred.

Whoooo said that? Alice cast about, and there, in a neighboring (till recently, nonexistent) tree hovered that conspiratorial Cheshire Puss.

"My head?" Alice asked.

"Yesss," purred Puss, "it took so long to lose it, as it is."

"And yet, I'm so very accustomed to . . . having it."

"High time, then," Puss averred, "you find out how to do without it."

"But, how do I do that?"

"Lose *yourself* with it," returned that Cat. "The way, some say, a lover disappears into a kiss . . ."

"Well, when you put it that way."

With a measured step, half-convinced, Alice turned back—and there, invitingly enough, rose that shapely Caterpillar 2: "Come," said she, "shall we . . . disappear?"

"Ohhh," Alice ohhh'd, "but it's taken me so long just to appear. I'm not sure I'm ready yet to disappear."

A subtle and mighty O, ascending, floated, fit right around her sniffly nose. She couldn't let that in. Or could she? . . .

Never, never once in her life, had she considered what it would be like to set aside all the talk in her mind, all the expectation that bred all the regret. *Could it be useful, actually, just to relax?* (And if so, what would that mean for *him*? To set aside the eating cares? To feel more of a peace with himself than with his fear?)

"One puff," proposed Number 1, "and all one golden afternoon."

For him, too? The thing was, those cool-kid Caterpillars sure seemed sure of themselves. "But will it really?"

"You tell us," puled lovely Number 2.

And with that "us," Alice leaned—as if recollecting some dream in which she'd leaned—inclining herself toward some fruit of wisdom so delicious, Time itself would stop; and in that pause, she'd let her head drift off. *Yes.* She'd let all of it drift, all the niggling thought, the ceaseless self-questioning, all the continual *consciousness* . . .

With that, she . . . puffed. *Oh whoa!* Her head—the head she'd always held so dear—went lifting, hovering, surging—

"Kachhhhhhhhhhhhhhm."

Kachhhhhhhhhhhhhhm? And now some plank in Alice's reasoning broke. Just when she'd been finding such sure footing (in her mind), suddenly she found herself falling, falling through some realm of blue—thudding up against and plunging back into some too-too-grounded world.

"Mmm-hmm?" she mm'd.

"Kachhhhhhhhhhhhhhhhhm," a raucous throat, declamatorily cleared. A knownknown voice, following up: "My gloves?"

A familiar-seeming figure, Alice seemed to see. Someone looking quite perturbed. *White Rabbit? Oh no. Quick! Snap to!*

"I believe you have my gloves?" he asked again. Barely containing his consternation.

116

"Whooooo, me?" asked she.

"You *don't?*"

"I do. I must."

But those Rabbit eyes seared through her. "Me, I've been waiting for our scene."

Our . . . what? She tried to recall. She did try.

"Come, come," he snipped, "you know the bit. 'The Crash of Broken Glass'—the big 'Alas.'"

No no no no clue. She had no clue.

"Our bit, I say," said he. "The page you skipped?"

"I did?" she gulped. Not doubting him. But *what?*

He Rabbited in, insistent. "When your hand is just so big you knock down my entire house. And I call you Mary Ann . . . ?"

Ah yessssssssssss. That bit. In truth, she was never unhappy to skip that dippy scene, where he called her "Mary Ann." But braving it, her smile said, "Haha, yes. And you send me off to fetch your gloves and fan!"

"I'm frantic for them, actually."

"Of course. So sorry. Sorry. I suppose I . . ."

"Got distracted?" cooed that canny Caterpillar 2, winding her budding way, redundant, toward Alice—ring after marvelous ring of that bluer blue.

Now, see. In all the rush and wooziness, Alice had forgotten that caddish, and that smoldering, new companion.

Alarmed, alert, her Rabbit jerked and twitched, his vellicative paw brushing her hand: "So, shall we?"

He drew himself up. Like some neurasthenic thespian. Whiskers crimpling, as he (all derring-do) leapt into the scene they'd missed: "'Oh, Mary Ann! Mary Ann! Fetch me my gloves, this instant.'"

Still woozy, Alice barely could handle it. "But is that really why you've come? To fetch your gloves?"

"And fan?" vamped Caterpillar Number 1.

And now those two (1 & 2) wound their countless legs together, taunting: "As if you meant no more to him than random Mary Ann."

"Oh, Mary Ann . . . ?" cooed Number 2.

And Number 1: "Back a bit, where we began . . ."

White Rabbit twitched, his stoical ears in a total snit: "Where *what* began?" His whiskers, paws, tail, and nose aquiver. "Time, time, I have so little time. Oh, why did I come down at all?"

"Perhaps I'm looking through a different glass," Alice postulated. (Trying, she was trying. Gold Star for that.)

He fidgettwitched—so anxiously, so antsily—as if he kept

using each fidget to dig, then to deepen, some river between them.

"Come," she goaded him. "You followed me, now follow me."

"No," he retorted, "follow *me*."

Waistcoat collar tight hot itching, Rabbit hopped into his umpteenth recitation of that celebrated book bit. "'Oh, Mary Ann! Run home for me, this moment, please.'"

Alice stood, just stood and stared. "Come, aren't we a bit too big for this?"

His look darkened. But now, through fumy rooms of blue, she reached; she took that hookah, and she held it out to him—knowing the more she unsettled the bunny, the more she'd be tempting the boy. "But, *this* . . . stops time, it does."

"It does?"

"To whom Time may concern, it does," she confirmed.

Poor Alfred-Bunny. In a puddle-muddle, so perplexed. Wavering so uncertainly. Waffling—wobbling—oscillating, really—he stifled a thump and met her look.

Tenderly, Alice offered: "Just—one puff? You'll know no time. You'll breathe again."

He did not budge. But Alice sensed, she knew, he wanted it. More nearly toward him she leaned, as he teeter-tottered. Toward her he leaned, then away, then to-to-toward . . .

All at once, his nose bunched up, in spasm: "But it's not *us* who puff." Tilting his head toward Caterpillars 2 and 1, he offered as proof: "They're *them*. We're *us*. We can't be . . . other Characters."

"Can't try on other selves, you mean?"

"Be other than ourselves?"

At that she smiled; but answer made she none. At a loss, White Rabbit watched; every nerve within him tingling, as she puffed . . . as she . . . peaked. As she exhaled one lustrous cloud—tempting, tickling him with something so exultant; meanwhile, near-burning his bunny olfactories.

Against his flinching underlip, she rubbed that hookah, as if it were some wish-fulfilling lamp: "Drink me."

"What?!"

She couldn't not grin, assuring him. "Come. That *is* the scene."

The Honorable Mr. W. Rabbit seemed to feel himself go numb—meeting her look, sending a quick chill thrilling through Alice, a sense of nascent exaltation. Till it felt like they both might rise right off the ground . . . Then, suddenly, he (or his overwrought, rioting mind) cried stop: "Oh, my dear, dear fur and whiskers! The Queen! The Queen! She'll have my head—you understand?"

Skeptically, Alice eyed him: "She will?"

"She will. As sure as ferrets are ferrets. Executed."

Feigning bland indifference, Alice let him simmer. "Then go."

"I will," his eyes, his words, his petrified fur affirmed.

But he did not move. He could not. Straight-faced, Alice asked: "And so?"

Poor Rabbit trembled. Hemming-hawing. "I am rather fearful of losing my head."

"I know," said she.

"I'll go," said he.

Almost, he did. Almosting it. Half a pace he took, with half a rising wish . . . But, a brawling voice abruptly butted in and punctured every bit of Wonderland: "*Absolutely*, you will go. In fact, the Orderlies are here. First stretchers go to the soldiers, then it's you."

Alice stopped her recitation cold. And stood, speechless as those old cylindrical walls, which rose into view again, like some ghastly caricature of Dover's cliffs. Blankly she stared about: no wonder, no Wonderland, anywhere. No sungorgeous clouds, only Angus Wilkins's opium. No luxuriantly lounging Caterpillars. No watery future "Her"s (certainly not in concrete-dusted skirts like hers)—just her. No White Rabbit. But—*Alfred?!*

Ah, there he was, behind that starched, stranded curtain. All else a wash: nothing but the one unending Underground. Nothing but the wilderness of cots. As if, or so the burlap insisted, life should be merely *physical*, now they were here. (But of course it wasn't. Surely, their real life took place in their minds. That was where "events," good or bad, landed. Where they mattered, really. Where everything lived on—in memory—in all she imagined . . .)

In the meanwhile, that Platform-World rolled on. Irrefutable. Belligerent. The monstrous Red Cross Nurse pivoted; and sweeping that quarantine's curtain closed, she addressed the waiting stretchers. (Those stretchers being sent somewhere else—to gather *someone* else.) "Now move it!"

Clap clap she clapped her ruddy hands. Each clap, like her clamorous tongue, resounding through the entire Tube station. Her starched-white armor glimmering in the aura she wore, the halo-glow she had absorbed from the chokes, gasps, screams of all those sadly expiring souls she'd cared for, seemingly without a care for them.

Listen to me, Alice thought, *attacking some old Nurse. Surely, my wit's diseased.* But she so was at a loss for how to resist her thought—for how best to help her friend. Caught up in her own obstinate questionings, she'd let her story slip. And she had no word, no refrain she could catch, no refrain that would bring it wordlessly back. For she only truly had it, having him—telling, retelling it, to and with him.

Maybe, she concluded, the White Rabbit had been right to be so wary; maybe she'd lost her grip on the tale by *changing* it? She searched her heart—from blank to blank, without a thread; without a narrative to stitch one supposition to the next; her every other thought a page she'd skipped. Or perhaps like a page she'd read (as she so often did) without paying any attention to it.

Thankfully, Tabatha had been paying keen attention, intent on everything untold in Alice's tale. She prodded: "So, did he? Lose his head?"

"Did . . . what?" asked Alice, at a loss herself.

"Your Rabbit."

"They can't take him," Alice stated, definitive. "I won't let them."

The Red Cross Nurse turned—one Red Cross look. "He will go, when and where we send him. Wherever we send him. Now, do I have to strap you to that bed?"

To a child like me, thought Alice, *every grown-up is a giant.* But this Nurse rose so high as just to be colossal.

Clap clap, those Goliath hands clapped: "Lights out, in ten minutes."

On the woman went. *Whew.* Alice peered, through the half-extinguished light, toward that closed curtain. *Closed indeed*—like a page she no longer could read, by dint of staring so long at it. Yet—what could she do but *look*? All the while feeling, acutely, how each look brought home only the distance between them. (When, in fact, one shared glance might hold so much—so much food for further thought, so much tenderness . . .) Really, it was like that Nurse had closed a door, just so she could close every possible window.

. . . Only some months ago—six, maybe seven months—was it? Though it all seemed so remote as to belong to someone else's life. (Some world, some life, before the nightly hail of the bright bombs began.)

That stolen Sunday afternoon with Alfred. He, only just "well enough" to go out again. She, only just approved to accompany him.

The Giraffe House, Regent's Park. In the gelid light of some enduring, if crueler, April day. Together they'd stood, in a wondering silence, as once they'd stood so many years before. He,

124

extending a leaner forefinger toward their favorite giraffe. (Still there!) "See, Alice? His tongue—dark as ever."

"And not a bit sunburnt," she'd kidded, echoing her exact words from all those years before.

He nodded, grown quiet with remembering. But his smile half a frown already.

"We'll be careful to keep our mouths shut," she gibbered. Wanting to luxuriate within their shared remembering but sensing some more solemn spell come over him.

He nodded toward their long-necked friend. "Casts a longer shadow, these days, doesn't he?"

Meaning? *she near-challenged him. But some stronger instinct told her just to let be, just to listen.*

And he continued: "He's like all those things most near to us—sadly, all too dear to us. All the stuff of circumstance, in the midst of which we eat and drink and live—things like my illness, say; or, which train shall we take to get 'poor Alfred' home again?—all that seems to loom so large, its shadow takes up all the room in us. Till everything that matters most becomes so small. So nebulous. Nothing but an after-dinner dream . . ."

Oh, but it does not, Alfred. It will not.

This, though, this surely was no dream. This Underground . . . diminishment. This sitting, here, broad-waking—on some unsleeping cot. Her whole psyche so emaciated, she felt like one of those Giacometti sculptures, really. Her body like a terror to her. Her arms, her legs, without dimension. And he, the wiriest wraith, mere silhouette of all he'd been, exhibited upon some quarantine bed. And . . . everywhere else she would look, nothing seemed quite to include or surround either of them.

Vigilantly she listened. No coughs now, no wheezes. "So did he?" came some odd meow, drifting down and down.

"Whoooooooooooo?" inquired Angus, just as abruptly. A poof of azure smoke hovering, wafting through.

And now, a spray of fresh, familiar, and still disconcerting voices:

"Oh, you know who. We all know who."

"Him, that's who."

"You-hoo!"

Mamie, Dodgy—it must be. Alice knew, without even looking. The two of them, in their persnickety two-of-them-ness, always insulting. Chittering, chattering, always interrupting. What she wouldn't give to distill all that unintelligible talk to a single intelligent thought.

Still. Once more, Alice peered about: the world still there, without her all the time. That painfully ordinary platform, that customary Cot-Land, where not a dot, not a jot had shifted. Still, as always: the soldiers wailing; the hepped-up Harold leaping, ducking about; Dodgy doing dress-ups (wound in his woolen, but as in some profusion of silk and shawl); and of course that nimble-marmoset Mamie, she, who'd tossed a tarot deck with Lady Asquith, blandly disdaining to play Whist (let alone, Go Fish) with the likes of Nigel; he, who—to her annoyance—kept blunting, nubbing, and ink-smudging his cards' ends, rub-a-dub-dubbing them from neck

126

to chin, murmuring under his breath, "This is it, it's the end. It goes dark in the end!"; as Angus sat, wielding his manly, ash-speckled deck, pondering the nothing—except, perhaps, the life he might have had, the life that might have made life worth all this.

And yet. Something had changed. But what, if nothing had changed?

Alice sat, so unusually self-possessed, so consumed with her own searching thoughts, it was as if she were alone with them: her only task, to sift through them. Yet, even as she did, there came the most querulous, cicada-like sounds, issuing from all those chirruping, largely indistinguishable mouths:

"So, did he?"

Some feigning mouth deigned to comment, as if with disinterest: "Lost his furry head, did he—for the sake of that one puff?"

"See, see, here here!" Harold Pudding exulted, riffling through his sketchpad pages. "His funny bunny ears, right here—puffpuffing up with every puff!"

What a soldier you must have been, Harold.

"She *kissed* him?" inquired Miss Van Eysen.

"Do tell," Dodgy cooed. Condescending to profess interest in someone other than himself: "*Did* he . . . puff?"

Alice nodded, half-against herself. "He did. And as he did, he . . . rose, floating from the stubble-ground with her, through that full-bare distance, up and on, through the kelly-green veil of the trees."

"Sounds like a brilliant high," observed Tabatha dryly.

"Me," that would-be pilot Angus spewed, over the

terra-cotta bowl of his otherwise ivory pipe. Pontificating throatily upon his favorite theme: "Me, I think that Caterpillar had a lot to give. Sure, they kept him there, wastin' away, arse-over-tit, on some shroom. Never lettin' the would-be pilot rise. Never allowin' him his wings—am I right? Still, he'll show 'em, one day—won't he? When the boy becomes a butterfly!"

"A sordid business, really," muttered Dodgy. "Such a beastly story."

They'd been listening?

A sudden rustling, from behind that curtain: "Beastly? No, no. It was . . . lovely."

The boy peered out, frail but sitting upright.

"Alfred?!"

His look brightened. "Do go on."

Trying to adjust her whole sense of herself to accommodate all she felt, seeing him upright again, Alice smiled. "Yes, lovely. *Yes.*"

And with that, the tale resumed. And it took up every bit of the room within her head.

CHAPTER XIII:
—
SUCH SUCH LOBSTERS

O, they puffed. And as they puffed, they both together rose. (Or so said the Tale, the Tale which had made itself a bed in Alice's ear.) *Together both, they rose, until . . .* from the uttermost tops of the tallest trees, the purplemist distance that surrounded them had also entered deep within them.

So high! They'd climbed so high, Alice could extend her hand and almost touch those clouds—not those fumy, near-forgotten blues. Rather, that golden promontory, just beyond the nodding treetops, where she stood with her White Rabbit, taking in the wonder of this land of afternoon. All the scenes that seemed to flutter from the illustrated pages of that book, which had become the book of her memory . . .

There, the Dodo and the Magpie, the Duck, Canary, and Eaglet, racing in their Caucus Race to nowhere. A race that never quite began, and yet never could it end. A race that Alfred and she'd first acted out, and madly run, within their common London garden. She could almost see him there still, beneath their shared wild-cherry tree, pleading so irrepressibly:

"Let me play the Dodo, too!"

"But you're already the Duck and Eaglet, the Magpie and

Canary," she'd countered, "to say nothing of the next bit, where you're back as the White Rabbit."

"But," he'd said, to end it, "you are still the only Alice."

And here she was, all these eras later, still so Alice. (Even dressed in her own Alice Dress!) Standing beside her true Rabbit-him, looking down on the ample lawns of an actual Wonderland. See, *there*: still barking, that Preposterous, Enormous Puppy! Pawing and panting, trampling who-ever came near. (Suffice it to say, that role too had had to be Alfred's. Still, she could see that twelve-year-old him: wag-ging, bow-wow-ing, chasing sticks, then bounding back on all fours, toppling her, near-slobbering all over her. Ahh, there had been moments, once he'd done with leaping, moments of him poised above her . . . when she'd catch some lively glint in those pale eyes of his, when she'd thought perhaps they'd linger, that finally they might . . . kiss? But, not. Not yet.)

And speaking of classic Alfred roles, *see*, there: those two in formal livery, bowing to one another, the Fish and the Frog Footmen, one of them forever grumbling and griping, stoop-ing behind her: the other, always rising, so pleased to greet her. Neither one ever letting her into the Duchess's house; and yet, both of them forever letting her out again.

And within the house—hear, hear!—the shrill, imperi-ous Duchess, burping her baby so brutally, serenading him with a violent joy, promising the pig-nosed thing some pep-per whenever he sneezed.

And there, just there, as if through the worn, phantom pages of her mind, she could see . . . the Mad Tea Party, more mad—"More tea?"—more riddling than ever.

And there, at the edge of a royal embankment, that large White Rose Tree, where cards Five and Seven were testily, if sloppily, painting every white rose red. There, that glorious Croquet Ground, with its endlessly curious Furrows and Ridges. And there, beyond the Flamingos and the Hedgehogs, beyond the lawn's clipped edges, she could almost make out, on that Legendary Ledge of Lonely Rock, her poor Mock Turtle wailing. And beyond . . .

How, Alice asked, as she took in those wonders—more wonderful still, for transporting her again to those first moments they'd *played* them together—*how*, she asked, could she hold so many memories? So many already! How, as she lived, and each day remembered, so many more, even commonplace, instants, how would she house them all? *And as she got older?* Was she to become one of those women she'd see—those solitaries in wan brown scarves on odd park benches—stooped from holding so much that they'd lived through? Their eyes no longer taking in where they were, as if it would cost them too much to have more to remember. Sitting so motionless, befuddled in wonder, near-turned into monuments themselves . . .

So, maybe she should start *Un*-remembering? *Seriously.* Should start concertedly unraveling all the years, all the feeling, the entire future she so had believed in. Truly, she'd trade in the whole life she'd lived—she would—if she could only be here. If she could only stop all the thinking and unthinking and simply be here, this moment, with him. Once more in Wonderland. From these mystic treetops looking on.

Really, she ought to be showing her White Rabbit, ought merely to be marveling with him, at all the intimate splendor below them. There he was, of course, all Rabbit-wriggled up, beside her on a broad and yawning branch; seemingly dazzled, himself, by that lone glimmering leaf—as if it were some mystic insignia of the spring (of which the first leaf is the tale of coming leaves).

Say something. "The, uh, treetops!" she marveled. "I have never seen the treetops!"

"Not *from* the treetops," wryly he replied.

She smiled. "And see, beyond that lonely rock, the Mock Turtle's Rock—"

"The Mock Rock?"

"Precisely," she agreed. "See—all the waves of the sea, lapping still, still so. And on that pebbled shore—there, that legendary Quadrille, the stately waltz of all those gorgeous Lobsters."

"Such such Lobsters!" he marveled. Then confessed: "I am finding myself oddly hungry."

"Not the Lobsters!"

And with that, she tapped his hand and, for the first time ever in Wonderland, had to suppress a certain bashfulness: "I mean, I do so love the Lobster Dance . . ."

"Yes, of course," he blinked, he batted back.

Lord, what a pause ensued. A pause, it seemed, they both were in, but neither knew just how they'd gotten in. *Oh dear oh dear*, thought Alice. Why must she always keep wanting something more from him? Tripping them both up, into some Absurdist pause, by all her rethinking, by her endless angling. In place of just letting be.

And *there*, where it seemed only Alice could see, there drifted some—what?—ears? Some mouth of cloud? Some Cheshire tongue releasing a fond familiar hymn: "Oh will you, won't you, will you, won't you . . ."

Was that a prompt? That child-rhyme from their book, it was. Hmm. Maybe she could lead with that?

Once more through blinkered looks, she caught his glance. And certainly, half-certainly, she chanted that old storied chant: *"Will you, won't you, won't you join the dance?"*

His nose twitched. His ears flinched. "But I'm not in that dance. Not in the book, I'm not."

"Not yet," that Cheshire purred—but only Alice heard—from that seeming mouth of tumbledown cloud.

And now, some irrepressible star seemed to rise in the grey lamps of Alice's eyes. She looked to the White Rabbit, surprising him with her own Cheshire grin. "Not yet."

White Rabbit flushed. A peony-pink blushing up rosered. And so . . . self-conscious. He could not dance. (Surely, she knew that.) (He knew she knew that.) (Sure as sure, they both knew that.) He *never* could dance! "You wouldn't want to, really—with these ears?"

"The dearest ears," she (pseudo) deduced, surveying them.

"But, I'm all paws."

"*Aren't we all?*" clucked that Cat-ical tongue. Letting a bit of steam out of the neighboring clouds.

"Well, I'm all soles and eels," an emboldened Alice ventured. Remembering forward, he smiled a bit. And so she smiled again. But still he nothing said—and so she nothinged back. *What next? What next?*

Well, you can pause and pause—and pause, Alice thought. Or maybe Chesh thought. But by now, all trace of Cat had disappeared. Only Alfred left. With the Alfredest look on his face, a look which seemed written in a language known only by her . . .

Ohhhh, but she could sense him, poising himself, within himself, upon some dizzy precipice. "Now, shhh," she pronounced. And resumed their chant:

> "*You really have no notion how delightful it will be,*
> *When they take us and they throw us, with the Lobsters,*
> *out to sea . . .*"

"Alice, Alice, we can't!" he protested. Half-against himself.

"Yes, we can. *Here*, in our own Wonderland, we can."

Knowing well the rhyme, he came back:

> "*But the snail replied, 'Too far, too far!' and gave a look askance—*
> *Said he thanked the whiting kindly—*"

"Please!" she urged, through laughter.

On he went:

> *". . . but he would not join the dance,*
> *Would not, could not, would not—"*

"Can, can, can." She lapped him in that laugh. And as he paused, she pointed. Down down they looked—farther than far, to where, below them, twirled the Lobsters. Printing a golden path in the still more golden sand. With her Rabbit rapt in wonder, Alice curtsied and discreetly took one gloved paw, then another—in her ungloved hands.

And a music crept upon them—from the waves, perhaps, from all the weltering shadows of those wavewhite mermaid waters, which seemed to lap their darkness on the sand. A music which they could not comprehend, and yet which somehow comprehended them.

> *When you partner*
> *With a Lobster,*
> *All the world's your shore . . .*

With that moody flood of words and notes, with the twining stresses, two by two, the Rabbit seemed to lose himself (or almost) in those dulcet sounds, which, on his spirit, made a music too. Music, like a melody from the other side of memory, a tune she also seemed to hear, which held her spellbound too—as she led him, paw in hand, from that chandelier of tapering trees onto a carpet of air, a carpet that unfolded from a cloudless vault of heaven. And there, within the blue beyond, she held him near. They waltzed. He, with a brisk titubation of those dearest ears, displaying a surprising mastery of each step; maintaining, even as he moved, that gorgeous immobility one sees in world-class waltzers—

WAAAAAAAWAAAAAAAW!

A siren wailed—some air-raid siren. *But . . . here?* Like a cry from the broken world, through the spine of night, sending some sonic rip through Wonderland.

Alice grabbed for her White Rabbit—every illustration fluttering below them; every paragraph sputtering; each phrase loosed; whole chapters, spewing raw their drawings from a wash of rained-on colors—as he groped, groped madly, madhotly, for his pocket watch. His proper watch. *Was it only that, then? No actual siren, only his alarm bell going off?* An alarm on a pocket watch? Indeed, it was. Awful, hectic, clamorous, loud as loud. (As if bell after tormenting bell were battering the belfry, breaking down the bellman from the tower.)

One impertinent watch he yanked out—struggling to contain the anxiety that came rising with it, enormous as Time. A nightmare, from which he could not wake. Something fierce as History, defying him to shut shut the screaming off, to shutshutitdown, *shut it up!*

Stopstopitwatch! Pockpocketwatch!

Keeeeeeeeening! He clamped the glowworm watch face. He pressed the pin, each importunate button. No luck. He yanked out another impudent watch. He clamped. He

137

pressed. Still it kept sounding. From somewhere. Like a scream escaping, striating the sky. Infuriating! Out he yanked another watch. Pressed it. Hating it. Hating himself hating it. *Stopstopstopstopstopit! I beg you.* But . . . *no.* He tried another. *No.* Another. *Nonononono . . .*

Alice squeezed her eyes shut tight. So tight, and suddenly: the sound—*no sound?* It had ended? *Yes.* Without an echo? Yes. Only some bottomless moan from the sea below. Intently, she turned to her Rabbit, relieved—

But he, frantic, still so out of breath: "Oh, dear dear. So much—such a muchness still to finish!"

"Just . . . please," she urged. "One minute more, on this page."

"This page?! What page?! We're not even on a page."

"We can change what's on the page."

"No no," he cried, "*you* can change. The page can't change."

His chest and waistcoat heaving—with a spasming arithmetic—stumblingly he started off.

"Please! No!" she cried. "One more minute!"

"Oh, we all know about minutes," he contended, every word suffering its own conniption fit, recoiling back upon him, "how they start out merely minutes—*seeming* minutes. Soon, each second, it's a minute, and the minutes run like seconds, till they're hours—running, slipping—years and years—gone, gone, gone."

"But they're not," she reassured. "Not *here*, they're not."

"Gone. Gone. *I'm late! I'm late!*"

"For what? Croquet? I'll come."

"*Alice*, stop. Please," he urged. "This isn't just some silly game. I have no time left—not for this."

"There's time. There will be time."

"No," he mourned, more gravely still. "If you knew time as I do . . ."

"But I don't. I only measure time by when I'm with you and when I'm not."

Violently, the Rabbit shook—and, with that, shook some earth-cry loose. A siren screamed, and the screaming held across the sky. Then Alice, too: *"Stop stop, please!"*

All at once, she lost him—lost him, falling. She, too, with him, falling, falling, down down doooooooownnnnnnn, through the fiery clouds, those colder embers of the dying day.

Still falling, through the oncegolden sky to a world of night. Toward some siren keening, crying for night.

The two of them, falling—wordless—like the night. Or was it, rather, *they* who were bringing the night? The darkness spilling from them, suffusing Wonderland. Or . . . had this archaic, broken-spined night, dotted with dust-bits of parchment, *ever* been Wonderland?

Regardless, still they fell. Fell falling past those fleet, Third Reich death-gliders, rising as high and bright as the phalanx of stars. Inscribing bright trails with their smoky flight, leaving smoke turrets and spires and towers behind them. Until, it seemed, all the silvered architecture of the city-night had been transposed to the sky, and the dark veil, which once had made night of that sky, now obscured the widowed face of the darkworld below.

There, as they tumbled, lay London. But a London blacked out. With all its conscience-riddled streets, impatient to resume their world. There, the East End, only blistering embers. There, King William Street, in ruin. Not a light in Piccadilly. Nor on Fleet Street. See, the Marble Arch in darkness. The Westminster Bridge, the Houses of Parliament, Buckingham Palace, too—so dark. So dark. They'd all gone into the dark.

Only there, beyond—the parched horizon slit by glittering tongues of fire. As if the eviscerated city were some charred and fiery log, just struck, which sent forth innumerable sparks: like so many grisly auguries of future cities under siege, of refugees to come, of children hanging from wrecked tanks or playing dolls on stacks of shells . . .

Down down down. A city ripped from silence. By this sole unholy siren. Not a chime from a single cathedral. Not a tower tolling some reminiscent bell. Not a telescope gazing up into heaven. Nothing, no one calling. No train running. No world, no sound, of London—of all that hum that made it London.

Darkness. Not a searchlight even—not a car light—only those white markings on the curbs and bollards. No one out—no, only her Alfred and she, falling toward those blackened streets. Just bodies wholly body, falling. Down, through some bunkered shelter, where children huddled among vaults of corpses.

Down down, past some huge-mouthed tunnel. Through the catacombs, it seemed. Through a monastery of dead monkish bodies . . .

Down, through some wasteworld unearthed below—
past a layered crypt of Anglo-Saxons. (Their bared heads an
oblivion within those lost bone-houses.) Below them, ancient
Britons; and all they were was ivory—their bodies, wooden
shroud pins. No more pearls even for eyes.

No, only . . . layers of mold, below them: loam gone numb.
No maggots on those dry white bones. Only Roman relics
and remains, with nothing beside—and still below . . . the
empty heaps . . . the void and formless deep; the infinite emp-
tiness, boundless and bare.

On, on, still they fell, through the lampless night, with the
wounded and dead, to their birthgrave of Mother Earth.

"Till *here*," Alice said. And pointedly paused. Her recitation paused.

A mouth, from the gloom, Nigel wondering: "'Here'?"

Dodgy: "As in?"

Angus: "Just . . . *here*?"

Alice sat, too paused to ponder. Still too nowhere. Then
she felt her head start nodding: *Yes*.

She looked about—and here she was. Within that
browned familiar Underground world. Upon the cot-webbed
platform once again. She in her bed; he, in his. Once more,
here: amid the clammy walls, the dismal scents, all those treasured, dog-eared pages scattered on the tracks. The sleepers,
too, still there—sleeping somehow on, beneath the screeching siren so unending.

CHAPTER XIV:

—

A THIEVISH PROGRESS OF DARKNESS

SURELY the worst of it, with a siren, was the after-shock of silence. The waiting, Alice thought, the charade. The mad denial—of all it truly meant, of what would come next. *There*, that mongrel-Nurse, maintaining a studied calm, but back on the prowl. (Like some corrupt friar, preaching and condemning, casting her spells—meanwhile, banishing everything truly spiritual.) And there: Nigel and his thumb, rockrocking, muttering, "Mummy, this can't be it. Not yet it. Not not like this!" Meanwhile, Miss Mamie, restacking her solitary holiday trinkets, protesting that no indeed, the world could not be at an end. Not yet! On Thursday, Auntie Beardsley was throwing her a birthday party—at Liberty! The entire civilized world was to be there. Naturally. All the while, as she chirpedchirped on, Dodgy, mockmocking, tepee'd in his blanket, with his haughty chin held high as high, holding some imagined phone in hand: "Roger that. Adolf? Dodgy here—listen up. It's Mamie's birthday—and the bombing's such a bore. Could you put a pin in it?" The while, Angus puffpuffing on his yellowing pipe, saying how much he hated the sound of the siren fading away. Hated knowing it was headed somewhere else, that it soon would be sounding for someone else—someone he might never know, somewhere he might never be . . .

And . . . *Alice*? No denying she, too, was waiting, mute, inattentive, uncrumpling her thoughts like some school-paper wad. And so deliberately dithering. Lost on some map of what-ifs. Like on those ghostcold nights she wouldn't dare climb out of bed, for fear she might never get back there again. All awkward, without any ballast, unwashed as her blouse, on this dismal cot. Impersonating herself, for herself, again. She, whose shadow surely ought to be endless. Ought surely to extend beyond that curvilinear Tube-station wall, beyond that white-glazed round—far beyond those cold glinting tracks. But it did not. Merely sat there, stiff and inhospitable as she.

Some moments, sure, she'd sat. But since then, since she'd paused—since she'd become a sort of pause—how long? Mere moments? Hours? Whole stretching cycles of years? Years of this, her Night Nine Self, sitting, straining her comical neck, to make her periodic checks on him. (With no return but that blankcurtain glare.) In the meanwhile, clocking the wastrel crew, who'd remained all winter in London, as she had—to get through "these dark days together, in the bosom of the family." All of them huddled, as she was, beside the coldshoulders of those shadowy tracks. All of those motherless tykes, with whom she could soon be blown to bits. Each of them, like her, alone in some room in their head . . .

. . . *Like all those lonechild faces beside that railway station,* Alice remembered. *A year ago, September, wasn't it?*

With the dismal brown wind, like some hollowmouthed radio announcer, howling about the effect of the war on the weather.

There she'd stood, beside those coldshouldered tracks. With Alfred, watching those queues of ghosteyed children. Children soon to be evacuated, armed only with gas masks and diminutive suitcases. Mere children, sent from London, dispatched from their families, in order to escape the nightly sieges. Homeless children, really.

Could as well have been Alfred and she, boarding a train without their Dad or Mum, departing to who knew where. Through some cracked (assuredly, unhinged) window within her, an icecold child hand seemed to branch into Alice's chest. Gripping so hard her knees near-buckled under her.

"Come, Alice," Alfred urged, catching her, setting his firm warm hand on her shoulder. In reassurance that their world, and they, were there still.

"Come now, home now, Alice," he prodded, "your Mum must have you home with her. If a raid comes tonight, as of course it will . . ."

"Of course, yes," she mustered, and started homeward with him. Only to feel those icefingers within her, and to turn right round again: "But where will they all go?"

"To Somerset. To Derbyshire. To some rural somewhere. They'll be safer in the country. There'll be fewer raids, or no raids—"

"But they're children!"

"Yes. And they'll be safer there. They'll know their parents love them, and soon they will be home with them."

"Then, should we go there with them?" Alice had challenged. "We'll be safer too."

"No no."

But she pressed on, the words like some warning voice escaping her. "Or should we singly stay on in a city grown so barbarous, it could cast out helpless children?"

"Come, you're talking round in circles now. It isn't like that, Alice, and you know it. It's their parents who decided."

"Yes but, Alfred, the injustice!"

"Is it? Parents doing what they think is best—everything the government will let them? Maybe there's a mercy in it too."

"Why can't their parents go with them?"

"Everyone leave, then?"

"Everyone!"

"Alice, someone has to remain—for London's sake. Someone has to 'aid and stir,' as Churchill says, to stand up in resistance."

"But why does that have to be us? You're still recovering, Alfred. You're in no state to be standing up for London—not at the moment. First you must get well again. The countryside will do you good. The dust alone is so hard on you."

"It's hard on everyone."

"That may be, but—"

"Alice, please. My Mum and Dad, they want me home. As your Mum wants you."

"But it isn't the same."

"It's exactly the same. I'm no worse off than you."

But that wasn't remotely true. Still, what what to say—in the face of the look he gave her? A look of regret, of indignation, but so powerful in its restraint she could not meet its gaze for long.

"Alice, we can talk all day. Your lips are blue from cold. Come with me. Home."

With such words, with such a world of care, finally he'd steadied her, and led her past the heaps of splinters, weary brick, and black-ash rubble. There, behind some scooting rat, amid the debris, she spotted a bewildered school-edition of Euclid. The blasted pages of his Elements fluttering, flummoxed by the breeze—as if leafed through by some god, who murmured on: "A point is that which has no part . . . A line is a length which has no breadth . . ." Just beyond that demiurgic murmuring, some awkward-sad recording of Tommy Dorsey, sounding: "I'll never smile again . . ."

On they went. (As if walking through a time before there was any accounting for time.) On, past a crumpled, old old woman, in a Turkish robe and slippers, wailing from the ruins she would not go to a shelter. Why, she keened, why had life been spared her? Why not take that, too? She had lost her home, her everyone, her children, her grandchildren . . .

Through all that, he'd walked her. Had seen her home, and stayed on—through that night and all the next day with her. He had held her hand in his, had read to her, as she lay shaking. Pale and shaking, just as he lay shaking now . . .

. . . And had they gone—as she'd proposed? Had their parents actually set them on a train, like those children with their gas masks—all those months ago? Had she trusted her own inner voice, had she simply insisted—to her Mum and to his—that they both be sent from London, they would know no part of all this. They would be well out of it. In Derbyshire, perhaps. Or Somerset. And through the long temperate days there, he would know the sun again. There, he would find himself again, and he'd have rest. She'd read to him, and he would be well again.

But what to do, beyond remembering? Beyond hosting her soul at a retrospective of all the bad choices she'd made and now could only second-guess? Meanwhile lying here, utterly restless, in this fetid Tube, consumed with care. What to do, but let be. To move past her belittling self. To buck up, and ignore the lumpy demands of this bed. To scrawl again within her old-friend notepad, with the dwindling nub of her dwindling pencil, a kind of acrostic. (Just a young girl's jottings of her war impressions, and consequently meant for publication!):

> *An auto stopped for me one night,*
> *Lit by a lone Red Cross,*
> *Its colors camouflage; and I thought:*
> *Can we please just not?*
> *Eternity is for the gods. I'm wounded, but I am not . . . lost.*

Or was she . . . *not?*

"Hmmm," someone hmmm'd. (Taking the word right out of Alice's mouth.) But who? And was it meant in judgment on her acrostic?

Leaning forward, pressing the offending poem to her

knees, Alice sent her look scouting about. There: some shameless grin upon the stagnant night air, lingering. A sort of scar. And behind it? *Cheshire Puss?* Needless to say, that would be a bit strange. *What would a Wonderland Creature be doing in the Underground, anyway?*

"Dear, dear, everyone and everything falls apart so queerly around here," that cryptic grin observed. Growing conspicuous now, agleam on that Cat's unmissable mouth.

Once again, Alice peered about—no one in medical uniform prowling about. So . . . why should she not let her thought out, to that fugitive feline? Besides, it wasn't every day, some actual fictional character made its way down here. Shouldn't she at least reply to it?

Holding all that in mind, Alice summoned a sigh: "Yes, well, it all keeps disappearing. The pages turn so quickly."

Chesh nodded, her brindled tail like a freaked question mark, peering from behind the cracked-oval clock. "The moment you're *in* the story," she meowed, "you find you're *out* of story. But perhaps that *is* the story. Always parting, always greeting."

Always parting, always greeting—the exact thing that that fantasticatical Cat was the emblem of. *But parting from whom—to be greeted by . . . what?*

Maybe, Alice thought, part of what reassures us that the world still exists, even without us, was simply that the things within it stay there, that they don't dissolve into our seeing them—that they remain there so long as our gaze does. But, the fact of that Cat seemed to refute exactly *that.* For, although Chesh had the look of something that liked being

149

looked at, Alice could never quite hold on to the fact of *seeing* her. Could never quite catch up to herself in the act. It was, rather, as if the Chesh was always dissolving just beyond her perception of her. (As though there were nothing anywhere out there that Alice could hold on to. Nothing she could count on still being there—on *staying* there.)

She was right there, Chesh was—wasn't she?—and yet, still *beyond* there: that toothy, teasing grin, like so many sorry syllables, disbanding, discombobulating, "Always parrrrting, yes, and greeting. At least you can't complain you need a change of scene."

Mentally I shake hands with you for that answer, despite its inaccuracy. "But . . ."

Gone. No sign, no symbol of her. No trace of who-or-whatever, fictional or factual, had actually been there. (In any event, Alice asked, can there be anything, so quick to come and quick to go, as the frank affection of a cat?)

And again, the siren—like some barbaric, yawping echo of that Cheshire meowww—wailing even as it waned. *Yewawwawweeweewaa . . .*

Pertly, Miss Mamie turned to Dodgy: "Maybe Adolf missed your call—about my birthday?" Then: "On Thursday?"

"Thursday?" Dodgy yawned. "We'll all be gone before the night . . . Still, one day when they dig us up, we'll be immortalized . . . Pray God, I haven't aged too much."

Yeewawwaaaweewaooooaa . . .

Suddenly, Pudding. Bolting upright. Shaken. His bad eye palpitating. As if he'd just heard reveille—or some Alarm for Troops to Turn Out under Arms.

150

"Pudding, sir! Harold Pudding. Present and correct."

Waawaaw, the siren waaw'd. Not to be outdone, that hemispheric Nurse drew herself up, aghast. Pivoting on her sensible heels. The definition of shrill: "Mr. Puuuuuuddddiiinnng?"

"Sir! Yes, sir! Before your Throne of Grace, sir!"

Angus, roused from his roost, satirically called out: "Right, right. And I, I, too, shall not cease from this mental fight, nor will my erect red Sword, my heated Meat Puppet, sleep . . ."

"Hehehehahah," Dodgy giggled (while Angus guffawed godawfully). "His red Trouser Snake, the boy means!"

But Harold heard neither—heard no one—too alone he was, to take in any ventriloquism outside him. Standing at attention, in a shuddering vigil—like the last man standing in some mad dance of marionettes. Giving fair warning to his imaginary friend, his lost companion: "Put on your flak jacket and helmet, Freddie! Head down in your trench. *Doooowwwn!*"

Startled and sad, from a sadness as large as her past, Alice watched every last silhouette stop. All except Harold's, that was.

With a nod of the head, Pudding made sure his imagined mate was there, still there—as he clasped his good Pudding hands in good-soldierly prayer. Brusquely he shouted again, *"Dooooowwwwnnn!"*

A grim whistle blew. The Nurse, it was—summoning an Underground marshal.

"Come, Freddie, that's us!" Harold urged. "There've been whistles enough!"

"Abso-bloody-lutely, mate," chirped Angus. Abruptly out-Freddie-ing Freddie: "Out of this dust, let us rise and be touched!"

But Harold did not hear that faux-Freddie cry, nor that heckling grunt. Prone on his belly, he'd ducked under Mamie's cot and lay there now, utterly still, shoulders hunched. While Mamie herself ducked under her blanket, still holding, still minding, her precious gilt cup.

"See, blokes like me," argued Angus, "failed volunteer blokes like me, we don't fly. No, we climb a great ladder." With a near-canine chortle, he ruffled Mamie, with a rough hand, through her blanket: "Muck-ups like me, it's easy-peasy—see, we put out the li'l girls' fires. But soon soon our ladders will be cryin' for water! *Haaaaaaah!*"

Shrilly that Nurse-whistle sounded. She herself drawing nearer, crying after, "Fire Guard! Marshal!"

But on Angus had gone. Pocketing his pipe, he clamped that same presuming hand on Alice's back. Swaggering suggestively: "Let that Queen call her dogs and her Marshals. The real enemy's in our pants, isn't he, darlin'?"

"Alice," a voice rasped. *Alfred?*

It was. Yanking his curtain full open, the boy peered out palely, wildly.

"Alfred Hallam," the Nurse cried, her own eyes wide in alarm. "Close that, this instant!"

"No matter what—if we lie down, or don't—it will come!" Angus cawed.

"No! You! Don't!" cried Alfred, rearing himself forward from his precarious perch.

"Ah yes, we can keep to our sad separate cots, still all those Kraut-bombs will fall. Fall like some pestilence," Angus prophesied. "Explode here, above. Just a matter of time, till they're all close enough. Till that water main bursts, and all your fine tunnel is smothered in sewage and gas."

"It will not!" Alice retorted. "Mr. Churchill would never have let us come down here. He knew it was sound. And it is. All of us, we'll be safe down here—"

"From the *Drip*? Do you think—"

"Let her be!" Alfred shouted, heaving himself farther forward, his feet near-skidding from under him as he hoisted his frail form toward the floor.

Keenly whistling, bounding suddenly toward him, the Nurse called out, "Hallam!"

Alice saw: "Alfred?!"

But Angus snorted, holding her hostage, staying his burled arm on hers. "Don't get your knickers in a twist."

"That's enough out of you!" hollered Alfred. Running, trying to run, his knees foundering. Hurtling himself headlong toward Angus. "Fear-mongering thing," he cried. "Half-priest, half-pilot, are you? Setting yourself so above—looking down from your fear? Men like you, you're the reason we're down here."

"Oh, do you think?" Angus challenged.

"Let her go!" demanded Alfred. And he lunged, all at once, grabbing Angus, breaking Alice free with the force of his fall.

Yes. No. That moment, falling—once again—*Alfred!* But the stalwart Angus held on, with rough arms breaking that fall. Holding him, catching, resisting, as Alfred kicked, struck, and balked, wheezing and panting and heaving for breath.

"Give me him," commanded the Nurse, pressing her own

stalwart flesh into the mix. Grappling Alfred, still convulsing, into her arms, she glowered at Angus: "It's you, brought this on. You Hothead Fool!"

"Opioid-induced Hyperalgesia," the Good Doctor interjected, fixing his (indifferent) congregation with a mad pulpit eye, "this was ever, seemingly, a paradoxical phenomenon, ha; but—"

"Dr. Butridge!"

"Whaaaat?"

Rebuffed, half-repentant, like a shamed reprobate, still Angus held on. Striding beside the Nurse, helping her lug the still-protesting Alfred back to his tent. There, with a firm, callous hand on his chest, she wrestled the boy's wasted limbs onto the bed.

Across the grizzled room of the Tube, Angus looked bluely back. In self-abasement. A look of pure apology, a sort of open ovendoor to a soul in regret. But Alice was taking no guests. Straining, stepping toward Alfred, shaken by the sight of him—as if some deathly chill had caught hold of him—still she could not catch a breath.

And . . . that moment, Harold Pudding leapt like a cricket caught in the kitchen. With a sudden shudder of his shoulders, swatting his neck with his scarred open palms. In a frenzy. Alarmed to conniptions by Angus's outburst. Chilled, sweating, yellower than yellowing grass, the dazed soldier vaulted about, to the consternation of every cot, sparking an "Ouch!" and an "Ow!" and—from the just near-again Angus, a "Hey, mate, look out!"

"Careful," called Alice.

154

But he did not turn. With a brisk disheveled bound, down down the platform went Pudding, caprioling.

"Pudding? Harold Pudding?" Old Doc Butridge queried, as if he were just, fortuitously, awakening.

Still so distracted, that Private related: "'For God's sake, Pudding,' they told me—with the blood still spurting down Freddie's face. 'For God's sake, Pudding, take hold of yourself.'"

"My thought exactly," the Nurse commanded. "Just where do you think you're going?"

"No weapons, sir!" that good soldier returned. A broken syntactical plea: "My presence will be with you. Even when you are without me. And no weapon turned against us, never will it prosper."

Like a panicked colt, so confused it kept running back into the barn on fire, Harold cantered—pouncing on each stair, coursing past every bugaboo'd sleeper, near-whinnying as up up he leapt, he went. The fraying pages of his sketchpad fluttering onto the platform.

"Your book, Harold!" Alice called.

With that word he stopped, with that word he looked— some faint blossom of a look put forth to Alice. Like a thing set free in a sharp wind. Like some green life within the scorched tree which still housed him. *Quick, quick*, said the look, as it also said goodbye.

And . . . Just as quick (too quick for any fresh word from her to interrupt) he turned, he went. Like some candlelight, by which he'd read and sketched within that book, flaring that much higher. *Before going out forever?*

"Hey, cool the borrowed brass, mate—there's a raid on!"

cried Angus, with an abrupt burst of dust, toiling after.

But nothing surfaced further from the soldier, as on and on he bounded: "To the breach! To the breach!"

"Pudding, dear boy," Dodgy deigned to call after, "do come to your senses!"

But on on, regardless, the untented soldier went. Still shivering. "'Thank Gawwwd, our Harold, our youngest, is well out of it . . .'"

"Come back here!" the Nurse yowled. Her cramped crabbed feet chasing after.

"Stop! Stop him!" cried Nigel.

But on, toward the loudpounding night, Pudding went. Evading the Nurse and the winded Angus's grasp. Stair after stair. "'Chip! Chip! Chip!'"

"Pudding, this minute!" the Red Cross Nurse demanded.

But *on*, as if into his lost comrade's arms, Harold ran. On and out of the Underground.

"Pudding—nooooo!" Dodgy bellowed after, discarding his usual guise of disinterest.

But . . . gone. His shadow gone. Not a footfall left.

The entire world, it seemed, staring itself into shivers after him. A world dispossessed. Till finally, the Tube station drew in a breath, as if ready to participate in the sensation of living once again.

"Oh my God, my pearls!" Mamie shrieked suddenly. Ripping her blanket from her, near-toppling her teacup. "Where are my pearls?!"

"Your neck, darling?" posed Dodgy.

Mamie checked. Still there. Sigh. "Well. All right, then."

And the world was itself again.

And she? Not herself, not just yet. Searchingly Alice looked up the platform to Alfred. There he lay, flushed, chest heaving still, but with such relief in his gaze he seemed almost content. And yet, and yet. She feared what all that exertion had cost him. Was it only her delirium—or was his chest still trembling? As if his body was now too weak to keep secret how sick he actually was . . .

. . . An oral quiz it was. History class. In the stale air of their staler schoolroom. That barrel chest of Alfred's, ballooned toward her—so full of life. So full of him. As he insistently pointed and pounded his thumbs toward his breast. His gaze so ardent, beneath those lank copper bangs.

"Alice Spencer?"

That snub-nosed stickler, Miss O'Shaughnessey. "Yes, ma'am?"

Alice, alone. Standing, knock-kneed, in front of the class. And falling, free-falling—all of Newton's stupid Laws coming back to haunt her (all that force, mass, and whatever the rest of it). As she tried tried tried to sort how, when, and why those Angles, Saxons, and wretched Jutes had first invaded Britain—in AD 880.

Miss O'Shaughnessey, nose-wings aquiver: "Shall I repeat the question for you, Alice?"

Show no fear. "No, I've got it. I believe."

Alfred, from third-row center, watchwatching. Wanting, so keenly, to feed her the answer.

"Then?" Miss O'Shaughnessey jabbed.

Near-bereft, Alice swallowed, breathed: "Who led the

157

British troops to victory in the legendary Battle of Effandune?"

Ah, the aching contortion of Alfred's sweet face!

"Ethandune," Miss O'Shaughnessey coldly corrected. "But yes, that is the question."

Thank heaven.

"And the answer?"

That was the question, yes.

"Alice?"

Never once, in all those thousand years, since the Battle of Effen-Ethandune, never had a single Angle or Saxon gesticulated so urgently as Alfred did then. Cupping his hands on the crown of his head.

Ah, the crown! "Well, it must have been . . . the king," Alice conjectured.

Miss O'Shaughnessey, unimpressed: "Namely?"

What what were those Alfred-thumbs trying to tell her? Jabbing again toward his chest.

"King . . . Chest-er," Alice tried.

"Excuse me?"

"King . . . Me?"

"Alice!"

Then it hit her. Eureka. "King Alfred!" . . .

. . . "Pudding? Harold Pudding?" Dr. Butridge quacked, with a wary, mysophobic air. That quack transporting her, as such quacks do, back to the Limboland world of the Tube (that unmapped space, located somewhere between the gloom without and the gloom within). There, upon the blurred tile-horizon, that delusional Doctor still tracking

Harold—like a dentist chasing a traumatized patient who'd fled to the waiting room. His madmedical clipboards rattling, coldly pinching the air. No pinch in death—they seemed to brag—so sharp as this.

But as the echo of that rattling brass mournfully died away, some strange, articulate silence settled upon them all. The Nurse drew closed Alfred's curtain, and a slow awareness dawned, that that damaged infantryman had just run, half-senseless, into the rain of shells and the fiery night. Still, the wordlessness, and the awe, lasted only so long. Then, that familiar beast, Adolescent Hubbub, reared its head once more.

"Maybe he thought those bombed streets needed company?" Dodgy opined.

"Quite right," Mamie cooed. "Good of him."

"But what if he? . . . If he's . . . hit?" mewled Nigel.

That dire, flattening siren sounded a kind of amen, and again all eyes peered up those stairs. But . . . to no end. Not a word from Pudding. No one there.

Only that Red Cross requiem, that whistle resounding through the night—and all their insomniac ears—as she summoned her Secret Thugs, aka the Orderlies. With a heaving-and-ho-ing of her stalwart arm.

Just watch her, Alice thought. Must be wanting only to throw up her hands, to sit and weep—for the shadow of death, falling on all of them. (All of them, like Alice herself, so rude, so resentful of her. As if, despite all the Nurse's care, she could never inspire love in any of them, only fear.) And still, she had to stay in command. To marshal her strength, show no weakness, bring order again.

"The imbecilic, that numpty, Harold Pudding!" the Nurse decreed, then commanded: "Bring him back. Immediately."

Thankfully, not a body, nobody, was propped aloft on a stretcher, when those Orderlies dropped everything. (Effectively abandoning Alfred—*thank you*.) When they bolted down the platform, toward the stairs. A thievish progress of darkness spreading over the station, like the ominous, shuddering shadow of horses, fleeing, bewildered by lightning.

"All right, lights out. Everyone. In. Their. Bed."

With that, a stirring of blankets. A listless or begrudging moan, here and there. That was that.

Till, once more, Hubbub, with its thousand whispering tongues, could not restrain a single one of them:

"How dare he? To up and leave?" "Who?" "Pudding!" "Oh. Did he?" "Who?" "Abandoning his mates again, isn't he?" "I begged him not to go—you heard me." "Are we really bothering to blather about that half-wit?" "They'll be bombing!" "Bedwetter!" "I did everything I could. You heard me."

And Alfred, breathing more easily, was he? His body restored to some calm again? Or not? What had he done to himself, to his health, by lunging from bed to help her—*only made himself more flush, more feverish? Or had the expense of all that spirit reassured him somehow? That he still had it in him?* She could not see or know, only hear him dimly. As she chanted inwardly for him, thanking him, her true friend, thanking him . . .

160

CHAPTER XV:

—

SO LITTLE ABRACADABRA

NIGHT Two, it had been. (Though, "the weeping lasts only a night," Papa always had said.) And yet, a tear-riddled Night Two it had been, in this Underground station; with Alfred, though wounded, still here, just here, on a cot beside hers. It was before he'd begun the worst of the wheezing, the most frightful coughing. Before that dire Nurse had taken him from her and set him behind that insignia'd curtain. Till then, till that night, it had seemed like this whole horrid war was a thing that somehow had happened around Alice. A thing that, however acutely it grieved her, would one day make sense, if she only got through it. But this . . .

On Night Two, he had still been so him. His spirit resilient. Consoling, cheering her, telling her tales. In spite of the effort it cost him, regaling her with faux biographies of that whole Underground crew. (As if everyone else existed only so Alfred and she could create legends out of them.) Till she could do nothing but swallow her useless tears. Admiring again how inventive he was, how unflagging his care and attention to her. Naturally, he'd reserved all his wittiest bits for his recitation about their Dame Nurse. Affecting, all through it, to sound like some BBC programmer, while his head rested gamely on his pillow, the faint electric fire of his eyes still so animated.

"At the proud age of eighteen," he began, "the brilliant if unruly aristocrat, Agatha Heathcote-Drummond-Willoughby, had been formally presented to the Queen. To whom she reportedly quipped: "'Why is it only the women who have to wear gloves?'"

"White Rabbits aside," Alice replied.

He, duly noting, continued: "Educated at home in Kenilworth, for discretionary purposes until her Mum and Dad had had their fill, the girl continued her schooling at the Convent of the Assumption in Paris. That is, until her expulsion therefrom. Due to . . ." (And here he paused, for effect, or at least to ponder what to say next.)

"Do tell," Tabatha ventured, eavesdropping from her crevice above.

"Purportedly due," he complied, "to her catastrophic liaison with some notorious Czech race car driver, and the subsequent traumas she inflicted on a half-dozen young, trusting nuns."

"Oh, he's good," opined Tabatha.

"And so, back to England—back to the family manor—she went?" queried Alice, her mood lightening, knowing so well the (invariably) Jane Austen—esque form of his fables.

"To Kenilworth, yes," he affirmed. "But then, finding their Agatha all grown and home again, what were Lord and Lady Heathcote-Drummond-Willoughby to do? What with her flooding and moating their formal dining room, what with the forts she constructed from the Louis Quinze settees as she did battle with Imaginary Vikings? Where could they possibly send *the girl? What career could contain her? What lord (or lady) ever would have her?"*

Unsure about that, Alice and Tab chose patience and waited.

"Thankfully," the boy resumed, "those parents' heartfelt prayer was answered with the outbreak of World War II."

"All right, lights out. And silence," that omnipresent Nurse abruptly brayed.

His voice remaining gentle and low, as ever, the mischievous Alfred continued: "To the relief of all, and the surprise of none, Lady Agatha insisted on marching directly to the front. And while her genteeler sisters—"

"I said, silence, Crickets," Nurse chirruped. "Why is it I hear you, but you can't hear me?"

Let her speak, Alice thought, catching the Nurse's eye. Offer some bland smile; soon enough she'll mosey on.

"Indeed," Alfred pressed on, in a whisper, "that very evening, Lady Agatha spied a placard at Paddington Station: FIRST AID RED CROSS LECTURES. *Within moments, Her Ladyship was memorably in attendance. Impressing one and all, with her vivid classroom interactions—"*

"I said!" And there that Actual Nurse was, her sudden stern hand on Alice's shoulder bidding a halt to all this nonsense. Encroaching, once again, on everything them.

"You will wear the boy out with your chatter! Now lie down, as he has—on your bed. Let the poor ailing thing be. Time. To. Sleep."

Reluctantly, Alice settled back, set her preoccupied head on her pillow, her blistered arms under her blanket. And she

remained there, at anchor. Trying to convince herself that the
Nurse was moving on, like some ruinous angel passing over.
(An angel, like the one Papa'd told her of: always turned toward
the past; but seeing there only one heap of debris. Wreck after
wreck after wreck . . .)

And now, through the monotone drip from that water main,
she could feel her sensation waning, some new silence absorb-
ing her mind, as if she might finally melt into night . . . But
there, like a balm, came her friend's rebel whisper: "With the
barbaric intensification of the Blitz, that newly certified Nurse,
who had anticipated the most heroic of front-line adventures,
found herself assigned to a lowly Tube station. Disheartened
but undeterred, she applied the steel wool of her mind to main-
taining that station like a Spartan military operation . . ."

And still, Night Nine, it was. The ninth of nights, in this
Underground-now. But had it *ever*, she wondered, been other
than now? Other than lying here? Other than praying that
ungodly Doctor (so certain in all his certainties) would not
hear the tracheal moan through Alfred's cough—and would
not seize on that as medical evidence . . .

Yes. It had. On those blessedly thought-free lawn runs,
behind their houses. Those times the morning seemed so
transparent. *On offer.*

But how when where was all that greenshade now?
Where—on Night Nine, with the spring of her mind winding down? Consigned, as she was, to hearing again those
nightboots of lead creak across her diminutive soul. She,

sitting restless, stiff as this creaseless cot. Surely, she'd been exiled to some Land of the Lost, where she fed from a trough of regret, on the hum of a train, which never quite came, and that singular, simpering drip.

And there, somewhere near. In some pool of the dark, not far, that artful Dodgy stirred. See, draping himself stealthily, in his semi-rheumatic flannel blanket. Seemingly, for no one else, alone with himself, he preened and posed, he positively glowed. (Let those doltish do-goods languish in their doom and gloom, content with their obscurity. That boredbored boy intended to party!)

"I said: Bed," the Nurse bayed, strong-arming the negligent Nigel (who'd been busily saying the prayers Mummy taught him). Done with that, done with him, she started round, inspecting, would-be protecting, and when need be, forcibly flinging her restless charges in bed: "One day, dears, you'll thank me."

Consumed with this, her righteous mission, stripping from the children this last vestige of that petty thing, Liberty, she did not notice Dodgy, dolled-up Dodgy, trailing his floor-length behind him. Behind her. Would-be bedazzling, as he sashayed down that dreary platform in her wake. All lightness, himself, all chiffon. (As if she were merely Night's bridesmaid, he the true bride.)

With a haggard gasp, the Red Cross Nurse paused. Affronted. Scandalized by something. *Not Alfred.* Then who? Some truant? *There!* That blue-blooded debutante, nattering-on—*upright?* "Miss Van Eysen!"

"Sorry, it's Mamie."

"Excuse me?" the Nurse reproved her. "What do you dream you're doing?"

"Me?" the frayed Mamie riposted. "Sitting up."

"That much, I can see. Really, the more I do for you, Miss Mamie, the less you do for yourself."

"All right, then," Mamie agreed, "I'll just amuse myself here. Meanwhile, you go fetch us some Breakfast Tea."

"There is no tea."

"Only three Tube stops to Harrods, or so they tell me," the pale girl retorted, saluting the Nurse with her chipped gold-and-shell-pink teacup.

Baam, those Cross (kleptomaniacal) hands clamped down on Miss Van Mamie and her contraband cup. More intent, frankly, on claiming a win than on correcting any real sin.

"Ohhhh," Alice thought aloud, "how I wish I could shut myself up like a telescope."

Wonderlandwords bounced straight back at her: "Too late, Pig."

Alice looked about, puzzled. Only to be struck by a fresh bit of verbiage: "Come, Piggie," a weirdly familiar mouth frowned. "Come to Duchess."

The Duchess?! From *Wonderland*? That Imperious Dame, with the wattling neck and snout, who would so savagely beat her pig-infant and fling him about? Who so crassly chastised the Story Alice merely for thinking aloud. ("Think too much, my dear, and you forget to talk!")

What was that deadly Duchess doing here? Had the Underground been so battered, and left so bewildered, that now it was letting whatever Wonderland Characters in? (Alternatively, had London been so thoroughly deluged, even storybook characters were taking refuge in the Tube?)

No time for wondering. A mere two cots away, Nurse Cross was so consumed, attempting to bury the spit-and-polish Mamie in rough wool, that that Underground Duchess was free to grab at Alice, to dandle the child to her withering breast: "All grown up, are you?"

"Not *all*, my Duchess."

"Not what I hear. Pig!"

"From whom?" Alice demanded.

"From *youm*. Wallowing through your story-afternoon, trailing bunny tails, doing Caterpillar fumes and shrooms?"

"But—" Alice tried, "the Caterpillars—"

"Blaming insects, dear?"

And with that, adopting the indignant manner of that cross-dressing Dodgy, that vehement Duchess gave Alice's bottom a smack.

"What are you doing?"

"Rule Forty-Two"—La Duchesse scowled—"you know it, dear. You so, 'Oh I know it all by heart!' *You have no right to grow here!*"

"But I can't help it."

"Can!" she demanded, thwacking Alice again.

"Really," sighed Alice. "I'm too old for this."

"Exactly," the Duchess proclaimed. "Now you're all too big to be my pig!"

"I never was your pig!"

"Pig!" the Duchess spat. "You made yourself too big! You skipped my bit—your cherished Chapter Six—entirely. Set a bookmark on my heart, but don't mind me."

Whack, she smacked the girl's tail end.

"Ouch!" Alice leapt from bed.

Round the Duchess circled, her enormous skirt swooshing and swirling on the yielding air, till the Red Cross Nurse jerked about. Through the murk of senseless darkness, her trained eyes discerned some laggard behind her. "Who's that?"

"Mummmmy!" wawled Nigel. Suddenly, demandingly, grappling the Nurse in his weakened arms, stopping her cold in her tracks. (Like an infant crying in the night, and with no language but the cry . . .)

The Nurse stiffened, tightening her smile; but then let

her arms, suffering all, slowly fall, and suffered this child to embrace her as Mum.

Almost Alice was touched—to remember how lucky she was, that one day, when all this was done, she would again be held by her Mum . . . For the moment, however, she was too consumed with this redoubtable Duchess.

And she, said Duchess, was entertaining no interest in some blip of Underground tenderness. Merely she glared at Alice: "Now what have you done? You *piiiiiig!*"

"But, shall I not get any older than I am?" a defiant Alice asked.

"Wretched Pig," swaggered the Duchess, offended. Her words rattling: "Grew yourself such breasts and hips, my lovelies sagged, just watching them. You broke my heart, you selfish tart, and now my day's just fart fart fart! And so I'm left—with no one left."

"But, I never—"

"You stole my soul and made me old, you pig! You stripped the sheets, and stole my sleep, and left my youth a dream. I'll see you at the Trial!"

"The Trial?"

"Exactly. You think our Tale—and that bouncy bunny tail—belongs to *you*? To hold on to, to linger, to rewrite as you choose? You *pig!* You *piiiiiig! Piiiiiiiiiiiiig!*"

"*Dodgy Dawkins?*" the Red Cross Nurse abruptly blared, near-burning a hole in the Underground air.

"Oh please," came back Dodgy. From somewhere near.

"Don't tempt me." Catching hold of the scoundrel, the

Nurse peeled him from some blanket not his. With a sneer, "Back! To! Your! Bed!"

(*Really*, Alice thought, the day this war was done, the woman should be named the Patron Saint of Sleep, in recognition of her sermons about "Back to Bed.")

Fortunately, before that (saintly) Nurse could draw too near, the dastardly Duchess had disappeared. But . . . to where? Or had Alice hallucinated the entire encounter?

Never could she quite riddle it out. For, soon as she set herself back in bed . . .

That Nurse, striding on to the quarantine curtain summoned her watchdog: "Doctor, join me here."

What now? Let him sleep, can't you? You're the Queen of that. He just needs sleep.

On came Dr. Butridge: mumbling, clipboards clinkclanking in his blundering forefingers and thumbs. Utterly oblivious to his own blundering. *Unfathomable*, Alice thought; the way he came sputtering on, eyebrows scrunched, squinting like some half-blinded tailor, reducing the infinite world to the needle eye he struggled to squint through.

Still, as she squirmed, Alice tried—truly she did try—to do that so-difficult thing of imagining someone elderly young again. With a spring in their step. With an ennobling purpose, some real investment in a future which would benefit others, which could rock the world a bit. But try as she might, the man was like an oyster she could not get open. An image she could not get past, of a life spent in service to archaic, materialist ideas, administering a medicine for the human machine, while utterly neglecting the soul.

170

Huffing and puffing, finally that Doctor steadied himself beside that mordant Nurse. "Hallam. Alfred Hallam," he murmured.

"Yes, Doctor. See. Some frightful chill's come over him. That'll show him, jumping out of bed."

What?!

In the Doctor leaned, and inspected: "Oh my. My. The lad has plunged."

Plunged? Because of what he'd done for her? No no no no no.

At a brisk brusque look from the Nurse, the Doctor grimaced. Less for the sake of Alfred, it seemed, than out of fear he'd neglected to put on his Glacial Mask of Doctorly Distance. Getting a colder grip. "Blood-tinged phthisic sputum," he pronounced.

Meaning what?!

With a grave and graver look, he so offhandedly asked: "Is there family?"

Nurse replied, dutifully: "None found."

"I'm like family," Alice cried, bolting upright. "He has me. He'll always have me."

Swatting such buzz-a-buzz from her, the Almighty Nurse chastised those beleaguered out-of-breath Orderlies: "Did I not say move this boy? Ward D. Immediately."

"No!" Alice shouted, jumping from bed. "He's here with me."

As if in some dark-karmic response, Alfred erupted in violent coughs. A harsh gasping sound. So loud!

"Alfred!"

But the Nurse came charging like a boar in heat toward

her, grabbing hold of her: "I said: Let. Him. Be."

"No!" cried Alice. "Let me go!"

But, her words made nothing happen. (In this war-torn, refugee world, even the best words held so little abracadabra.)

Skidding across the unswept concrete, Nurse Cross dragged the unrelenting girl back. "Be grateful I haven't expelled you from the shelter."

Before Alice could so much as murmur, nervily that Cyclone Nurse turned, threatening to drown that whole scandal-mongering crowd: "Not a word."

At that word, Alice battered, kicked, pounded; half a scream screaming out of her, when . . .

As if in response—thank you, enemy planes!—a Scalded Cat raid suddenly splintered the night above. A brisk marauding foray by multiple planes, evading anti-aircraft fire. And with that impudent attack, the crack began. Some wound, some trembling which Alice could sense, from above but also beneath the tracks. An abysmal chasm opening—just as, once before, it had: sending her world tumbling down. *Not again.*

"Everyone—under your beds!"

All at once, everyone ducked—Nigel, Mamie, Angus, even Dodgy (but so slowlocomotively; as if by some horrid bureaucratic accident, he'd been booked on coach, instead of first class). Everyone but Alice, down down, on all fours, and breathing hard.

But Alice could not move. Only she felt the earth within her tremble, mourning with her. As if this whole dark world, and wide, were sensing some coming wound. Were knowing

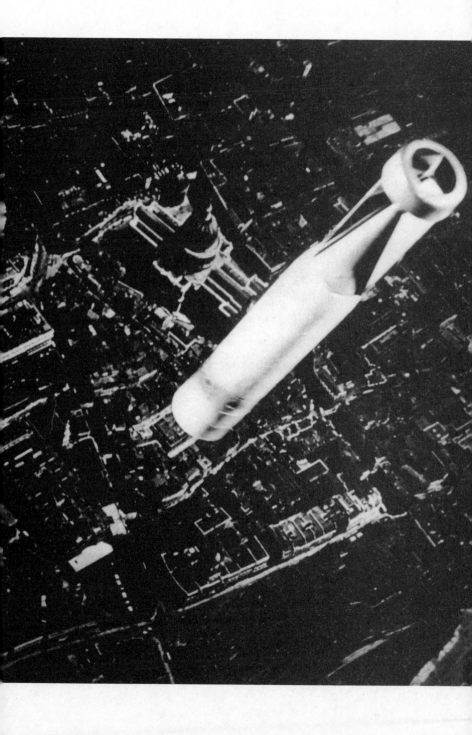

some groaning intimation: soon there would be chaos come again. Once more, the tremors, those pillars of fire falling, zigzagging their dark lightning through the night. The windows of London shaking, dreadful; from Brixton to Islington, all the sisters crying; from Clapham to Greenwich, all the lost papas; from Stepney to Shoreditch, all the young mothers, turning down chairs in their shelters, chanting some broken tune to distract their infant from the dreadful roaring of the sky. To keep those hornets in the sky from becoming once more the hornet in their mind.

A meowing from the crevice mouth: "Pudding. Poor thing, Harold Pudding."

Harold Pudding out there, still? Running as the bombs come falling? He, too, soon a body on fire? Fleeing, screaming. Running through the pages ripped from all the books in all the world. ("Every page," as Papa'd say, "a grief dispelled, now turned to . . ." *something else?*)

"Alice, on your knees. *Under your bed,*" the Nurse blared, darting below-cot herself. "Pray God, we all get through the night."

That was all the cue Nigel needed; he began murmuring feverishly, "Our Father, who art in heaven . . ."

Toting her treasured tea-trinkets below, Mamie struck a rather diffident tone: "Pray to God? After what he's put me through? I wouldn't even invite Him to my birthday."

"God is dead," pronounced Dodgy blandly. Examining some disastrous bacon-like bit, stuck to his lower lip. "Meanwhile, I'm not feeling so well myself."

With that, Alice dropped onto her chafed chafing knees, surreptitiously crawling across the shadowy platform toward Alfred. Taking advantage of a world distracted.

For the moment, only the stopped breaths and the dull tin-tinnabulation of the hollow Tube station. All else silent, till . . .

With an antique toke on his Sophistical pipe, Angus theorized: "At this point, God's only excuse is He doesn't exist."

"He doesn't," Tabatha hissed. "We killed him."

Maybe, Alice thought. Either way, this was no time for theology. With a final lurch forward, here she was. And now, and now, with a quick covert flick of the curtain, she peered up from under the quarantine tent. "Alfred?"

"'Hush! Hush!' said the Rabbit." In a low tone, through half lids, Alfred recited from memory: "'Hush! Or the Queen will hear you!'"

"Alfred, calm yourself," warned Alice.

Barely did he seem to take heed. No, his face was sealed to her. Pleased as he clearly was to see her, he did not seem surprised or relieved. (As if he'd known she'd always be there.) *Still*, something so unsteady within him. As though unready for that back-and-forth world of "won't" or "will," he relied on long-known book words: "'He sent them word I had not gone; we knew it to be true—'"

"Alfred, you're skipping to the end. That's the Trial."

But on he went: "'If we should push the matter on, what would become of you?'" Then, dropping all pretense of playing, he struck so plaintive a tone: "What would become of *you*, Alice?"

"I—" she faltered. "I'll be Alice still, and chasing after you, my 'Dear, oh dear!' White Rabbit."

"No," he answered squarely. "I won't be here again. We must, must end before I end."

"Alfred, catch your breath," she cautioned.

"No. I have to put a period. The sentence has no meaning if it does not end—"

"It will. Again, again," she assured him. "We'll go there still."

"*You* will. And for you to carry on, you must care less for me."

"Never. No."

He looked to her, as if through a world of pain for her, and answered with gravity: "Then, I'll make that easier for you. Although it breaks my heart, I'll help you let me go."

Alice stared at him. Unsure what to think.

"I followed you," he said, "now follow me." And with a flicker of his pale ailing hand, he summoned once again their one rosegolden sweep of Wonderland.

CHAPTER XVI:

—

"COME, WE LIVE IN RIDDLES, CHILD"

CLOUDLESS the sky stood, over the cloudless land. She, once more, standing beside her White Rabbit—she, in her Storyblue dress—before the house of the March Hare. That notorious house, just as detailed in their book, with its chimneys "shaped like ears," and its roof "thatched with fur."

For, here she *was*—yes, look—with Alfred here: transported, at his word, to their cloudless land again . . .

But was this, in fact, her Alfred—or was it the White Rabbit? Dressed in the Rabbit's plaid waistcoat he was, wearing those fine gloves—holding that dottering fan. But with some inner tremor, some Alfred-tremor; as if he still had something to prove to her—some thesis he needed her to believe in.

"There was a table set out under a tree," he intoned raspily. But no table yet appeared.

With a curious, maybe compensatory flourish, he gestured, the most official of White Rabbit gestures; assuming the mantle of Storyteller, summoning the fantastical scene. Meanwhile, pulling himself up, drawing himself apart.

And *she*? No matter how tightly she held on, she felt him glide out of his glove. Leaving her nothing but five empty cotton fingers, which were quickly losing all their warmth.

"The table was a large one," he declaimed, "and the March Hare and Mad Hatter were having tea at it, with a Dormouse seated between them, fast asleep . . ."

And now, like some magniloquent master of ceremonies, the Rabbit beckoned. And there: a terribly long, terribly formal table, covered in the finest cloth of dust, descended from the rose-fingered heavens and wobbled onto an endless verdant lawn.

There, the Mad Hatter (or a Harold Hatter, was it?). Seated, most regally, at the table's head; his rakish hat, his hair, his collar, thick with rubble and thicker with dust. A lazy Nigel-lidded Dormouse napping on the tabletop before him. And look—a random dusty page drifting from some dragon-ish cloud. The Hatter nabbed it, dabbed his lips with it—just as if there *were* tea in his chip-chipping, gilt-edged pink cup.

And *she*? Near-lost in the weird new wonder of it. Once again so absorbed. As if she invariably hovered at the brink of becoming the thing she beheld, disappearing into whatever page was before her. But now, it seemed, it was Alfred turning those pages, commandeering the look of the illustrations. (Determined, as he'd said, to make everything "easier" for her—by making her somehow care *less* for him?)

Speaking of. Staring intently at her (near-daring her to object), with a brusque tug-tug removing his gloves, the boy suddenly, utterly transformed. Casting off that dapper White Rabbit attire (and with it, his entire Rabbit About Town manner), he assumed the airs of a common Hare.

Alice went slack jawed. "You? But you're not at this tea."

"But the March Hare is," her Rabbitical friend came back. "And today he's me."

Alice looked to him, bewildered. And his tone altered entirely.

"You must, must carry on," he said plainly. So plaintively. "Without me, Alice."

"No!"

"You must. Come, follow me."

"But where exactly?"

To which, he nothing said. But his eyes seemed to probe her—to pose her, *to* herself, like some questioning musical phrase. Like some riddle he knew she never could answer. *How to look back?* Perhaps with the only look she had left. A look like the arrow in that Paradox: that useless arrow which could never reach its target, because in each moment, all motion is motionless . . .

But what did the Mad Hatter care about any of that? With a brisk peremptory twitch, he leaned, conspiratorially, toward the March Hare. With a fobbed-off flick of the wrist, indicating the Hapless Alice: "Do we see that little tweeb, just there?"

"My dear, what have you done to your hair?" the March Hare maffled, fussing like a maiden aunt.

"Don't be rude," retorted Alice.

"Then don't offend us with that hair," the Hatter sneered.

Ouch. What, should she just disappear? Like that girl in the big red painting by Degas, becoming nothing but the bother of her hair, nothing but the tug and the yank and the brush, till nothing remained that was surely her, only one vaporous redwave of the air.

But no. Better simply to sigh and set her ill-mannered bangs aside, like a book too important to be looked at just now.

With that, the Dormouse peeped out—but only to yawn, and to set off a yawn from the Hatter, who presently set off a yawn from the Hare.

And now, all at once, a trio of yawns. Open mouths, all around.

But why must they yawn? As if to display how tedious-to-be-with she was? But *no*, that was harsh. Perhaps it was just that—like everyone home in London—they'd all grown so hopelessly tired, and tense, from the lack of sleep, night after night, what with the interminable sirens, and taking shelter under the teetering dining tables, while all shattered London shook from the latest bombardment.

"The endless chain of days, you know," the Dormouse mulled.

Oh really? Despite all their sour-faced plaints, Alice knew she could be rather good company. Surely, she hadn't been away so long that she'd marooned herself from all her social gifts. Had she really so neglected her once-sterling wit and former, schoolgirl charm?

Intrepidly she approached. Terribly, formally, that March Hare sat up tall and blocked her from a thoroughly available chair. With a wave of one morbidly sensitive paw: "Sorry, no room."

"There's plenty of room."

Even the Dormouse snubbed her: "Not here."

"You give the goon some room," the Hatter observed, "the next thing that you know she wants your chair."

"Can't bear these chairs," the Dormouse declared.

Okay, rude. But what was she to do? Pretend she didn't want to play Pretend? Alice took a seat. (There were plenty of seats.) Immediately, the Hatter scooted one place away. The March Hare nudged poor Alice on, to where the Hatter had been, and dropped into the seat that she'd been in. *O-kaaay.*

But what to do? Here she was. Here they were. And her Rabbit was telling it *this* way. For *her* sake, or so he claimed. And so she put on a wry, patient smile: whatever the hardships, whatever the wonders, together they'd take a pretend toast-and-tea, and they'd soldier on.

And indeed. Only too pleased with his grubby new seat, the Mad Hatter reared a cup, except he no longer had a cup. "I'll have another cup."

Alice tried: "Of tea, you mean?"

"Chip chip chip!" the Hatter nodded, (in a rather Harold manner). Then abruptly demanded, "One place on, please."

So it went. At a glib, grating pitch. As the Mad Hatter pushed one more on, and the Hare nudged Alice on, as he flitted into the seat that had been hers—and made it his. *Like some insufferable game of Musical Chairs.*

"Did you hear how mean she was to Mary Ann?" quipped the March Hare, with a look askance at Alice.

The Dormouse, demure: "Love Mary Ann."

"I wasn't," Alice crisply replied. "She was. Mean."

"Then you should say what you mean," the Hatter chided.

"But I *did.*"

Once more, open mouths greeted Alice all around. *Blind mouths.*

And then the Hare pressed one seat on, and the Hatter one seat on, and the Dormouse too, one on.

"She means: she means what she said," the Mad Hatter said, meaning just what he said.

March Hare: "It was mean, what she said."

"It was mean what she *did,*" the Hatter punctuated.

"But then, that's how she is," deduced the Hare.

"*Hate* how she is," the Dormouse gloated, ever glib.

Talk about mean. Really, it was the most infuriating . . . *Or.* Was this, maybe, what Alfred had meant—saying he'd make it easier for her? Because he was being—and who wants to be with or be near someone who's being?—so unspeakably rude?

Although "rude," alone, did not speak it. The word was too little, the word was beneath it. The fact was, he was using this scene—one of their most beloved, time-honored scenes—to castigate her. To demean her. *And all because?* Because she wanted to hold and keep him? Because she wanted, still, Wonderland to be, forever to be, all it had been—for both of them?

The Mad Hatter lifted an imaginary teapot. Toting it aloft, he turned meltingly, and thereby all the more menacingly, toward Alice. "More tea?"

"One place on. And more tea, please," that Maestro Hare abruptly declared.

"But why do we keep moving on? In truth, there is no place at your table for me," Alice stated, trying to waken the kind, caring Alfred she'd known. The Alfred who must still be there, behind beneath that Mad Tea veneer.

"My hat!" the Hatter smirked. "She wants more tea."

Sorry? "But I haven't had any yet. So, how could I take *more*?"

"No," the Hatter whined, less than benignly. "How could you take *less*?"

"It's simple to take more," adduced the Hare. Doubling the dig. (Certainly more than their book ever had.)

"That is," is'd the Hatter, "when you've had none."

With a near-rhyming dig, Alfred dug further in, "You senseless twit, go taste regret."

Alice stood, beyond bewildered. Beyond offended. Seemingly abashed, he dropped the March Hare mask: "Hate me yet?"

Well, now that you mention it. "I never would or could," she said.

"You should," he said. So baldly said. Even as his eyes met hers, in a kind of involuntary plea.

In, toward Her Alice-ness, the Hatter leaned. But Alice cut him off. Defiant now, definitive: "Don't. I mean, you're all so mean."

"We do that," huffed the Hare.

"Must we?"

Something so urgent and raw in his look as it met hers. Imploring her: "You tell me. You keep coming back for more."

With a discreet dip of those dubious ears, he was, once more, Alfred: "Hate me now?"

"I wouldn't know how."

So, that *was* it. That was why he'd confined them in this punishing, this opprobrious scene. To make her hate him so much, she'd let him go.

Haughtily the Hatter hoisted himself up, toasting the air with a fustian hand: "So, shall we have a riddle?"

"Yes," Alice air-toasted back.

"Now she wants a riddle!" the Hatter whined, with a roll of his one good eye.

"That, and tea," said the Hare, declining to care.

"Loathe tea!" the Dormouse dully declared.

"Come, can't we move on," Alice urged more than requested. "Just one place on—from all this nastiness, this name-calling."

Seemingly repelled by her goody-two-shoes attitude, to say nothing of her fiendish ingratitude, the Mad Hatter scowled at Her Alice-ness: "All right, then. Since you insist: Why is a raven like a writing-desk?"

"You tell me," she replied, tight-lipped.

The Hatter blandly adjusted his hat. "Well, I haven't the faintest idea."

With a maddening laugh, the Dormouse gawped, "She knows that."

The Hare could not hold back, "And yet, each time we see her, she still asks it."

"No. *You* ask it."

The Mad Hatter, pulled up, indignant: "And always and forever, she insists I give her the same answer."

"That there is no answer," Alice said, pointedly averred. "I think you might do something better with your time than waste it asking riddles with no answer."

The Mad Hatter glowered. He glared. "If you knew Time as we do, child, you wouldn't talk of wasting it."

Alice grimaced at the March Hare. "You waste time by not spending it."

"I daresay," the Hare dared say, "you have never spoken to Time."

"We have spent so many years with him," the Hatter alleged, "and you, you are just meeting him."

Gamely, the Hatter beckoned the March Hare. And up, together, they bounded, buckjumping from seat to seat. *Just like Harold leapt, cot to cot,* Alice thought. Articulating every jaunt of every vault, till they clambered onto the tabletop.

"White Rab—Alf—do be careful!"

Unflappable, unanswerable, that dynastic duo stood. Assuming now the statuary poses of certain pious politicians. (Without podiums, but with no less a mission.) His Madness the Hatter faced her down, as if from a lectern: "Time for you to riddle yourself home."

"Prithee," burped the Dormouse, "pass the scones."

"Leave us alone," the Hare droned.

Well, there it was. Still, Alice stood her stubborn ground. "No, I won't. It's you who talk in riddles."

"Come," balked the Hatter, "we live in riddles, child, and sometimes there's no answering them."

Wordless, Alice looked to him. From underneath his riddling hat, some wounded Harold Pudding-look came back: "What leaves home as Mummy's hero, then crawls back a less-than-zero? Like a teacup chip-chip-chipped, like an egg God dropped for kicks?"

Alice stared, unsure. As if meeting someone so long forgotten, he no longer seemed familiar. "You?"

"Ahh," the Hatter sighed, "but I am no longer me."

Indeed.

And on, sorely on, he went: "My mate, you know, was drop-dead funny. Then he dropped dead—isn't that funny?"

"Indeed," the Dormouse seconded.

186

"Indeed," concluded the Hare.

A proper pause ensued. For, never had a silence sounded, never had a sentence felt, to those tea-sipping souls, more eloquent. Till, finally, the Hatter seemed to snap to. And was his Hatterself again. Thoroughly insouciant, he turned to Alice: "More tea?"

The Dormouse: "Hate tea."

That Pretend Hare, once more, tête-à-têtely to her: "Hate *me?*"

"No!"

"No tea?!" the Hatter spluttered, aghast.

"She," caviled the Hare, "and her incessant need!"

"The next thing you know," the Hatter dryly affirmed, "she'll be demanding herbal tea."

Alice shook her head, in disbelief: "I don't like herbs."

"Or Herb?"

"Or tea," said Alice definitively.

"No tea?!" In mock-shock, the March Hare snarled at her: "Sooooo, you tell us now you've got a thing for tea?"

Oh please. At her limit of mock talk and tea and mad venal mockery, some abyss, some growling maw, erupted within her—words spilling from her. Words directed toward Alfred, as if to exorcise the merciless Hare from him: "You can't do this, you know. Can't change what's on the page."

"Like you, you mean?" replied those ardent Alfred eyes.

And she, with her own X-ray glare, consigning him to a skeleton life: "I hate you—you know that? I hate you for getting sick. I hate you!"

What's left us then? she had time just to wonder.

For now, and now, Time seemed to tumble from its stilts, shattering the great clock of the world. Splintering their Tale—annihilating all they'd made. Scuttling all the King's horses and all the King's men. All the toast, the tea, the chimneys, toppling; the emerald lawns and fountains scattering; all the bright, beckoning gardens, fallfalling into the dark. Ripping the rug of her life out from under her. Leaving only one sea-blood sunset, like in that painting of the exiled Napoleon. A universal blank surrounding him—the color of fire and ice and solitude. Everything, their everything, slow-motionly rupturing—as that Hare, her Alfred, fell fell, free-falling onto that table.

"Stop! Stop it!"

But there was no table to stop it. No Hatter or March Hare. No cloudless afternoon or fur-thatched roof. No, in the place of that book of Knowledge so fair, only that less-than-nothing hub. The dreary vertiginous Underground. Like some blank horizontal in a crossword, without any letters to hold the view together.

Alice looked: there, beside her, her Alfred. But lying so lifeless, in his soiled hospital robe, on his sooty cot. Wheezing so raggedly. So drawn.

"I didn't mean it, Alfred," she insisted, trying so hard to assure him, feeling how much with each word she kept losing. Losing *him*. "You know I didn't mean it. I couldn't!"

"Ward D," the Red Cross Nurse declared, sponging her way in. Eager to manage some fresh catastrophe. With a ruthless hand uprooting Alice, yanking the girl away, as she

beckoned a stretcher. A renewed, tyrannical command: "*Him.*
This instant.*"

Him—to Ward D? Alice looked about, wildly. "No—you
can't take him! Alfred! I wouldn't!"

"Hush now," the Nurse commanded, grinding each word.
Punctuating each beat with a fierce fingersnap. "Say your
farewell."

There, look, just beyond: in the lamp-blank gleam from the
ceiling, Alice could make out . . . a *second* stretcher? An injured
young girl, staring glass-eyed from it. All bandaged, limbs
immobile—in splints. Her clothing torn to rags, her thick-
strewn hair, her eyes, her lips, full up with cement and dirt.

Suddenly, surreally, White Shirts mustering. The Orderlies! Holding a fresh bloodstained stretcher.

"Don't!" Alice cried. "I won't let you—"

"Shut it!" the Nurse ordered. Clamping some medical lid
over this too-too-unsanitary world, she cawed fresh orders to
the Orderlies (as if to prove, once and for all, how on top of
everything she was).

But Alice cried out yet again—catching hold of Alfred's
stretcher, fierce in both hands. Tearing that stretcher from
Alice's grip, the Red Cross seized her. *"Let. Him. Go."*

"Noooooooo!" Alice howled. Her lunge toward Alfred
thwarted by that Fascist forearm. "He's not one of those. For
Ward D."

With cold-blooded ease, that Nightmare Nurse did her
best to tear Alice apart from her hands. Then, with a brisk,
Florence Nightingale nod, she ordered those Orderlies off.
And away away those troll-faced minions went. Taking Alfred,

her Alfred, with them—divesting her of what little was left her, mauling every one of their oncegolden afternoons . . .

Possessed by some force, by some righteous fury greater than herself, beyond her will, savagely Alice broke free. And lunged—from that Scylla of a Nurse into some Charybdian void of her grief—only to meet there the Good Doctor Butridge. Blockading, assailing her. "Awaaaaaaaaay!" jabbered he. "From that Hemoptystic . . . Hare."

"What?"

"That, that . . . Buck Tubercular . . . With the Pneumothoraxic Paroxysmic . . ."

"Stuff and nonsense!" Alice said. "*You* away!"

"Beware!" he cursed. "Beware the . . ."

"What?"

As if his words fell silent, shamefaced to hear themselves, all the Good Doctor's babbling abruptly stopped. Dried up. (It was like he'd always been so convinced of the righteous, therapeutic strength of what he said, that his words seemed, to some, to have some impregnable weight. Some imperishable worth. Stripped of that pretense, those mumbles resembled only the dangerous nonsense they actually were.) He blanched, he belched, he burped—one insensible word from her book. "Brillig."

"Please!" Alice pressed.

"Tubercle Bacillic—" *Burp!* "Braelig."

"Stop it!" cried Alice.

"'Beware the Jabberwock!'"

"The Jabberwock?!"

Mouthless those lips hissed a hideous yesss: "Beware the jaws that bite, the claws that catch!"

"No!" Alice cried. "You can't have him. Let me by!"

"*'Twas brillig and the slithy lobes . . .*" The words came, fire-hammering, banging the decrepit Butridge right out of him. Summoning, from his customarily stooped form, an enormous Winged Phantasm. With an unctuous grating smile, trailing bat sails behind! Luridly, collectedly, leering. With sudden vulture nails—*what?!*

Casting his clackety clipboards aside, that Demon Incarnate, that Incubus, lurched and hunched and eerily drew himself up; louring, towering, out of his usual Doctorly slouch, lashing a lacerating tail, baring pitchfork claws, and four fanged front teeth—until he looked just like that child-mangling beast from her book *Through the Looking-Glass*. The very picture of the modern Jabberwock. *One more step,* his fang-toothed stare seemed to say, *and I'll claw off your face.*

Those hellion jaws opened: "Brillig braelig uffish-ness and cryptic diagnosis. Words mean what we say they mean—and that's the way it goes it."

Ah yes, Alice thought, it does make some dark sense. What was medical jargon anyway? Just so much dragon-speak, so much *uffish*-speak, to confound and inflame you. *So,* let him spew, let him *say.*

The jaws splayed wider, and before Alice could utter another whatever, those vast and *vorpal,* ingrown claws caught her, those scrofulous thorny wings clutched her. A renewed, relentless stream of Jabberish assailed her—with a seismic wash of unspeakable loss.

She fell to her knees. *"Let go of me!"*

But, the Beast did not, he would not. He, and the million-fanged, demonic minions materializing around him. Like Time grown old, every one of them, breathing their fires upon her—through jaws of death.

Like that fire decimating London, Alice thought. A fire so bright that, on nights when she'd raised her blackout curtain, she'd been able to read by it. And here it was, burning and blistering, blasting everything, everything from her. Virtually cremating her memories. Consuming every childhood street; tearing every stone from the heart of their common garden. Incinerating every chestnut tree, rooting out every elm beneath which they'd read; scorching every brick they never dared skip on their faux-Croquet walkway; reducing to nothingness all those turrets and eaves where, one year, that light,

Peter Pan snow had fallen . . . All that, all of that, stripped from her, as those iron claws gripped, suffocating her, draining her, subsuming every syllable, every name for her grief. All of it nothing but idiot jabbering. As if every treasureword within her were part of a love letter mutilated by government censors. A dictionary cut into Christmas ornaments. Nothing left but mangled, meaningless gibberish.

Tighter and tighter, those *slithy toves* held her, the *gyre* and *gimble* (to speak in Jabberwocky-speak); the teething-mouthed *mome raths*. See, the *frumious Bandersnatch* had her—he had her—choking the thought-chortled life-breath out of her. Cold hard medical hands clamping down. Holding her down down down. Confining her. The infernal *Jubjub* night, closing, *beamish*, over her.

CHAPTER XVII:

—

"'PLEASE' AND 'PUSS'?"

SHE'D slept? Perhaps she had. Sleeping unsleeping in Wonderland time, in a Looking-Glass night. She'd dreamed? She had. Waking, wiping some nightmare like gunk from her eyes, she'd stood in what seemed like a palace of twilight. But then that palace, too, had disappeared.

No one but she now. Opening her eyes still to see . . . a barestript Wonderland, such as she never had seen. A terrain robbed of all its tics, of all its vertiginous hills and ridges, all its near-delirious specificity. All that now a kind of blur. Only one spineless meandering stream between two deserted lawns. Like a book left open, so long unread, unremembered, that its every page had gone missing. No leaves, no wind. Only one red-golden sky, like some mirror of her mind. Bare outline only, of one solitary tree. Still no leaves. Only the unintelligible babble from a brook she could not see, a brook that, in fact, seemed rather grammatical and yet could not tell her the secret of its sorrow. For, Alice had as yet admitted no true sorrow to her depth and still had no firm notion of what real loss meant.

So, she stood. But where was *he*? Some disconsolate wind passed, chafing the tree, chafing her cheek. She would simply stand and wait here. Would wait, till her fear dispersed, dissipated like the dust, like so much ghostblack ash on the London wind.

Or no. She would not. She would run again—into the volatile night—just as she'd done on that catastrophic night, running from her house on fire. Again, now, she'd find him. But . . . how to run and *where*—when there was nowhere *there*? Only some blank Eveningland, where it was not even evening yet.

But, *there*—beyond that lone-tree branch, in some insubstantial morning light, she caught a glint of . . .

"Cheshire Puss?" Not a whisker stirred. "Cheshire Puss!"

One faint caliginous gleam appeared. Alice pinned to it what hope she had: "Oh please!"

Just enough mouth lingered, to emit a milky meoooooow: "'Please' and 'Puss'? I like that."

Maybe so. But Alice heard, within those words, such a world of desolation. She had to get round it. She would! She'd launch herself forward, no matter to where—back, back, to that swarthy, thick-ribbed Underground, even to that Underworld Dungeon of Ward D.

But now, that Chimerical Kitty materialized, like some harvest moon suspended, growing humongous before her.

Sudden fangs—halting her! Alice ducked—tried to duck. But, there was no scooting under that low-bloating belly. *On!* She pivoted—*Quick!*—and pressed *on*.

Lo! an endlessly lanky tail caught her. No Cat, just tail there; slinking, wagging, cowling-and-uncowlinging sulkily around her. Clinging. Alice shuddered: "He needs me, don't you see? Let me past."

That disembodied mouth snarled (once there was enough mouth there to snarl). Impressing on the air its toothy glint, and leaving it silvering there—like the mirroring rim of that Tube-station clock.

And with that cracked ticktock, Alice feinted left but bounded right. Only to watch enormous paws dislodge, spreading so vast, absorbing their own spread into the vacant air. Fur-flickering, darkening like some darker understanding of herself.

Alice froze: "Don't!"

And now, Alice darted left, only to meet chaos in that calico mouth: a pair of sky-scraping incisors, the most monumental premolars. Looming. Mocking. *No fun. Not friendly.* When all Alice wanted really was to . . . *run? But to . . . where?* The unmapped space of some glowering nowhere?

Whoknewwhoknewwhoknewwhoknew.

For despite all the thoughts she might think about everyone else, in the end Alice felt so inevitably herself. And there was nowhere she could run that she would not find herself—even in finding *him*. Nowhere that she would not soon again be thinking and rethinking, expecting then regretting, mouthing second thoughts like this (forever caught in sentences with "I" in them). Nowhere she could *be*, that she would not be confronted, by some floating dental image of the world's unyielding grin. *And so?* What was she to do to address that blank, armored resistance, those cat teeth that were (for the moment) her mirror and were rearing such defensiveness within her?

But, *what?* She had to believe in the usefulness of *doing*. In something she could Do, in some way she could reach him. What else was the point of all this feeling, if not to make known, to make eloquent, at least to herself, who *she* was? She would not, simply would not, be a riddle without meaning.

Determined, Alice spun about: "Cheshire Puss, please. Tell me, which way I ought to go from here."

The Cat Mirror chose to reflect nothing of what Alice chose to present—only her own classic grin: "That depends a good deal on where you want to get to."

"To *him*."

Alice waited—but only that insolent grin came, scintillant, back: those teeth like so many trace bullets, dissolving into the night, leaving only their trails of serpentine fire.

All right, be like that. But where *was* she to go? "In truth, I'm now so lost."

"Then does it matter, really," those incisors asked, "which way you go?"

"Yes," Alice said. "Of course. It must." *It only made it matter more.*

The Cat sighed, done: "Well, I'm sure you'll wind up somewhere."

"Where?" She had to know. She had to ask. "It all keeps disappearing. The pages turn so . . ."

"Quickly. Yes."

Alice foundered, "Why can't he stay?"

"The question is, when someone needs to go, 'Whoooo are you' to make them stay?"

"But there's so much left still—of our story!"

Through the ember-like boughs, through the stellar pallor of the sky, that bare grin spread wide as wide: "That is the story, love. Always parting, always greeting."

So wide, so narrow now that grin, it seemed just about to disband, like some last indigent reef of evening cloud—

"No, don't!"

Feline lips parted in speech: "It isn't hard to say hello, it's how we say goodbye."

"All right, then," Alice decided, rousing herself. "'I shall find that golden key,' and bring my Rabbit with me, 'into that loveliest garden, to run among the flower beds and—'"

"Alice," the mouth growled. "You cannot keep believing impossible things."

"Sometimes I've believed in as many as six impossible things before breakfast," the misremembering Alice replied.

There followed only a Cheshire Purr, without a word. Like the hum of thought evaded in the mind—something lingering *because* it had already gone. (A further intimation, if she needed one really, that only what departs from us can ever truly call to us.)

Still, Alice took the hint: "All I want is time with him. More time."

"It isn't how much time," Puss clarified. "It's how we use the time."

"But he is always out of time."

"Perhaps he hasn't much to give," the Cheshire hissed.

"But—"

Once more, that low low Cheshire purr: "Alice, pause, and let the picture in."

"And then?" Losing all patience, Alice chided back: "Like, to be there, is to be in Wonderland?" Then, with a resolute shake of her head, "Enough of that."

And with *that*, Alice turned her back on the stupefied Cat, and went. Startling a crack in the Looking-Glass.

And out out, like some last candle of twilight, went that notorious grin.

CHAPTER XIII:

—

A TERRIBLY GRAND TURTLE (I SHOULD THINK)

A SIMILARLY somber mood mantled the imperturbable camp, where Alice sat. Stranded in that ruminative Underground gloom. Trapped in some faded black-and-white illustration, after all the color pages she'd just known! But back, she was back. Suppressing every perception of the furtive rumbling aboveground, ignoring its warning of some fresh attack ahead. Finding (still finding) herself, unable to believe in anything, in *anywhere*—Here, There, or Otherwhere. And, therefore, finding herself unable to *tale*.

Oh, but *someone* among them still believed in tall-taleing. She, that ever so sensitive, that will-o'-the-wisp Mamie. She, too, stricken by all the fresh horrors without explanation. Under the cover of Lights Out, she nattered on, taking refuge from her utter inertia in the drone of her unending monologue, her monogrammed hankie busily shivering—like a sparrow who'd arrived too late to migrate, "At my Mum's— you know, in Warwickshire—my Governess would say, 'for children, all stories are true.'"

"*All* stories?" probed Nigel. With pointed scrutiny as if trying to distract himself from everything unnerving and unlovely (for example, that renewed, pre-raid grumbling), he perused the poker hand which Angus had dealt him—a pair of Threes, plus a useless Ten, Six, and King. "Three for me," he requested, testily tossing his reject cards toward Angus's deck.

Casually, over that deck, that gadabout Angus taunted the lad, "Hear that? That plague of Fritzy fighter pilots—gathering again? In their big-bad Heinkels and Messerschmitts? Let's go get 'em, shall we?"

"Children," that handkerchief resumed, "are always caught up in *what is*. Consumed by what's in front of them—and never by what they've left behind or what's just ahead."

"Not *her*," contended Dodgy, with a silent-movie eye roll toward Alice. Alice, who sat so rigidly silent, it was as if Talk itself had walked out on her. Chewing on that, on Dodgy went: "She's always looking ahead, but with her head in her behind."

Can we not, Alice thought. After all, it wasn't about which stories were true. It wasn't even about the truth. As her Nana'd said: "If nothing is written or said, then there's nothing false or true. There's *only* what is."

"So, it is," that haranguing hankie concluded, "that children have no real sense of future or past."

It was always like this, wasn't it? When one was waiting for someone, one felt them, their absence, so profoundly, one barely could bear anyone else being near . . .

Then again. What was it Cheshire Puss had said? "You can always indulge in some Magical Study of Happiness" . . .? But what was she to do with that? What but imagine him still on that cot, with those futile fig biscuits still as sweet as their past? . . .

"Up here."

At that improbable purr, Alice stopped. (And just when she'd been telling herself such important thoughts!) But now, her eyes roamed the station, surrendering bit by bit to the hard fact of remembering it there again, obdurate as ever. Without her, again.

"Up. Here."

Alice looked more profoundly into that gloom-penumbra. And there, above, across the track, she could just make out that near-familial gleam . . .

"How are you getting on?" the gleam asked.

Squinting a bit, Alice checked: were there ears enough there to hear? Even as she did, Tabatha spoke again:

"Join me, while I look for him."

"Where?"

"I'm sure he's wound up somewhere."

"Alfred?" Alice stared, bewildered.

"Pudding. Harold Pudding. Red Alert out. They'll be bombing any minute. Him, poor naked wretch, gadding about. Crying to his Freddie to 'guard the rear!' He won't know where or what he is."

"But I can't leave him."

"Who? Your Alfred?" that sandpapery tongue clucked.

"He'll be back. Soon. He will."

"We will, too. I've done this, often enough. We'll get you back safe and sound. Back to your story, from just where you left it."

"My story? No. Not without him."

"Alice."

"*No*. He wouldn't want to skip a scene or miss a single beat. There are so many of his favorite bits still to come. The entire Trial, for examp—"

"Suit yourself, then."

And with that, the glint went. Imperceptibly as summer, as some twilight inclination that one bats away. Some glow-worm blinkering out. No one but Alice even noticing, as into the furnace-night above, that intrepid girl slipped. Leaving no bandaged grin.

Always parting, Alice reminded herself, *always greeting.* And yet, with each goodbye, she knew, something does abide. Some *sensation sweet,* as Papa'd say, *felt in the blood and felt along the heart . . .*

"Good night, Alice," Mr. Hallam had said, with a reticent smile. "Good night, good night." In that odd, husky whisper, every word like a still performance, seeming to offer but not offer her some mysterious blessing.

He'd surprised her, actually. On her way out. Stooping benignly beside the banister—the hair on his wide head, standing up, recalcitrant, on both sides of its part. As he bid her that good night. As he clasped her hand, with a sudden singular warmth.

Again that whisper: "Thank you for coming today, to see Alfred. For today, for all the days." He swallowed. "Till tomorrow, then?"

"Of course. Yes."

"It cheers him up, you know. It helps him so much. Even his rest. You do know that?"

"I think. Yes."

Rising, with a valedictory nod, he led her to the front door, without a look back. "I don't know where we'd any of us be without you, honestly. These last months. Well." *He paused and looked to her. Meeting her look, as if from a well of tears.* "You're all he talks about, really."

Mr. Hallam, then. *And now?* Buried, scorched, in debris. *Good night, good night . . .*

"*Ayy meee!*" came a cry, echoing through the hollow Tube. *Mamie?*

Once more, as on those gutted London streets, Alice seemed to catch the refrain of someone else's grief. (Grief, which sat, a moment, beside one Londoner, then beside another.) But then, what had *she* known of grief—beyond her book?

"*Ayyy meee!*" *Nigel, no doubt.*

With new-washed eyes, Alice shivered off her glooms. And sat relieved. After all, as Pastor William would preach: "Every tear is an intellectual thing, and every sigh, the sword of an Angel King . . ." *Meaning?* Maybe that our tears are weapons, really; shields to protect us against thinking we are everything.

Was that what Harold had meant, then—when he'd proclaimed, "No weapons, sir!" Was he simply saying he'd run out of tears?

Harold. *Yes.* She must go, help look for him. Certainly, she didn't want Tabbie alone out there, exposed to shell fire again. "Tabatha?"

No answer. Alice's gaze prowled the track, the steps, the high cold empty chink . . . No one.

"Tabbie?"

Not a meow. And now, Mamie it was (as always it was)

who noted Alice noting the absence, and then just couldn't stop noting it: rattling the entire atomic make-up of the station with a prissy "Look who's not," then a pithy "Guess who went . . ." Until that entire vagabond crew got caught up in it. Their bored eyes scouring above, beyond, and about:

"That Tab!" someone concluded.

"Running high tail after him."

"Ayyy me!" some unknown voice bemoaned. A doleful moan.

Meanwhile, on the sassy set gabbed: "First, Pudding deserts his regiment—"

"Not to mention, his Freddie."

"Then, *us*."

"One less bedwetter."

"Ayyy meee!" *Who was that—Angus?*

"Just shhh," Alice wanted to retort, "no use grousing." But, it seemed, no one but she could hear those sad "Ayyy Me"s. For, they all kept blithely on, like a chorus of talk that had subsumed all thought:

"And still that Tab goes after him? To what end?"

"The East End."

"To lead him," Mamie stewed, "to that hideous House of Abandoned Children she first ran away from."

"Serve her right if she gets bombed out, too."

"Boo-hoooooooo!"

Alice peered into the murmurous gloom. Remembering— or imagining, rather—and for no good reason really, those inconsolable sighs from her dolorous, old Wonderland chum. "Mock Turtle?" she called. "My Mock Turtle?"

At that unintended summons, she watched him—it must be him!—her Mock Turtle, suddenly near-numinously assuming his old familiar form. (And yet, inexplicably, stooped like that stammering Doctor; with chin erect and neck extended like Miss Mamie.) His carapace shell, ripple by ripple, manifesting his inimitable Mock Turtle–ness. Though not, as in her book, situated upon some lonely distant ledge—not all all alone beside the wide wide sea—but instead, just *there*, beside her filmy cot. In shadowy magnificence. With his moony calf's head and ears, just like in the classic illustration from her book. But in place of those classic calf's hoofs, with (rather more turtle-esque) flapper feet spread upon a sort of glowing night-light of a rock.

But, how odd it was that again, there—in the Tube with her?—this Wonderland Being was. "Turtle! My poor Turtle!" Alice called.

That woeful Magnifico looked back. All dolor. Sighing as

if his heart, and flappers, too, would break: "Turtle? *Me?*" He sobbed portentously: "No, I am no longer a Turtle. Only a Mock Turtle."

Longfamiliar words—but how unlike themselves they landed on Alice now. For, wasn't that what she too had become?

She, and all the others huddled near. In equal ruin and mocked by all they once had been. What had they become, if not mock-thems? (Like grumblers left behind in some museum of their former lives: just they and those ghostly, Goya-like portraits, left in the dark after closing time.)

Oh so morosely that Mock Turtle mourned. "Oh dear dear me," moaned Alice responsively, in an involuntary show of empathy.

"You mock me!" the Mock Turtle chided, retracting his heavy head under his shell.

"Oh, no, I assure you."

His head tucked halfway out again. His wide bronze eyes blinked skeptically. "Then . . . what brings you to this grievous rock? This desolate grey reef?"

Given that Alice had not in fact departed to some desolate reef, and had no plan to anytime soon, she pondered how exactly to reply. Then began, brokenly, "My friend's been taken . . . but I'll be with him soon, I pray. There's so much left still—of our story."

"Ayy me!" the Mock Turtle fired back. "I told myself that too." His bare shell heaved, a prehistoric heave: "If only you knew who I *used* to be."

Down, down, Alice called to some rising sob within herself, as she gazed at him, admiringly. "A terribly grand turtle, I should think."

"A *baby* grand, perhaps."

Hahahaha, Dodgy laughed grandly, and Angus's chortles echoed skeptically after. And were those Miss Mamie's pearls, tittering, twittering?

Alice clocked those chortles and gestured dismissively. Seemingly, persuasively—for the snickering largely settled—or grew less acrid, anyway.

Must be some joke of their own, Alice surmised. For surely, they had no notion of that Magisterial Mourner, that Soulful Sea Reptile, bellowing just beside her. No more than they ever could know the mourning within her—the mourning for how little she actually felt. Even now. She, who'd always kept so distant from herself, never truly participating in her own experience—effectively living as if she were someone *else.* Meanwhile, consoling her bandaged soul with some revisionary tale: about how well she'd done, about how good she truly was, about how loved she was. And therefore how well, in the end, everything would work out.

"Such a salty story, really," the Mock Turtle sobbed. Such a salt-sea sob! "I can't tell it."

"Really?"

"Not a word until I finish," he scolded. *"Please."*

It was all Alice could do, really, to sift through the summits and terrible plummets of his Melancholia, to discern some muttered word. All the more trying, as she was trying so hard to resist a mourning all her own.

But on the Mock T sobbed. No words for his grief—no way, presumably, to articulate its enormity. Still, Alice tried to nudge him politely: "Sorry. I don't see how you can finish if you never start."

At that, he whimpered, wailed—swallowed and subdued by each Sisyphean sniff: "Once . . ." *Sob!* "Once when I, like you—"

"Not me," resisted she.

"Once when I had my *Tortoise* still with me . . ." he sobbing sighed, the silt dribbling from his eyes. "Well, we called him 'Tortoise,' because, of course, he taught us."

Alice nodded. "My friend and I," she just managed to say, "we went to school together every day, though now our school's been blown away."

"Ayyy meee!" some new mouth wailed. Assailing the void and vacant air—to say nothing of *her*.

But, who could *that* be? Weeping-and-wailing, a ways away, so plangently! Whoever it was, the Mock Turtle redoubled his sobs, as though not wanting to be outdone.

"*Ayyyyyy meeeeee!*" he echoed, elongating each vowel, his hard shell rattling from all the chest-banging.

But who, exactly, had heaved that first "Ayyy meee!"?

Alice dispatched her gaze. And *there*, beyond those ever-hovering smoke rings, slumped some second Mock Someone. On Mamie's cot, or rather, on some pile of stony rubbish, some seat of desolation, just beside. Never had Alice seen such a splendid, sulking thing. "Now, who is he or she?"

"*Ayyyyyy meeeeee!*" the Mock Turtle sighed. "A *Mock* Mock Me. A mockery!"

And now, what a competing flood of sobs burst forth from that *Mock* Mock Turtle. Such cloudy, lugugugubrious ululations!

"I knew Tortoise, too, you see."

"Yet, it all began with me," Mock Turtle evinced, in rival grief.

"Nay, *me*," the Mock Mock bawled defiantly. "In truth, he thought you were a Drama Queen."

"*Meee?!*"

A cry of chortles issued once more from those dusky corners. Anonymous lostchild chortles, from within that palpable obscure. Kerfuffled, Alice peered around. Trying hard to make out—from the muddle of umber faces and forms— some little touch of Nigel, some defining glint of Mamie, in the night. All of them so hushed in some congregation of silence. (Like openmouthed angels in that medieval Nativity painting; their features so pale, they seemed more stone than angel.)

With a wave of her half-dreaming hand, she turned again to the Mock Turtle. But for one weird mirrormoment, she seemed to see only herself there—moaning. As though she'd fallen asleep reading about him and had woken to find she'd *become* him. But no—surely, she was the one listening, or mock-listening, not the one moaning . . .

And ohhhhh, the cries that now arose! All the baleful bawling, kvetching, and intoning. That Mock Mock sternum throbbing so pronouncedly, as he (or she) declaimed (so conspicuously): "Ahh, the life my Torty and I had—before the Crash! How huge we hoped to be! . . ."

Ayyy meee. Had Alice's whole world become some Mock Mock Turtledom? Had all of London been grieving so long that its citizens had been turned to stone? Had constructed, each one for themself, some unfeeling *shell*, some polar-block version of themself, beneath which they could recede and sleep in peace?

Maybe so, Alice thought. But not *she.* Yes, her world might be emptied, but not she. She would not become some Mock Me.

And still. Amid all those jitters and jeers, some quiet pulse of a loss still to come, some quickening surmise of grief, seemed to course through her, to touch some sense of loneliness she always held somewhere else, like some goblin whom she skirted in the dark, afraid even to see. A sudden fresh palpitating wail: "Ayy mee!" But who was this?

Some stooped Mock Mock Mock Creature, peering from under a yarmulke and tallit of foam? Moaning cantorially: "I was halfway through my Haftorah when my Tortoise plopped. Swept out to sea! Oy me!"

"Ayyy mee," came some infernal Throb. And the entire station thrummed, between two roaring crowds: "Nay, me!" "Nayy, *meeeee!*"

"Enough!" cried Alice suddenly, her voice breaking with the cry. "No one has ever loved like me. I've . . . lost everything. And now, I've lost him, too."

"Aha!" the Mock Turtle retorted with a told-you-so groan: "You see, we are a we."

"But . . ." Alice searched for words. "I don't know how to let him go."

"Don't," the Mock Mock Turtle preached. "If you never move forward, you never have to leave your friend behind. Simply give into your grief, live and breathe your grief, like—"

Breeeeeeeeeeeeeeeep. That Dread Cross Whistle. A frenzy of torchlights, and a rampage of shoulderless shadows, swept across the platform, bedazzling the rafters. And, ever-mysterious, there she was again—Tabatha. Recoiling from the passing gleams and toobrightstares. (Like a thing so long familiar with the dark she couldn't do for long without it.)

"Tabatha Dedwin," growled the global Red Cross.

The most disingenuous meoww: "Ma'am?"

"Where have you been?"

"Nowhere. Ma'am," retorted Tab.

"I said."

But, that rum-tum Tabbie couldn't have cared less *who* said or *what* they'd said. "Me, I'm the girl who went up, then came down without eyes," she purred. "Not a light on, up there—you could die of the truth out tonight."

"Yes, indeed," Mamie sniped, "that's rather why we all stayed down here. And left you to chase after that half-wit."

Dodgy puckered his pursey lips. Freed now, it seemed, to gossip to his heart's content.

"Harold Pudding. Exactly."

"Puddinnnng? Harold Pudding?" Dr. Butridge came on mumbling—as if some long mustache were muffling his mouth, except he had no mustache.

Ignoring the man, the Red Cross Nurse abraded the renegade Tabbie: "And . . . Pudding?"

"Couldn't find him. Anywhere."

"Well, what did you expect?" the Red Cross Nurse countered. "That he'd be lounging on the neighboring curb, cross-legged?"

"I looked down every street," reported Tabatha. "Rows of flats stripped of their backs, like so many broken dollhouses. Row after row of four naked walls, just staring at each other. Their roofs blown open, revealing stairways to nowhere. All those furnished rooms, emptied. Littered with busted beds and cupboards. A plate of unpeeled potatoes, left on some plaid tableclothed table . . ."

Another lone echo mourned, seeming to arise from somewhere within Alice: "Ay me!"

"I called his name," Tabbie pressed on. "Nothing. No one. Some crusty, drunken bloke by the alley stood bragging, how many shops, how many houses just down. Like it was worth keeping score. The gloomy pride of the just bombed, you know."

"*Ayy meee!* . . ." Alice felt as much as heard.

"I asked every shadow I met—all the anxious worried women in their doorways, all the grime-smeared lodging-house keepers, all the men too old and unsettled to stay in the shelter—had they seen my soldier? Some rouged-up street-walker squawked back, '*Yours*, dear? Gone and left you on your lonesome? I'll take care of *that*, then.'"

"*Ayyy meee* . . ."

"Then, who can blame the lady her willies?" Tabatha went on flatly. "So many soldiers wandering about, like stars gone out. And what can you ask from a man just back from combat? It's like he's returned from the Land of the Dead. All he can really say is: 'You cannot imagine.'"

"And the rouged lady?" Dodgy deigned to ask.

"Oh, her," Tabbie replied. "She shrugged. And waved her torch and showed us heaps of broken glass. All the latest style in litter! Oh, and those scattered body parts in rubbish sacks—"

"Tabatha Dedwin," the Nurse blared.

"What? How else do you sack up the dead? How else recover the limbs—and pitch the bodies blown to bits?"

As no answer was forthcoming to that, Tabatha resumed her former track: "I wanted to thank that Cadaverous Lady: 'If you knew what your torch, or a hurricane lamp, what a lit window meant—to those of us out on the streets.' But she'd gone by then. Leaving no lack of void. As though all those Messerschmitts had finally managed to shoot down the moon. To blot every watery star from the deadman's sky. Nothing but the nothing left."

"No Harold?" Alice couldn't not ask.

"A van marked 'Dead Only' passed. But no Harold, no Pudding among them."

But, he had to come back. At least for his sketchbook. He couldn't become just some swelling of the ground, some rock, rolled round as the earth rolled round . . .

"I'll be seeing you, in all the old familiar places," the sardonic Dodgy crooned.

Harold, he could never be like one who fought and died. More like, one who died but still was fighting . . .

Accustomed as she was to swallowing sentences whole, Nurse Cross seemed unable to handle the lump in her throat. Alice could almost hear the woman thinking: *And all for what?* For what—the exhaustion, the late nights, all the ceaseless caring about every detail? For what? For them, her charges, who were always so resentful, or frankly indifferent? Only for them, too, to wind up dead on the streets? "Ah well," the Nurse said, "he's not the first."

Doctor B suppressed his spittle, as if to attest to his powerlessness. If, in the end, the patient will not listen, if he will not follow his prescription, what is a doctor to do? Meanwhile, the Doc put on his best nod. "At least we've spared Ward D another lad."

Silently the Red Cross Nurse set her face in her hand, and with that, a terrible lamenting arose on the air. A sorrow, larger than London, that bewept itself: *"Ay meeeeeee!"* As if some grand Bereavement Group of Mock Turtles were having it out, right there on the platform: grieving the good grief, gnashing their absent teeth about how lost they were, beyond recall, and, worse still, how normal that, too, had become.

Having none of it, insistent, siren after siren sounded. This time, in rapid-fire succession. And still, the roaring of engines drew nearer. Like evil heralds, announcing the coming scarring of heaven; that nightblue heaventree of stars decimated, shattering into a darkness so hideous no darkness could comprehend it. Once again from the battered world above came the shrieks of the dying, crying without wisdom, unregarded, from the streets. And there, from below words, some menacing sense of an ultimate, idiot silence, a wordless sense of hopelessness, began to settle in—to steep itself in everything. Like a sigh from all the small things of the earth, the books and the identity papers, the garters and school ribbons, all the greatcoat buttons, guarded by loved ones in cupboard drawers, somewhere . . .

And yet. There, just there, in the very material of her mind, in the depth of her ear, below those anguished chords from the impious Nazi war on heaven, Alice could make out some slow buzzing hymn. (Like in Chopin: some return to D-flat major—after all that throbbing darkchord drama!) She could feel, she could sense, some windy grandeur soon to come sweeping round.

Surely, she thought, *Churchill must be on radio now*, rousing them all through this darkest of hours. Soon, sometime soon again, the "All Clear" would sound, commanding with invincible sound. And from every corner of this still-sceptered isle would come Butchers and Bakers and Candlestick Makers, would come Clerks and Clerics, Typists and Tailors (and in from the suburbs, Wheelwrights and Tolltakers). All of them, striding victorious over bomb craters, until they came clattering, down down the Tube-station stairs. To queue, as one does, for the late train—home again.

One night soon, Alice knew, she would walk up those long stairs with Alfred. Not tonight, to be sure. But once this awful war ended, they would stroll again through Westminster, along the Embankment; the lamps of all London would lift their frail lanterns again—glimmering, half-blued, from the opposite bank. The Thames running softly on, as some passing tram captured their face in its brightening glance.

They would linger, they would, beside those rain-worn Victorian sphinxes, in the shadow of that Ancient Egyptian Obelisk. And there, they would know that they too had stood, that they too had survived. That they too now were part of that monolith, which had stood through so many eras of dark hateful fire and yet still pointed in peace toward the still evening sky.

CHAPTER XIX:

—

THE DEVIL'S FERRIS WHEEL

"THE Devil's Ferris Wheel, that's what they call it, Alice." So Alfred had informed her, as they peered out from under his blackout curtain onto the London night robed in fire.

Just a little more than a month ago, was it? Only a month? His eyes so alive with that firelight, his cheeks flushed, his breathing tight, uneven, as he beckoned her nearer. "All the colors, Alice! The orange, the magenta, the purple-pink-green flames, see—like souls in bliss, riding that wheel into the brimstone pit."

Well, she couldn't disagree, looking out on that kaleidoscopic night. Only color wheeling after color; each one lavishing itself, long and wide, like another blood-ribbon in flight. As bullets sprouted erasures, and as bombs tore open the sky— scattering shrapnel and shells, rattling the roofs, and pounding every disfigured street in Bromley.

(What, she asked, what was going on in the mind of the sky? Was it bewildered by the delirious fire? Or awed by the dazzling display—the latest style in Nazi fireworks? Or neither? Somehow it seemed so . . . unperturbed.)

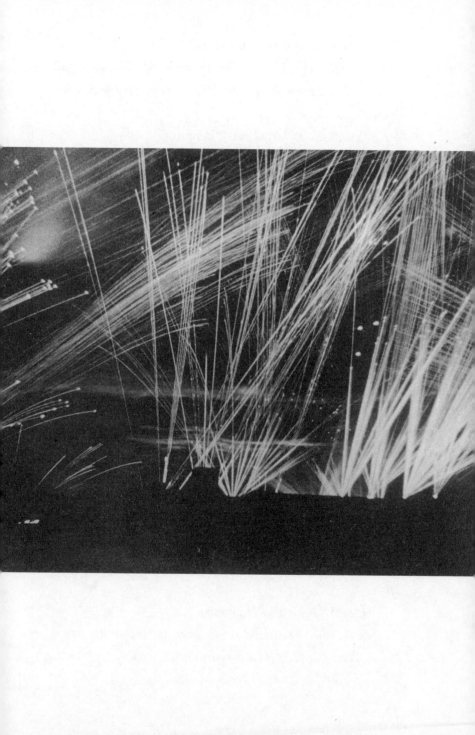

"We must close the curtain, Alfred."

"We will," he said, no affect to his words. His gaze still fixed on that darkpane of light. "Father says, they've bombed the zoo again."

"Oh no!" Alice blurted out. "They have?"

Faintly on the window, his grim reflection nodded. "One of the zebras was sprung. And a host of monkeys. Our squirrel monkeys!"

"But they'll find them. Or the monkeys will run home again. They'll be hungry," she assured him.

"Me, I envy them. Honestly. Despite how frightened. Despite the sky on fire. Better, one last fanciful dance . . ."

"Yes." No. No.

"Better that. When you look what's happened to the fishes!" he expostulated, his agitation rising. "All our carp and perch and eels—"

"Our soles and eels—like in our book!" But she saw how gloomily her lightness fell upon him—disheartening him. "I mean, yes. Mum told me."

"All lost," he moaned.

"No, some were moved, to room with our Flamingos."

"But the Python, Alice. He's been boxed up, sent away."

"For a while, maybe. But they can't keep a Python down."

"And our Tortoise—our Mock Tortoise! They've sent him off, too."

"He still has his shell, I promise."

She watched her friend recede once more, into his fervor. "Sorry, Alfred, let's do close the curtain."

He watched her draw across the drapes—in long, runged folds, one layer after another—fixing his blank inner gaze upon her.

She felt him watching. Something so resigned in him, as if some inner clock, each moment, measured what it cost him—to be part of that from which he could well be departing.

Without warning, words came tumbling from him, mute, secret words: "If they should have to send me somewhere, Alice—"

"Send you?"

"If."

"But they've done with the evacuations from London. You, you won't be sent."

"But should I have to go. To leave you—"

"You won't. Ever. Don't be horrid."

"But my doctor—"

"Stuff and nonsense."

But his look was like a plea still. And she softened. "Come," she said, quoting their book: "it sounds 'uncommon nonsense.'"

But his eyes paced restless, over the shoulders of those shadowy draperies.

"Alfred?"

With a patient sigh, his gaze settled once more on hers. Letting all he had not said remain so. All that which she'd just interrupted. "Do remember this, Alice. This night of fireworks. The sky so full of our proud plumed Pythons, our starry-eyed Peacocks, our runaway Flamingos ..."

"They must miss us. Our Flamingos."

He half smiled. "In any event, do think back on this and remember."

She had. She would.

In fact, no matter where she turned, it felt like she was, forever, looking toward that window—from his lighted room. On the darkpane before her shone the reflections of the world still lit behind her. Every single object in that room. Still, still there before her—between her now and everything she viewed.

There again she could hear it, they all could: above the darksome air of the Tube, that sinister sawing. (Like some German church music, played night after night. Forever, the same bass line and chord progression, but nary a trace of melodic variation.) Soon, so soon, she knew, the rude whistling would resume, then the deathscreams from those Jericho Trumpets, the propeller sirens of the dive-bombers. Soon soon, those shrieking incendiaries, sending sparkles like eyesight, cascading the night; ruckling the pavements like crazed baby rattles; the maternal groaning of the gutted earth to follow.

"It's a buzz-bomb—hear that?" Angus half-deduced, half-conjectured, as if tamping down his cowlick weren't enough to distract him. "Br-r-r-r-r-r-r-ruum—hear that? That pulse-jet pulsing fifty times per second!"

"Under your bed, Wilkins! Not a word!" came the Red Cross Commandment.

A sudden blast from that sky of hell shook the walls. Violent bits of broken tile and concrete, scattering over the shaken crowd, the stairs, and the platform.

"Alfred?!" Alice cried. Reproving herself for the cry. While, admittedly, wanting so badly an answer.

Not a shrug came back from that emptied quarantine, nor those unlistening tracks. Nothing from the shadows over the rails, where the frailest children still hung, in a hush suspended.

And so? So, she held to herself. Thinking of all those children above, in their supposedly cozy homes, huddled under bed frames, beneath rattled windows, so terrified, even in Mum's arms. While beyond their flimsy bedroom walls, the rising ruins of London glimmered around them; searchlights, lighting the first lights of evening—like some low-hovering galaxy of powdery stars.

Still, all children cry out, don't they? From their beds at night and through the daytime—when separated from their Papas, as she had been, that time in Kensington Gardens. Every statue, every sculpture she'd run past, even that abandoned bandstand, acting as if it had never known her . . .

"Chip chip chip!" someone pipped. Mamie? Yes. Looking utterly distracted from her wit, crimping and uncrimping her lip over the cup's trembling rim.

"Shall we have a spot of cream, then," a composed Angus tossed in, "in honor of those missin'?"

And of course they all cry—from their toppled tricycles, from those rude swings lifting, heaving, chucking them . . .

"If you can even call it cream," Dodgy drawled from under his unseemly bunk, "and calling makes a thing."

Setting her hypersensitive hankie aside, Mamie lifted her ramshackle cup: "In honor of our dear, departed cream."

An instant after, a second savage blast rocked the station. Brattling the cots, hovering like a goblin damned over the vibrating tracks.

"I want my Mummy, I want my Mummy!" cried Nigel, wrapping his arms ever tighter around him—as once his Teddy might've done—only making his pocket pen bleed all over again.

With a deftly lifted brow, Dodgy dripped: "Appalling."

Mamie simpered, smiling darkly: "London Bridge is falling." *They all cry, still. They do. Even when grown. At the beastly injustice. At the interruption. At the sense that this, their story, will not work out as it might have.*

"Bloomin' listen," Angus countered, rising, "we're not squealin' for peace. We're lettin' it come, we're resistin' 'em." Then brandishing his pipe as if it were his broadsword, "They'll see we're not British for nothin'."

"Wilkins!—Spencer!—For the sake of God—under your beds!"

Denying that cry, Alice remained upright. Mindful that to move, even a bit, could be to topple from her resistance, from those silver cliffs of her remembrance.

All she really had to do, she knew, was duck to her knees, to lie prone on the platform, to submit to some greater destiny *of.* To accept that this crisis *was*—and that soon she too would be *gone* . . . But no, she would not. She had cried long enough. Had longed, for too long, for an answer outside herself.

No, Alice thought, she would not be caught, at some stultifying rim of where she actually *lived,* with all things future and past threatening to collapse. Into what? Some "fate" she could blame? Some supernal shuffle of the inhuman deck? Some domino-drop of her redbrick block, toppling to white-powder death? *No no*, though much had been taken away, still more of her—and more of him—remained. That which they were, they *were*.

Why would she, why should she, give herself up to the ruthless, ceaseless bombardment, when *there—hear?*—in her own golden ear, a trumpet sounded. The Trumpet of a Prophecy. *TatatataTaaa!* A blowing hymn. *There*—an ecstatic clatter sweeping over the platform. There, as the whole of the coward world crouched, a pack of proud playing cards, subjects of the immortal Queen of Hearts, came marching, life-sized, along the track. *Why couldn't those Tube-squatters see it?* All those pusillanimous souls, like so many discarded cards, lying flat on the ground. *Really*, thought Alice, we all should be rising and regally bowing. To that festooned, faux-royal deck. To that Knave of Clubs, that Knave of Hearts, clanging fantastical kerosene lamps. Dashing lads, dashing about. Announcing: "The Trial! The Trial!"

And . . . *there*. With a bat of her blearying lashes, Alice once more looked about. And saw, or seemed to see darkly, someone there, down the track. Just beyond those life-sized, paintbrush-wielding playing cards. Someone, just there. Like a phantom form in the night, beneath some unlit lamp. Some frail gleam of someone before her. Yes. Trembling, pale as an apparition, in his fluttering hospital gown, stood . . .

"Alfred?!"

CHAPTER XX:

—

ISN'T IT A TRIAL?

MIRAGE or a miracle, was it? Or a riddle made visible? For, everywhere around Alfred and her spread the shadowy platform, and yet, it was as if this strip of Underground station had been transformed into some undiscovered corner of Wonderland.

See, up from the glinting-steel tracks, toward the trains, which, these slow-traveling nights, never passed; over the cold, umbrageous platform; over the empty cots; along the station walls; and curling luxuriant over the rafters and railings—bloomed the most resilient and royal white roses. Their faces peering argent from the dark, in silent protest of all the barbarous London loss. Roses. So many spotless white roses. Making of the makeshift shelter a kind of marvel: a subterranean wartime garden in bloom.

But Alice could barely take in the wonder, so struck she was to see him. Her loved friend. "You're here!"

"I had to," Alfred insisted. "To finish it. With you. We could not end like that."

Alice nodded, felt herself nodding, gone mum. How pale

he looked! Tremulous. His gaze seeming to swim toward and away from her; with a swerve of such self-conscious regret. The look of a soul that has to stay where it is.

"Alice, come," he beckoned. "The Trial."

"What? No!"

"We must," he entreated. His breathing heavy from the effort it cost him.

"No!" she said again simply, shaking her head, her matted tufts of hair falling in protest down her forehead. "I won't. I know what's next—*after* the Trial."

Setting a firmfrail hand on her hand, he importuned her, "Then, *please*. We're late."

"No," she said once again, allowing but not taking his hand. "I'm staying here. With you." *He had to stay—of course he did—if there were still chapters ahead.* "There cannot be a Trial without me there."

"Alice!"

"I shall never leave this page," she declared. "We'll simply stop the story here."

"Alice, I can't!"

But he could. She knew he could. *I can, he can . . .* Though now, it seemed, there was nowhere for her to look, nowhere that would not intercept his look; his eyes, so intent on hers, as if to look away too long would breed in him some thought too deep for tears.

"Perhaps," he attempted, "we were never meant to . . ."

"Yes, we were," she urged. "We *are*. We still can be. Forever. *Here*."

His face contracted, something crumpling within him. *Now what had she done? Oh no no.* Why must everything she said be like a spell? A spell she cast upon herself—and him. Truly, all she'd meant was . . .

Too late. Alfred spasmed. He couuuughed. A bruising cough, seeming to shut him out of the book of himself, spewing blood. And with each successive cough, every white rose turned red.

"No!" Alice cried, turning and turning, taking in, not taking in, the mark of blood on every rose.

"Alice. Please." He took hold of her arm. Imploring her.

"But, your roses . . . !"

"Yes," he said, so somberly. "They are as roses are. As roses, here, must be."

Because we paint them with our fear? Because we glut our sorrow on them? But *no*, not that. She could not taunt him—not now; she could not presume or demand like that.

"I've got to reach the end," he pleaded. Some hectic red crease suffusing his cheek. "Just this once more."

"I thought that when you knew a book," she offered, "you had the chance to have it as you always want to have it in your head."

Alfred forced a fitful smile: "It doesn't always end as books would have it end."

What then? she thought, but that too passed unsaid. As she caught again his rose-lit eyes upon her.

"I'm a rabbit in a waistcoat, really," he stated, so plainly. "Running out of time in Wonderland."

"But how shall I be here without you now?"

So near she was, she felt she almost could touch the frightened soul, the *actual* animating intellect, within him. Him just here, warm-kindled, beside her. She reached and he did not resist as she drew him to her. In the full rush of emotion such that she could not yet find herself in. She, ever so thoughtful. Ever so pulled up. So interminably self-interrogating. Forever hounded by her own identity. Where was *she* in this?—with *this*, her fierce desire meeting his faint embrace?

Abruptly he drew back. "Alice! No—you mustn't get too close."

She leaned closer. Summoning every ancient god and goddess within her, to be here now, to smile and descend in whatever golden chariot, to help her convince him. *Why why should life divide what their death might join together?* "Take me with you."

"What?!"

Still closer she leaned, demanding a kiss. Her first, their first, *yes. Please, please, just this.* "Drink me."

"No no." His eyes choking. "And lose you, too?"

"I'll be there. Always. With you."

"Alice, no. It's just me they want."

Keep me with you. "I hear them calling, too."

His eyes upon her did not turn away. *Let me ask him, with my eyes, to ask again.* And then he asked her, with his eyes (he did, she knew he did). And she set her arms around him—*still him, just him*—she urged her lips toward his. To

230

kiss him into roses, to wake him, more than wake him, to wander with him here, forever here. That moment she could feel her lips so near, just brushing his—

And he—that moment . . . stopped. Pulled back. Stiff. He stared at her. *Through* her. And his voice came, clamorous—like the twin of his vision. A peal as if from Gabriel's horn. The voice of the Trial itself: "Silence in the Court!"

What what was he afraid of? "Don't!"

But, that moment, a hideous, spine-chilling scream, some fable-shrinking shriek, rived them apart, sending a spidery crack through the mirroring air.

"Off with her head!"

No no no—not yet!

The Queen, the Queen. TheQueentheQueentheQueen! With one Reptilian look, seeming to drain every drop of their red-and-white blood.

Stop! You can't have him! You won't take him!

No guilty shame seized them. Merely they looked on one another. Abhorring the abhorrence. Each from themself recoiling.

And then and then, before Alice could blanch . . . With a zero-at-the-bone prompt from Her Majesty, the White Rabbit mounted the platform. Assuming his by-the-book role as Chief Royal Herald. With a grave and Courtly demeanor, announcing, "All rise for the Queen."

Look at him, like some palepale fist, all the red life draining from him. So alone with the alone, still in his shivering hospital robe.

On reflex, it seemed, he had summoned the tale again. To protect her from him, from the illness fast consuming him. (A tale now left so untold, a tale *no longer theirs, really*.)

Still. For all her reserve, for all her finely honed sense of comme il faut and Wonderland propriety, Alice could not but cry out: "Noooooooooooooo!"

"A page too late for all that, I'm afraid," the Queen of Hearts declaimed (which is to say, merely enunciated. For to proclaim, in so regal a way, was to reframe the world as your personal statement, to hear on every tongue, and in every refrain, nothing but yourself in solemn quotation).

Taking her King by the hand, ushering him toward the platform (but always one step behind and beneath her) on the Queen blandly went: "Love, love, love, love, love—make me puke."

Love? Alice pondered. *"Love"*—*really?* Never, in all her life, had she felt less represented by the venom being spit in her direction.

Alice paused, letting her glance travel over that Dread Queen again. Over her blundering form in those buttressing robes. Over those feet, too proud for the painted earth beneath. Over that prominent nose, each nostril so assured of the devotion of the roses and wind, the woman hardly needed to breathe to breathe in. She, with that Heart on her chest, such a still and awful red. *Why,* Alice thought, *she could as well be . . . that Red Cross Nurse!*

Surely, she thought, *Alfred could see it.* She looked—but he stood rigid. As if he were taking refuge in incomprehension. His eyes like polished Christmas windows (when there was Christmas still in windows)—artificially brightened, and beribboned. *What was he doing?* Just barreling ahead? Did it really mean so much just to get to The End?

Wholly oblivious to anyone having a thought or sensation other than her own, that Queen of Hearts fastened her low-lantern gaze on that negligible husband of hers. He, poor thing, some mere *he*, who could not but project what a sad thing it was to be King, if to be King meant to rule overruled by that Queen.

Eager to underscore that theme, with a nod toward Alice, the Cross Queen hissed at the man's shrinking ear: "Well, at least she brought her head."

Fearing perhaps to lose his, that sage King hmmph'd: "That's good."

Then, like some nearsighted troll, peering at Alice's throat, grossly the man grinned. (Picturing, perhaps, some sun-dream guillotine, on some historic scaffold, in some French and/or Russian Revolutionary Square.)

Not that that regal Queen cared. With an air of the sublime, and the certain sense that even the slightest flick of her wrist carried with it the Law of God and Control of the Deck, she lifted a pinkie, blessing the air. (And the sky behind her adjusted its light, to show Her Highness only at magic-hour angles and only from her better side.)

She paused. As one does. She took in each Heart, each Club, Spade, and Diamond, bestowing on each, in turn, her imperious glance—as if she were permitting each star to pass Go and succeed the following star in the dark course of heaven.

Good good, Alice thought. *Keep her occupied.* Better that the Queen overlook her completely. *But Alfred?*

"Well, I am proud"—that monarch swelled—"so proud, to behold this record-breaking crowd." Warming to her theme, with a petulant peek about, she demanded King-Lear-ially, "Which of you can we say loves us most?"

A royal pause followed. Not a word, not a perfunctory clap, not a "hmmph" broke the air. A perfect vacancy wafting toward Her Majesty—like the perfume of a world she was not made for—and would not endure. (A silent and indifferent deck? A rumored row of empty seats? Not a thing a Queen like she would bear.)

Ever politic, and knowing his dear, the King coughed fustily, nudging the Knave standing near.

And. The. Knave. Just. Stood. There. Curling his profiled self into a kind of mustachioed curlicue.

Pivoting, nailing the King with a mad-red glare, the Queen importuned, "Yes?"

At an understandable loss, but doing his husbandly best, the King began, "Never has there been . . . a Queen . . ."

Sensing that sentence about to fall off a cliff, the Queen glared more glaringly. "Mm?"

"Who has accomplished"—that royal Adam's apple bobbed—"so much."

"And?"

"And . . . and . . . who has done so many . . . things."

Such a speech was not soon to be recovered from! An ecstatic cheer swelled from the crowd. In voices numerous as space. It washed over the land, bringing forth flowers of every hue, and a shade greener than green from the lawns and trees. A redbreast whistled, and a choir of birds stood witness, choiring—with every harmonious cry imparting to her Majestical self something still more ineffable. Her Majesty smiled: Queen again.

What next? Alice stood, still as still, unsure; like a creature of some strange new race, wrecked solitary here.

Pssst, she heard White Rabbit psst. Blankly she stared at him—*what was he doing?* Blankly he stared back—*what was she?* For inasmuch as yes, he was capitulating, she was completely stalling. This was *their* book, and she was the one, after all, who'd convinced him, had conducted him here, to do it with her. Their last chance.

And yet, her look said, did they have to *end like this?* Couldn't they just turn back a page? Couldn't they flip boldly back through—and do all those celebrated bits she'd so recklessly skipped? They could spend all afternoon, they could, just doing them? And maybe, then, each moment would offer not only itself, but also the means of their keeping it . . .

Or would it not? Could *they* not? Stories had laws, after all. And perhaps every book, even their book, held something inviolable. How could she transgress against her own myth and expect any good to come of it?

(And beyond that, Alice knew, every good book requires so much. Demands so much. First, from its writer, who never is up to the task of fulfilling their book's egotistical demands; then, from the reader, who's left to contend with something in herself she can never understand. Some discontent too exquisite to tell.)

"Alice, quick!" the Rabbit warned again, his fur like a bundle of shivers. As the Queen leaned dangerously near. Surveying Alice's delicious head and neck . . .

Finding herself in a place not her own (and worse, not really of *herself*), and meanwhile being less than royal, and not exactly an invited guest, Alice reasoned that, despite whatever slights she'd incurred, she ought to approach, ought even to curtsy—to acknowledge, with some bob of her knees, those florid, High-and-Mighty Cards. And so, she did.

"Your Majesties."

Pursing her lips, the Queen of Hearts swatted that blue stumbling buzz from anywhere near: "'Majesty'? Oh please. They've bombed my home, too. The north-by-northwest wing, anyway."

Utterly confounded, Alice looked to Alfred—but he did not seem to see her. Or, would not show he did. For to show himself at all was to show such feeling. To show *fear*, she thought. His fear of an ending.

She wanted to cry out again, but before she could summon a word, that Queen usurped, slurp slurp, all verbiage: "Come back for another look, have you? And found yourself too big for picture books? Too huge for fools like us?"

Sorry, what? Alice's lips parted, buuuut—

That Regal Tongue would suffer no impediment. Indeed, one dared not try to apprehend—rather, one simply *was*, and did—whatever the Queen said. (Why, even to speak the Queen's English was to trespass upon her property, really; to admit that even one's thoughts belonged to her.)

And yet, Alice couldn't help her humble self: "If you please, Your Majesty—"

"I—pleased?"

"I just want—"

"You want!"

Finding herself now in some sorely drifting boat, already leaking, on Alice rowed: "I wanted . . . just one moment—"

"You shameful girlish thing," exclaimed the Queen, burying a multitude of chins in her goitered stole. "You hate the part that's tiny still in you. And yet, you want to hide within the child in you."

Not true, Alice thought, that royal color flushing through her, making one crimson of her flowering cheeks. *Can't we hate our refuge and still use it?* "Hide? I don't. I won't."

"You can't, you mean," the Queen declared. "You can no longer not know what we mean."

But what did that mean?

Alice searched out her White Rabbit. There, he stood—swaying uncertain beneath those fretful ears—like some wavering palm at the end of her mind. No no answering look. No, not a word to defend her. He was scared, too scared.

With a lacquered flick of those fire-fangling fingertips, the Queen commanded; and that Royal Herald's horn sounded again. And now, as Alice watched, the grandest marching band appeared. A faux-splendid card representing each and every splendiferous instrument—each shimmering tuba, saxophone, and flute, each trombone and clarinet. (On the back of each card, an advert: "Buy War Savings Bonds and Stamps.")

Where is there an end of it, thought Alice "There is no end," that drone seemed to answer.

With a near-rocket flare, the Conductor Card seized his baton and set off a Huzzah. A score of broken intervals. A twangling thought-music that evaded human meaning, though it played, or seemed to play, upon the very stuff of reason:

Isn't it a trial?
No child can stay a child.

Before Alice could lodge an objection, that courtly oblong throng, all those Knaves, Eights, Kings, and Threes, let out a groan, joining that trilling Queen. And the White Rabbit tooted his trumpet along with them.

Where, where an end? "Must you, really?" Alice tried.

But her words found no net on that wind. Oh no, the Queen and her unshuffled deck merely exulted, jubilant:

> *The story never told,*
> *How Wonderland grows old.*

> *Oh, isn't it . . .*

What if it never did end? What if this horrible jangling of everything sensible, of everything heartfelt, never relented? Sure, she had wished to stay here forever—with him. But not like this. Not with him toadying up. Not like this, in this unchanging goldenglare—with the baabaabaa blaa of the Tuba blaring on, and the tralala-ing of all the Queen's men. As if Silence, and Alice, would soon be decapitated. Not like this, with that savage, sense-eating Queen sizing up Alice's head for the block. Extending her savage hands for Alice's neck.

CHAPTER XXI:

—

"FIRST THE SENTENCE, THEN THE VERDICT"

"CONSIDER, my dear," mewled the King. "She is only a child."

"And?" unmiffed, if unmoved, the Queen demanded.

"And the, uh, spectacle of such a pretty, headless child may well reflect ill on—"

"Who?"

"My dear," the semi-congested King a-a-answered, "the song is near its end. You must applaud, you'll need your hands for that."

"A little water wipes them clean."

"Come come, you're *you*, my dear. Even Queens must curtsy to Courtesy."

Zwapp. With a rabid rip through the thankless air, the Queen drew back her hands—and abruptly turned left from Alice's neck. Her ageless, lapidary eyes boring through that anointed King: "Lock it, Leonard. Or it'll be your head."

And O! every mouth cried O! With a sudden falling sigh, as the royal song concluded, with a burst of rocketfire. All those ribbony stars melting gold green silver through

the afternoon haze . . . And Her Majesty the Queen condescended to smile. To grace the huddled masses with a single
celestial glance, as she clapped her serene, ceremonial hands.
Like a portrait of savage benevolence.

Whew.

"A cat may look on a King," or so the proverb went. Or
that's how Alice remembered it. But what happens when a
King condescends to prowling, to mulishly meowing, like a
common alley cat?

Amid the corrugated crowd, at the foot of those royal
stairs, still Alice stood. Watching as that sorry King trudge-
clumped about, muttering "Buuuttt"—then followed that up
with "Buuuttt whaaaat?" As if this latest trauma had reduced
his syntax to dust. Had left him, superfluous, under his hollow
crown.

(Another bare, unaccommodated thing, shaking off fear
of himself and his Queen. He who would lay himself down to
sleep with grief, and then still wake and be King.)

No surprise then, that this shell of a King gesticulated so
tepidly. And still, with that gesture, a trumpet sounded royally.
Immemorially. *A trumpet of solitude, really.*

Seemingly startled by the sound, the White Rabbit,
who'd sounded it (in his supporting role as Royal Herald),
immediately unrolled a crumbling parchment scroll and
read from it: "The High Court of Her Majesty Against the
Heartless Alice."

No matter how little he'd intended it, no matter how
briskly he'd proclaimed it, still it was *he*, hoisting that charge
of "Heartless" like some scarlet flag, flapping on high.

"Heartless?" Alice asked.

No answer. Not a waver in his steely regard, in that Rabbit's compulsive commitment to paying attention. As if, in taking on the role of Royal Herald, he'd somehow multiplied himself by himself. (If only she could get to the square root of him!) Oh but no, he merely enlarged on the royal charge: "For, Alice Has Committed Two Treasonous Offenses. Recklessly Rewriting the Tale to Suit Her Selfish Self. And, Breaking Rule Forty-Two—"

At this, that fulminating Duchess pressed her prominent neck from the madding throng, to pin the outrage of aging on Alice: "You Have No Right to Grow Here!"

No?

Well-nigh convinced by the Duchess's mere declaration, the bloodthirsty Queen and her bloodless King exchanged a rapier-like look and closed in on that Heartless Suspect, Alice. The Queen, with a snap of her thick-knuckled fingers, demanding to hear and know all: "Item."

The Rabbit, *her* Rabbit, all riled up. Wanting so much, with such a muchness, to reach The End: "Item," he heralded, "she went reading, then proclaimed she'd dreamed us."

"Who did?" Alice challenged.

"*You* did," snapped the Queen.

"And the Verdict is?" demanded the King.

The Queen merely glared. Withering that Royal Sir with a single stare: "Pay attention when your Rabbit's reading." Then, to put a period, snapping her fractious fingers: "Item."

"Item," the Rabbit came back, putting on a brazen front: "First she bragged she brought us here—"

242

"Louder!" brayed the bellicose Queen.

Louder: "First she bragged she brought us—"

"Faster!" she demanded.

Faster: "First she bragged she—"

"Funnier!"

"First sheeee—"

"Guilty!"

Alice sent forth a sigh: "Well, this certainly is a trial."

"And the Verdict is—" came the Pronouncement from the King.

"First the Sentence, then the Verdict," the Queen reprimanded (her logic impeccable as ever). Clearly, this Trial was too big a to-do to conclude so soon. "Item!"

Alice bristled. "Why *these* items?"

"Now, she wants to choose her items," jeered the Dormouse.

"Mad," the Hatter came back. "She's mad."

"I'm not!"

"You're here," someone reasoned. The Cheshire Cat! Materializing like a painted wonder, over the King's ermined shoulder. "They make us all mad here."

"Not me," Alice declared.

"Oh please," the Dormouse squeaked.

"You little tweeb," the Hatter preened. Capering about, finding this a particularly fine time to stick up his hat, along with both sides of his hair.

"Guilty!" the Queen declared (as if such a thing had never yet been declared). "Item!"

"Item," the Rabbit-Herald resumed, "she went chasing tail—"

"But—" Alice tried.

The Knave butted in: "Well, she certainly held my Hedgehog, and wriggled my Flamingo."

"Child, I never!" blustered the Royal Mum.

In a rough stage whisper, Alice called to Alfred, "How can you bow to their madness? Why did you turn the page?"

How formally, how sorrowfully he nodded. (As if some Herald of Sorrow reigned within that Herald of Heartlessness.) "That is the story, Alice. Time to close the book."

"But—" Alice began. But that "But" went nowhere, swallowed by some omnivorous "Shhhhhh!" sounding, seemingly, everywhere around her.

And now, from every nook of the known, from every dark cranny, every undiscovered country, swarmed the most clamorous horde. (So many, Alice had not thought her book contained so many!) But there they were, everywhere: myriad wigged jurors with clipboard-like slates, lean solicitors (with their beneficent pet spiders); untold crowds of bespectacled spectators marking down each mistake, let alone each linguistic misstep, she made—and indeed had ever made. Numberless, their glares, redoubling until, it seemed, their insect-like, mirroring eyes would absorb the whole of her—and she would nothing be, but countless slightly differing images of some storybook thief.

"Excuse me, but? . . ." Alice challenged the crowd.

"Suppress her!" the Queen decreed. "Acting as if she were some mock me?"

"A mockery!" the Mock Mock Turtle keened.

"A royal Jabberwockery," the Cheshire Cat deemed the entire proceeding.

"She thought she was what was," espoused the Knave.

"Still does," the Dormouse brayed.

"The riddle?" riddled the Hatter. "She could barely even read it."

And with that most venomous charge—*Illiteracy?*—that swine-snouted Duchess brandished her spanking-truncheon: "Tit tot. You tart! You tit without a heart."

Knowing well, all too well, how to work the anxious cardboard crowd, that wizened creature shifted tone, winding her shelter blanket round her, letting the tears stand witness in her eyes. "She was my pig—I loved my pig!—and then she made me old and big."

"Indeed, she did," concluded the Queen, sizing up the Duchess carefully.

Dispassionately, the Duchess surveyed Her Majesty:

"Well, I'm hardly the only thing she's turned into an aging Queen."

With near-sweating labor, maintaining her posture of idle indifference, Her Majesty looked to the King for a word.

"And the Verdict is?" demanded the doddering King.

What a Queen, what a glare! With a bland, derisive toss of the chin, such as a sated jackal might cast, that Royal She turned and again condescended to bother Alice: "Now, we shall decide if you can leave here."

Alice, taken aback: "Do you mean you'd keep me here?"

"Someone write down 'duh,' and then add 'praved,'" the Queen instructed. With a wicked cluck, drawing herself up, monumental as Space, "I mean, really. Every syllable she wastes—"

"You age," the Duchess jibed.

"Off with your head!" the Queen ordained.

A bright, alfresco applause rose through the air. And still the Duchess did not budge, nor did anyone lift a finger against her. Wearily, the Queen adjusted her crown, as if it were made of thorns. "I cannot exert myself with another word."

Turning mildly, she nipped again at that Kingly ear: "You tell her, dear."

He considered. "Well, then." Clearing his throat, that castle-building King mused to Alice, "Every dream would love to hold its dreamer, it's—"

"—the dreamer who can't bear to know she's dreaming," snapped the Queen. Impatiently.

246

"But I'll know!" Alice was adamant: "I know the dream—by heart. This is my heart. My dream."

The King eyed Alice cynically, mock-Socratically: "Oh, do you think? Then—"

"—who and what are we?" quizzed the Queen.

"Part of it," replied Alice.

"You think?" posed the Queen.

"Then, where are we," the King asked Alice, "when you're not here? You think we just appear—"

"—because you read us?" inveighed the Queen. Then, with a faltering whine, to the King: "I can't. You deal with her."

Ever dutiful, the King nodded, his tristful eyes coming to bluer life as they settled once more on Alice. "The truth is, we are here, and sometimes—"

"—we let you into *our* dream," snipped the Queen.

"I won't believe you," concluded Alice.

The affronted Queen could not even fathom. "Do you think our dream needs you to dream it?"

"You, who are no longer you?" quandaried the King.

"You no one," denounced the Queen.

"I'm not no one."

"No one!"

"No no," cried Alice, pointing at every last Card and high-fantastical creature around her, "you, and you, and you are!"

"No, we're *Us*," growled the illustrious, two-dimensional crowd.

"You're some mere you," the Queen instructed.

"*We're* the book," announced the book.

"Your thoughts may come and go," explained the King. "We're here."

"And we'll be here," with inviolable voice the Queen made clear.

"No changing us," ta-da'd the Knave.

"We're the book."

Oh, are you? Alice thought. *We'll see about that.*

With a wave of her still half-dreaming hand, as if she were wielding some fairy wand, she summoned once again all those dusty dog-eared pages, the still-unbroken spine, the soul of her lost storybook. Once more she held it—held it out—for all those flabbergasted denizens of Wonderland.

With a jolt, she could hear every thought in their stiff, swarming heads:

"Well, I'm offended to my uttermost leaf."

"Unfeeling thing. Offering some ultimatum? To *Us*?"

"We, the text she loved! We, who bore the imprint of her soul—and elbows—on us!"

"*We*, the best illustration of how deep she is."

"Or *was*."

"We, who measured to the hour her solitude."

"*We*, who always gave so much, yielding more and more meaning the more she'd reread us."

"We, her unflagging support, when no one else was!"

"And now, she'd just shut and shelve? She'd extinguish, *Us*?"

"I mean, really. Does she think it's a one-way street—when the words allow you such familiarity? Can you know a book without it knowing you by heart?"

With those statements of the true dread every book feels—of being misread!—such a green chill settled over the trees, and a panting terror took hold of the painted lawn.

One step ahead, with a pointedly unironical smile, Alice taunted them all: "*You're* the book? Then, watch what happens when I close the book."

A sudden, frenetic squabbling broke forth—a railing, squalling, caterwauling:

"Close?!"

"The book?!"

"No—please!"

"Take my tea!" the Hatter cried.

"My cream! It's steamed!"

Even the Duchess deigned to plead: "Precious Piggie!"

But Alice dug her heels in: "Try and stop me."

As if she were casting, or breaking, a spell, she intoned those climactic words from the book, those which the Storybook Alice used to dispel *her* nightmarish Trial: "'Stuff and nonsense,' said Alice loudly—"

But her Dread Majesty interrupted, flinging open the hinges of her eyes, her pupils blistering like those fires at the end of time: "Guilty bitch! Suppress her! Get her head. Watch her shrink!"

"Watch me shrink?" Alice parried. "I don't think so. No. I've shrunk enough."

At those portentous words (soon to be struck from the Wonderland record) every eminent Juror and Jailer, every Judge, King, Queen, Knave, Duchess, and Tailor drew back in terror of Alice, whose body seemed now so vast as to trouble the sky. "You're nothing," she decreed. "Nothing but a pack of cards."

With that, Alice clapped her hands, slamming shut her book: *wwwwwwwhhhhoooooooooosshhhhhhhhhhh.*

And gone gone, at once, they were. All gone. Not a sight, not a sound. Not a card floating down from the clouds (as described in her book). Only some blank prismatic light upon those solitary fields . . .

Ta-ta. Good night. Good night.

But . . . her Royal Herald?

Alice cast about—all about. She searched the furthest tree, each slope . . . No White Rabbit there, no Alfred to be found.

Oh no no no! What had she done? Had she been so swept up, so mastered by the brute blood of the Trial, that she'd let herself neglect . . . that she'd . . . let?

"White Rabbit!" she cried. But not a thump. Not a sound. Oh nonononono.

And now, Alice's doubt rebounded on itself. Had she, in fact, used the Trial? Seized on it as a distraction, as a detour from some dark wood just ahead?

For, look what she'd done. Had run all the wonder out of Wonderland, that's what.

Perhaps the Queen had been right, then. In the end, she was no one. And therefore, had no one left. She, with a soul that was not a soul. Lodged in a room in which it never had fit. (Then again, how could it ever have fit—with just how little food and water she ever had given it?) She, and her empty mind, like some skull without eyes, scanning a book without print.

"Cheshire Puss!" she called out. "Cheshire . . . Puss? . . ."

Not a purr answered. Not a word.

But perhaps that was best. Better to be left on her own, with this no-one self. No longer tracking what page she was on, no longer counting how much or how little was left, with each page she turned, with each look she cast.

"Alfred?!"

No one there.

What now, what next? No answering that.

There she stood. On a blank Court Room Lawn, on a nonexistent page. Marooned.

CHAPTER XXII:

—

NO MOMENT OF FAREWELL

NOTHING left then. Where only moments ago had stood that imperial throng, now Alice stood alone. The majestical pageant faded—with all such stuff as her wonder had been made on. Gone. And she? Transported, somehow, somewhere else? (For, in a trice everything felt else.) Or was it just that some new locale was filling in around her? Like some fresh, lonesome background in the painting that contained her. Here, where now she stood. On some solitary riverbed in Wonderland. Some random stubble-plains, surrounding. All her fluttering pages gone—all those formidable cards, the maddest of Hatters, her Mock and Mock Turtles, her Duchess, King, and Queen. All ghostly, gone.

Nothing for it, thought Alice, *but to wonder at the absence.* To stand and stare in blankness at the still-blank sky; to wonder how the Wonderland sun held up, and why it brought no pain now to her eyes. How did that golden reef of cloud drift so goldenly on—for mindless hours, it seemed—all the infinite cumulous riches within one narrow room . . .

Somewhere she'd read, she was sure she had, something so strange about the sun. (Though why she should be thinking about some heavenly body right now, she couldn't quite figure out. Nor why, at such a time, she should be playing this game of hide-and-seek with her mind . . .) Still. What had it said exactly? That the sun, which was made out of light, could never quite look away from the light. So satisfied was it to be in the light, that it was content just to look and be looked on by it.

And the upshot of that? That nothing ever interrupted its view. That it was *continuous*. And thus, it never departed from itself—never found itself distracted; never paused to doubt itself; never felt *other than*. It simply *was*; and all it had seen and done remained part of it. So, nothing ever was lost. Nothing would ever be gone. What it remembered still *was*—and was always there.

Then, why was it that she, unlike the sun, could not stop herself looking back? To all those times Alfred and she would run behind their houses, within their common garden; all those afternoons, when he'd come again to play; when he'd leave her, by the end of day, with so many fresh things to ask of him. So many parts of him still to uncover. Still to desire. As if each new sun bred from her love a new love . . .

. . . *The Giraffe House, Regent's Park, that first, sunfreckled April afternoon. So long ago. Alfred and she, aged six—or seven, were they? Together, standing in a wondering silence. His child hand extended toward the fine, sloping neck of their long-standing favorite giraffe.*

"Alice, see!" he exulted, reeling right round. His loose fraying sleeve asway on the breeze. "Our giraffe—his tongue is

utterly black. Black as the spots on his back. It's to keep it from getting sunburnt."

"We'll keep our tongues in our mouths, then," she proposed. Sensibly enough.

"Forever Alice." Alfred smiled. And continued, with an authoritative glee: "Once, some years ago, the world's most acclaimed giraffe walked five hundred miles—with a royal consort, mind you—across the entire continent. Till it arrived in Paris. The Jardin des Plantes. There, the Queen of France was so impressed, she fed it rose petals from her royal hand ..."

"She did?"

He nodded, assured. Alice couldn't not be impressed. "How ever do you know all that?"

"My Dad," his shrug confessed. A slant of sunblue from his eyes, flecked with hope: "Maybe one day, when we're older, we can go and pay a visit? To our own royal garden—in Paris! We could feed our own giraffe." ...

... *Maybe one day, yes.* But not today, when not a soul was left, when even hope asked nothing more of her. Not in the blankgolden shade of this derelict, abandoned Wonderland. Beneath the unveiled sun—where now she stood. Knowing that no other Rabbit—no other Alfred—ever would come to her.

With a lingering sigh, Alice sent her look about: only these broad yawning lawns, the oblivious river casting its goldenblue over its lonely banks. Only those murmuring meadows of proud, silent flowers. Not a Tiger Lily calling her name—not as it did, so summarily, in her Looking-Glass book. Not a frownglowering Daisy remarking on how grown-flowering she'd become, or how she talked entirely too much.

No, only those blown souls on their unpainted briar remained. Only those voluptuous roses, each one rising, so fully itself, through the full expanse of its petals, to each of its outermost leaves. (Each rose, not preening exactly, but knowing the full freight of longing it held, within its petaling grasp, for so brief a spell.)

With every look, as Nana'd said, we are always saying goodbye. But after we have gone so many times—after we have left so many rooms behind—should it really be so hard?

Once more she looked about. The world around her suffused so with roselight, it seemed to offer itself to the view for the very last time. That moment every flower seems to glow most like itself, in that misting hour as the sun declines.

"Sorry, haven't seen your Rabbit," someone seemed to gossip. *"Not here, not today."* Alice cast about—and about . . .

No one there but her. No bird twittering, of the plain sense of things, from among the leaves. No bathers bathing in some homely stream. No rustic clippers clipping those majestical croquet hedges. No flamingos seeming to exceed themselves, being so pink. No hedgehogs there, hedging about. Another wondrous city evacuated.

But . . . *there*, some departing sound. Some iterated ellipsis of sound. Not unlike the dim rattling on distant roofs, that drizzle of shrapnel dropped so methodically it had come to seem part of the day to day. No, it was more like some odd, insistent ticktock. *Someone's clock?*

Uneasily Alice looked again—and there, on a lonesome rock, lay that Rabbit watch. His war-scored pocket watch! That worn silver moon, catching a breath on some sunlit ledge.

She stood, staring at it. Unsure how to extend her hand. Or if indeed she should. (For, like an instrument on which he'd played so often, it seemed still to vibrate with his touch . . .) Never could she reach it now, she felt, without some other hand joining her hand—as once his had.

(*Was it so bad,* Sisyphus asked, to want a little help in hoisting it?)

But . . . perhaps it wasn't his hand she wanted in hers, lifting that wornface from all she remembered. Perhaps it was, rather, the hand of the child she'd been. The child who'd stood watching him tap-tapping that flatglass, as if it might turn him into a Rabbit for real. The still-believing child who'd longed so to join him, just as real herself, in Wonderland.

Once more she looked. And there he stood—her White Rabbit. The light just catching the furred curve of his ears. So proud, in his frayed hospital gown, the perpetual afternoon of his eyes succumbing to the coming pageant of evening.

"You," she said.

His shoulders near-shivered, then shrugged, abashed. He, so polite to the end: "Still here."

Yes. Her eyes said, yes. As if she knew some deeper self, looking on him. "Somehow."

He nodded: "Yes."

A parting gift, she almost said. But hesitated. For she found herself most with him, only within the silences. And so, with no word said, she looked again. And saw him once again as first she had—battling the nervy May wind for control of his fluttering paperback pages. Every inch the White Rabbit already; in his double-breasted Edwardian jacket. His skin, both pale and flushed, against that bluest navyblue.

Now, here he stood, all those years later. *One moment more, still him.* Though he seemed to be fighting back tears. Tears which were not his. Or were, perhaps, not only his. The *tears of things.* As he said all he said, all he left still unsaid: "I can't tell you what it's meant, to come here once again, to run here once again . . ."

She felt herself nod. As if what she looked at were what she were *in.*

Don't let's say more, Alfred. Don't let's.

But he, again: "I hope you will remember how it was . . . ?"

She nodded, again.

"In the story," he said, "there's no moment of farewell. You know."

She knew. Hearing, within her, that hymn from the other side of memory; all of it, so silent and sad. The end-sound of a summer without end.

Don't let it.

He, once more: "And so . . ."

With no further word, he turned to go. But she could not. *"Please. Don't."*

And the back of him did not. Did not *go. He could not!* Not her Rabbit. Not yet. *However would the sun remain still there?*

But, see—the back of him, etched there, still there. The back of her Rabbit in his waistcoat. She would see him forever, she knew: there, by the desolate rock, forever on that hill in Wonderland.

Yet once more, he turned toward her. One last look. Her Alfred, in his frailer robe. Forever. *Look, there . . .*

Again, she looked and this time thought: *Alice, turn one page.* I loved him. I still love him. Yes.

CHAPTER XXIII:

—

"SUCH A CURIOUS DREAM"

BRADRRMMMMBRMMBRMMMM, she'd heard. And everything had gone one silvery blur. As some battery-electric Tube locomotive came rattling *Braadrrmrmmmbarr* down the track.

"*Our tea!*" someone shrieked joyously.

"Morning already? Ay me," whinnied someone else.

Her Mock Turtle? No no, not he, not *here*. Here, there was only . . . the trusty, gloom-laden Underground.

Like a late sleeper, resistant still to everything visible, with her eyelids half-shuttered, Alice wrenched herself about and saw—less saw than remembered—no curtain there now. No quarantine tent even. Only a barestript cot.

For how long, there? How long, till it too would be removed? Erased from the History primer—with all of them. All his thoughts, his memories, like pencil jottings in the margins: all those sleepless-night insights, reduced to so much eraser dust, blown to nowhere. Only the Tube-station walls to stand witness—speechless, cold depositories of the little joy he'd known there.

But then. "No child," Papa had said, "can ever be called

happy. They can only be congratulated for the hopes we have in them . . ."

So long she stood. So numb, it was as if she'd been turned to a pillar of salt. Till, at last, she roused and looked about again.

Through the veil of dark, the first rays of a profounder dark showed in scattered patches, in tinges of brown, near-touches of emergent grey. As if some prehistoric creature, with a hundred mouths, had just begun to rise, stretching itself yawningly from those still-mantled stairs. Scratching and licking its sleepy-faced forelocks (as always it had done, as always it would). Airing its belly and its airy umbrellas, testing its still-drowsing hind paws. Each morning-mouth grouching and grousing and mouthing some part of the air out of each other mouth.

"Bring us this day our toast and jam. Or at least some crisp baguette-y bread. Our coffee thick with steam, as our Dotty would have done once," that Mamie-voice sighed. "Ayy me, don't we all remember that loveliest of creamery butter—from our cooler? Gobs of milk, fresher than fresh. Got from our dewysilks in Devonshire. Our own gorgeous cattle, who loved us, who *knew* us, lowing in the meadows around us, part of us! . . ."

"Milk tea for me," Angus requested—from the large searching eyes of a mobile canteen worker. Settling his manly self at her tableclothed counter, taking pleasure in his morethanmanly order. "In exchange, I can offer my Meat-And-Two-Vegetables."

"Hahahaha," Dodgy cawed. But as the steady-eyed Canteen worker checked the time and briskly beckoned the next in line, he pressed no-nonsensely forward: "Two sausage rolls, please."

See, Alice thought: a just-awakening crowd of London life, queued before the opened doors of that train. The Refreshment Train! *That time already?*

Still-somnolent Alice peered around. Hardly a soul left on a cot. Even the sniffling Doctor and Nurse, already in line. Already fussing about how many meat pies, how many buns left, and slices of wartime pound cake . . .

Would Alfred want cake? Alice turned, almost turned to check, but caught herself and drew a breath.

Chomping a bit of mock cheddar, Dodgy drew up beside her. With a genuine intonation (or a passable imitation) of empathy: "Nurse Cross, she took him off."

She did?

Nigel nodded, from the tail-end of the queue, "In a better place he is."

From those warming tea-urns by the train door, Angus dropped his head casually. "Amen, then."

And then? Alice thought. Nowhere left in her thought.

For her part, Mamie held to her teacup, larking over her shoulder, while swilling the cloudless brew with her personal spoon. "Nothing to be done."

"For him, that is," Angus added in. "Me, I'll have another bit of bun." With a half-look to Alice, with a faint half-bow of the head, he loped to fetch it. But, passing Dodgy, paused: "By the by, cheddar, is it?"

A half-grin curled over Dodgy's lip. "In America, perhaps, they'd call it that."

Unsure where she was, or how she still stood, Alice thought she could count on one hand her perceptions. *As in*: Item, the stench of soot and coal dust. Item, it must be eggless, that sponge cake. Item, some few months from now, with Alfred's body settled in warmer ground, there would be thick clusters of his loved crocuses out, marigolds, too—perhaps a flush of those greenyellow daffodils . . .

"Milk tea?"

Hmm? Alice turned.

Dodgy it was—unprecedented as that was—proffering her a watery cup. Enamel cup, only half-warm. Like . . . something she'd known. And remembered? Yes! *Her cocoa mug.* Nana's ancient Liberty camping mug, always half-cooled, on that laminate brown linoleum counter. Set out by itself, before she'd even gotten there; as if to say how long Nana'd been there, waiting for her.

"Or . . . *no* tea?" Dodgy prompted.

"No—*yes*, I mean. Thank you."

Still barely catching up to herself, Alice reached for the cup—only to see, and remember, something she already held in hand. *The White Rabbit's watch.*

"Careful!" Dodgy warned, then complimented: "Handsome piece, that."

"Yes."

Taking the mug with her free hand, Alice strode, steadily, toward her friend's bare cot.

262

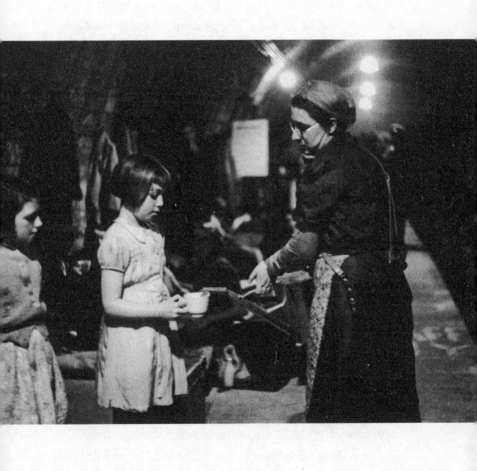

"Theobroma Cacao," the Good Doctor requisitioned, to the squinting dismay of the Canteen worker. Ever the gallant, gamely he proffered a pedagogue's thread through the maze. "Consisting of slab chocolate in an unmarked wrapper." *Ah,* her look said: Got it. Then, dangling his erudition like some forbidden fruit of wisdom: "Theo-broma. 'Food of the Gods,' you know."

"She knows. We all know. Cake, bun, and biscuits for me. I am faint," the parched Nurse protested.

At the edge of things, still unwoken, Alice addressed her absent friend, not lifting her eyes from the cot that had been his. The near-closing words of their book, as best she could remember: "And the whole pack of cards rose up into the air, and . . . disappeared . . . and Alice found herself again, seated upon a riverbank . . ."

"Let's be done with that, love," Angus proposed, saddened to learn, once again, that all good buns must come to an end.

"Boy is gone," Nigel reckoned resignedly. Grown restless in queue, and finding his thumb rather unsatisfying.

But Alice stiffened: "He wanted so to . . . finish it." She let her eyes shut and continued: "'And she told her sister, as best she could remember them, all her strange adventures.'"

Convinced that merely to observe was to sigh, the put-upon Mamie replied, "There she is, still reading to him."

"Somehow I doubt he'll be chiming in," Dodgy said, with a sympathetic vocal tinge never before heard from him.

"It isn't that the dead don't talk," uttered some voice above. "We've just forgotten how to listen."

With a hitch of her head, Alice made out not (as she'd expected) the ravishing gleam of that most enigmatical Cat, but rather the still-bandaged face of that street-tough Tabatha.

"Talk, do they?" Angus puffed. *"Talk?"*

"Through time," affirmed that evening-grin. "That's the riddle of the pages left behind."

Alice nodded to herself. Her thoughts coming and going in a silence of their own; "So, Alice sat, and tightly closed her eyes . . ."

"Dear God," Mamie balked.

"Shhh!" Nigel insisted. Scooching forward, frail arms akimbo, he implored Alice: "Go on."

She pondered a moment, unsure.

Pillowed on his fraying coat, Dodgy nodded. "Do."

And so, Alice did: "'Oh, what a curious dream I've had,' Alice said."

"'Curious, yes,'" Tabatha returned. "'But . . . wonderful.'"

An unaccustomed silence settled over the platform, a kind of majesty settling softly on the tea tureens, falling on the train itself, on the serried rows of emptying cots. Settling, falling on those few youths remaining, the morning all before them, and with nowhere much to go.

For the moment, only Tabatha watched, seeming to weigh Alice's loss. "Sometimes we overcome, you know, just by going on."

Alice let her eyes shut. Then opened them. Casting her look once more about the lightening station. "Light," Papa would say, "is a kind of reassuring." *World still there.* And

indeed, from the streets above, she could hear the brooms sweeping all the fresh shattered glass (what her book would call "such quantities of sand")—and there, the morning hammers, hammering again . . .

With a "Poor thing" sort of sigh, Mamie quipped to no one in particular: "Well, at least that book is done."

"No," Alice replied, "never done."

With that, she crossed, she knelt upon the platform, and with fresh resolution, methodically gathered the lost pages from her book, along with scattered pictures from the Harold Pudding sketchpad.

Just like that, she thought. She would bind them together like that, all the loose leaves of time present and time past. And in that composite book, all the pictures (all the sketches) from those Underground nights would look on and inform, would perhaps grow to mirror, all the conversations she'd had with her first storybook.

And perhaps in that composite book, in that weaving of blank misgivings and moods—from bits she'd learned, from all the thoughts she'd found and lost and found again—she would meet the child who once she'd been. Or rather, a composite child would arise from within her, would replace her, as she watched her White Rabbit forever running past—as she found and brought him again and again, down the hole to Wonderland.

CREDITS

—

Based on the stage musical *Alice by Heart*
Book by Steven Sater and Jessie Nelson
Music by Duncan Sheik
Lyrics by Steven Sater
Choreography by Rick and Jeff Kuperman
Directed by Jessie Nelson

Original New York production by MCC Theater
Artistic Directors Robert LuPone, Bernard Telsey, and
    William Cantler
Executive Director Blake West
Produced by special arrangement with Kurt Deutsch
    and Cody Lassen

BIBLIOGRAPHY

Beyond all my borrowings from poetry and fiction, I also owe a real debt to original source materials and contemporary works of historical nonfiction. Those works include:

Ackroyd, Peter. *London Under: The Secret History Beneath the Streets*. Anchor Books, 2012

Bell, Amy Helen. *London Was Ours: Diaries and Memoirs of the London Blitz*. I.B. Tauris & Co, 2011.

Harris, Carol. *Blitz Diary: Life Under Fire in World War II*. The History Press, 2010.

Harrisson, Tom. *Living Through the Blitz*. Faber and Faber, 2010.

Hodgson, Vera. *Few Eggs and No Oranges*. Dennis Dobson, 1976.

Nicolson, Harold. *The Harold Nicholson Diaries: 1907–1964*. Edited by Nigel Nicolson, Pheonix, 2005.

Orwell, George. *The Collected Essays, Journalism, and Letters of George Orwell*. Edited by Sonia Orwell and Ian Angus, Vol. 2, Nonpareil Books, 2000.

Perry, Colin. *Boy in the Blitz: The 1940 Diary of Colin Perry.* Sutton Publishing, 2000.

Spender, Stephen. *World Within World: The Autobiography of Stephen Spender.* Hamish Hamilton, 1951.

Woolf, Virginia. *The Diary of Virginia Woolf.* Edited by Anne Olivier Bell and assisted by Andrew McNeillie, Harcourt Brace & Company, 1984.

PHOTO CREDITS

—

Page xii: Photo by Anthony Potter Collection/Getty Images

Page 12: Photo by Popperfoto via Getty Images/Getty Images

Page 27: Photo by Felix Man/Hulton Archive/Getty Images

Page 32: Photo by Galerie Bilderwelt/Getty Images

Page 35: Getty Images

Page 44: Photo by Popperfoto via Getty Images/Getty Images

Page 52: Photo by Fox Photos/Getty Images

Page 81: Photo by Fred Morley/Fox Photos/Hulton Archive/
Getty Images

Page 96: Photo by Bert Hardy/Picture Post/Hulton Archive/
Getty Images

Page 122: Photo by Bill Brandt/ Imperial War Museums via
Getty Images

Page 129: Photo by Fox Photos/Getty Images

Page 145: Photo by Hans Wild/The *LIFE* Picture Collection
via Getty Images/Getty Images

Page 173: Photo by ullstein bild/ullstein bild via Getty Images

Page 219: Photo by ullstein bild/ullstein bild via Getty Images

Page 224: Photo by General Photographic Agency/Getty
Images

Page 263: Photo by Hulton-Deutsch/Hulton-Deutsch
Collection/Corbis via Getty Images

Page 266: Photo by H. F. Davis/Topical Press Agency/Getty
Images

ACKNOWLEDGMENTS

—

The author wishes to thank Duncan Sheik, Jessie Nelson, and all the (ever-changing) casts, crews, creatives, and producers who worked with us over the many years of developing the musical, *Alice by Heart*. Special shout-outs to Kurt Deutsch, Cody Lassen, Bernie, Bob, Will, Jessica, and everyone at MCC Theater; as well as Anthony Banks, National Theatre: Connections; Paige Price, Theatre Aspen; and Johanna Pfaelzer, Thomas Pearson, and Barbara Manocherian, New York Stage and Film. For all their work on this book, he also wants to thank his successive editors: Ben Schrank, Marissa Grossman, and Casey McIntyre (with a shout-out to Alex Sanchez). He also thanks his (successive) book agents: Simon Green and Mollie Glick, along with Olivier Sultan, Carin Sage, Tony Etz, Ally Shuster, and everyone at CAA. This book would not exist without the indefatigable efforts of his (also successive!) assistants: Jenny Lester, Josie Callahan, Abby Faber, and Elisabeth Siegel. Thanks, too, to his lawyer Ken Weinrib, and finally, to his personal support team: Alvrone, Lori, David, and Emily Sater.